Big-G City

By S. D. Matley

WolfSinger Publications   Security, Colorado

Acknowledgments

Thanks to the Walla Walla Rural Library System for filling my requests for everything from Amazon Warriors (the real ones) to Zeus; to Martin McCaw, who gave this book a thorough critique in his inimitable "Line Editor from Hell" style; to Bruce Matley, First Reader and first in a whole lot of other ways; to Carol Hightshoe and WolfSinger Publications for believing in me and the world of *Big-G City*.

Dedication

Dedicated to my readers, who want to know more.

Week One – Monday

David

David Bernstein and Clifford Essex descended the steep slope of Seattle's Madison Street, bound for the waterfront. Young Bernstein spoke with increasing frustration, his head tilted upward to address his companion, who was six-foot-nine.

"They've totally screwed it up," David said, shouting to be heard over the rumble of rush-hour traffic. "Thank Zeus they didn't tear down the whole Alaskan Way Viaduct. The traffic jams would be ten times worse."

The State Department of Transportation had finally agreed to replace Seattle's elderly raised highway (that many considered an eyesore) with an underground tunnel. The construction project had stalled early on and the result was far from scenic. David shook his head in disgust just thinking about it.

David had changed little in the five years since he'd discovered he was half immortal. His dark curls were still an untamed mop, his brown eyes still framed by thick-lensed eyeglasses, his body still wiry and slightly undernourished. But now David knew he was not twenty years old—he was something over 2,000, and his mother was not social worker Thelma Bernstein of Salt Lake City, Utah, but Hera, Goddess of Marriage.

"See?" David pointed downhill to the two-level raised highway, framed by office towers that loomed on both sides of the street. "That's the section where I first spotted Ralph."

Ralph was another immortal, a god of small-g status who'd been the one and only structureling assigned to disseminate his molecules throughout the Alaskan Way Viaduct. Structureling support was a technology Zeus had invented millennia ago to reinforce under-engineered buildings, bridges and the like, designed and constructed by mortals. The transition from molecular dissemination to computerized support, as led by Clifford, had recently been completed world-wide.

"So Ralph said," replied Clifford after a pause.

David wondered at the edginess in Clifford's tone. The same day David had discovered he was Hera's illegitimate son, Clifford had learned Ralph was his own father.

"Do you guys see much of each other, now that he's retired?"

David ventured.

"Rarely," said Clifford, his lip barely curled in what looked like a sneer. "He and Mum are stopping at Mount Olympus next week before they start their cruise."

Clifford and his mother, Briana, had also worked as structurelings, he in Seattle's Space Needle and she (most recently) in Big Ben. Briana, too, had retired. Ralph's rekindled romance with Briana was the talk of Seattle's immortals.

"Sounds nice," David said. He tried not to think of Hera, his own biological mother who had the nurturing qualities of an iceberg. Veronica Zeta, David's half-sister and new CEO of Olympus, Inc., had assured him Mom could be quite caring, but he had his doubts. Not for the first time David wondered if Hera treated him coolly because he was the fruit of her only known infidelity to Zeus.

"Ms. Zeta mentioned you'd be coming to Mount Olympus soon?" Clifford said, his voice eased to its usual British clip.

"This week," said David.

"Splendid. Your first time?"

"Uh-huh."

David had recently completed his double-major in architecture and engineering at the University of Washington, and he'd just been accepted to the master's program at Athens U! It was weird, though, because the program was keyed to immortal time and took two hundred years to complete. Veronica had told him to come to the City of Mount Olympus well before classes started, to adjust to life in an all-immortal setting.

They reached the bottom of the incline and stood on flat pavement.

"That way," David said, pointing left.

Clifford stepped into the street in front of oncoming traffic.

"Wait!"

David lunged forward as horns blared, grabbed Clifford's elbow and tugged him back to the curb. His heart, swamped with adrenaline, thudded in his chest.

"Sorry," Clifford said. "I've been at corporate so long I've forgotten mortal customs."

"No problem," said David reflexively, then flinched. Veronica had repeatedly asked him to drop the phrase from his vocabulary but it was a hard habit to break, especially when he was stressed.

The red hand on the crosswalk light changed to the white stick figure of a forward-tilted man. They crossed the street and strolled down the east side of Alaskan Way, under the still-intact section of the Viaduct. Speeding vehicles thumped and growled above. The damp summer air was gritty with Elliott Bay salt and the dust of ripped pavement. Ahead, beyond the raised highway's on-ramp, it looked as if a bomb had gone off. A large section of the Alaskan Way Viaduct had been demolished. A vast ditch yawned where the street used to be. Inside the ditch lay a monstrous, round machine, dubbed Bertha by the local press.

"Great Zeus!" Clifford said under his breath.

The underground tunneling device had been custom-built by a Japanese company for the "tunnel option" project—the relocation of State Highway 99 from the Alaskan Way Viaduct to a two-mile long tunnel underneath Seattle's waterfront.

Clifford removed a digital device from his tweed blazer's pocket and snapped some pictures.

"Incredible!" he exclaimed, sounding less than pleased.

"It's broken down—again," David said. "The project managers don't expect to start drilling again for six months, at least."

"How far did she make it?" Clifford asked as he clicked.

"Less than a thousand feet—of two miles!" David said.

"I don't wish to blaspheme," said Clifford, "but perhaps even the Big-G Gods won't be able to repair this situation." He turned and studied the brick buildings just east of the infant tunnel. "Clearly we'll need to deploy additional staff to reinforce these," he said with a wave of his hand, "and if the seawall fails I fear we'll have to call in Poseidon. Ms. Zeta will not be pleased with my report."

"How is Veronica?" She hadn't been in contact with David much since she'd taken over as CEO. Last month she'd sent a congratulatory e-mail and a one-way plane ticket to Athens International Airport for graduation, but he hadn't seen her face-to-face in a year.

"Ms. Zeta is—" Clifford paused, no doubt phrasing a business-appropriate response in his thoughts before speaking. "I believe Ms. Zeta is progressing well with every project but may be feeling the strain of full responsibility for Heaven and Earth."

David looked up and studied his friend's brooding, grey eyes. Five years ago Clifford and Veronica had been an "item." David had heard rumors (through other gods assigned to Seattle) that Veronica was now too busy for personal relationships. Clifford, though a small-g god who carried none of the blood of Zeus, Hera or their siblings, had been named head of the Architectural and Computer Services Department. He reported directly to Veronica. Their work relationship was close, but if he still carried the torch for her...

"I guess I'll see her when I get there," David said.

"If she has time, mate," Clifford said, his use of slang taking

David by surprise. "If she has time."

Suddenly going to Mount Olympus didn't sound like much fun. If Veronica was too busy to see him and Clifford was overworked and mooning, who would show him the ropes? His only backup was a heavily used copy of Edith Hamilton's *Mythology*, tucked into his backpack. He'd read it on his flight to Athens and learn enough, hopefully, not to make a fool of himself. But he was even more worried about getting there. Veronica had sent instructions for finding the portal to Mount Olympus, not the Mount Olympus mortals knew but a city that existed behind-the-scenes. Was he god enough pass the test?

"C'mon," David said to Clifford. He nodded in the direction from which they'd come. "Let's do Ivar's for fish and chips. My treat, and you can tell me what it's like at Athens U."

Veronica

Veronica Zeta scanned her oppressive surroundings and sighed. Monday had never been her favorite day of the week, and lately every day in the CEO office of Olympus, Inc., had felt like the cold, grinding start of an uphill battle.

Dad had removed himself as corporate head almost a year ago. Late last summer Zeus had finally pronounced Veronica, after years of working alongside him, ready to lead the organization that props up the mortal world. He'd turned over the top-floor office suite to her, said, "Go forth and save the world, Ronnie," and shaken her hand like an equal

She could still feel Zeus' grip, but his support had faded. They'd met to talk things over once or twice a week at the start, but then—it was such an odd thing—he'd become completely absorbed in babysitting his new grandchild, Hebe's daughter, Aster. These days it truly was, as the mortals liked to say, lonely at the top.

Veronica scanned the gloomy CEO office again, sighed again and turned her attention to the thick stack of paperwork piled on her desk. How had Dad stood it all those years—the mountains of interdepartmental memos, the monthly financial reports that required review and approval, the authorization forms from Immortal Resources to hire and fire and evaluate thousands of employees world-wide? She smirked. Knowing Dad and his lack of interest in proper compliance, he'd probably signed everything for millennia without reading it.

She picked up a pen and attacked the stupor-inducing pile.

Within minutes her eyes and limbs grew heavy. The air, spiced with a metallic, musty odor that pervaded the CEO suite, numbed her senses.

"Heaven and Earth," she mumbled.

Veronica stood and shook the dull ache out of her shoulders. She turned slowly in a circle, looking up and around, unable to see into the corners of the dark, high-ceilinged, windowless space. The light on her desk was the only pool of cheer. What had Dad been thinking when he'd had this place decorated? As soon as she had some extra time she'd meet with the plant supervisor and show him her plan for renovation, a light and transparent make-over reflecting her own style of management.

The black Bakelite box on her desk squawked. The sound made her head throb. Veronica sat heavily. She massaged her forehead with one hand and reached toward the box to depress a button.

"Yes, Stella?"

"I've confirmed your appointment with your eldest brother for tomorrow, Miss Zeta," hissed a voice laced with gravel and spite.

"Thank you, Stella."

Veronica released the button and cradled her head in her hands. Why had she agreed to keep Dad's executive assistant? Stella was a bear to deal with, had flat-out refused to convert from her intercom and vintage mortal telephone to the modern, efficient and quieter devices Veronica had proposed. How much longer until she'd voluntarily retire? According to Stella's personnel file, she was nearly 7,000 years old.

The handy touch-screen planner and communications device Hermes had invented glowed on the left side of Veronica's desk. Dad had resisted digital technology. The week after he'd stepped down she'd ordered Hermes' planners for every manager and supervisor at Olympus, Inc., world-wide. Veronica touched the icon for Tuesday and noted her appointment with Hephaestus. She tapped to Wednesday, then Thursday, the day she had a meeting with Hermes and Clifford to discuss the next major project.

Veronica smiled, thinking of her two hand-picked advisors. They were a true contrast—Hermes the charming trickster and Clifford so proper and formal—but both were brilliant.

Her smile faded. Much as she trusted Hermes and Clifford, she couldn't reveal one highly sensitive aspect of the new project to them, the project inspired by Dad's words: "Go forth and save the world, Ronnie." She'd share that information with one—and only one—ally she had yet to recruit.

Veronica set the touch-screen planner to sleep mode and

stowed it in a drawer. There was too much to do today without getting distracted by the future. She returned to the paperwork pile and signed Mom's voucher for the Marriage and the Media program—travel expenses for the program spokesperson, small-g goddess Candy Smith, who was due at Olympus, Inc., next week. Fiducia, the Finance Manager, had sent a proposed fiscal year-end closing schedule for Veronica's approval. A glance showed this was business-as-usual. She quickly applied her signature.

Next was a request from, Ares, God of War, written in red ink and marked urgent. Veronica gripped the paper with both hands and glared at it. From top to bottom it was a recital of wasteful military spending, like a list of toys a greedy child would send to the mortals' favorite demi-god, Santa Claus.

"Jets!" she spat. "He always wants more jets!"

Veronica snorted and pitched the request, unsigned, into the bottom drawer and shut it with a bang. The new project would take care of brother Ares, would that it were over and done! Her fingertips tapped her temples in a gentle massage. She'd start with Hephaestus, the Big-G God who liked explosions. With him she'd test, for the very first time, something Dad had passed on to her—a secret so dark she'd yet to speak its name.

Zeus

Hebe was late again but Zeus was just as happy. Until Hebe arrived to pick up Aster, Grandpa and his favorite girl could continue their joyous game of blocks.

Zeus and the toddler exchanged a smile.

"Excellent, my dear, excellent!"

The former CEO of Olympus, Inc., beamed at the primary-colored jumble of wooden squares, rectangles and curves his granddaughter had stacked in the middle of the den floor.

"And now—" Zeus' smile widened.

Aster took her cue and grabbed the edge of the blanket Zeus had laid on the marble floor to keep the chill off their play area.

"Now!" she shouted.

With one tug of her pudgy hand the wobbling structure tumbled to a heap.

"Hooray!" they cried together.

It was glorious, absolutely glorious to play with such a brilliant and daring child! Zeus wiped happy tears from his cheeks and took Aster's hand.

"Let's go to the kitchen and see if Cook's baklava is ready," he said.

Thoughts of Cook abruptly jolted his insides. Zeus glanced down at the red string he'd tied to his finger. Surely the chronometer hadn't chimed six already, but if it hadn't, how would he have realized Hebe was late?

"I fear Gam-Gam will be very, very angry with Ba-Pa," he solemnly informed the child.

Zeus had retired, but Hera still worked full-time and was absorbed by the demands of the highly successful Marriage and the Media program. Two weeks ago she'd insisted that he, Zeus, take over her responsibility of telling Cook what to make for dinner. Today marked the sixth time he'd forgotten.

The Ex-Lord of the Universe looked down at his drab house toga. Gone was the proud garment of white edged with gold he'd worn for millennia, a uniform of prestige now adopted by Ronnie since she'd taken his place as CEO. He hadn't meant to be entirely absent from Olympus, Inc., but when Hera's workload had escalated and Hebe needed a sitter—

"Ba-Pa, come!" commanded Aster. She tugged him toward the kitchen, her baby-toothed smile beaming up at him like a miniature sun.

Zeus' heart melted anew. What was power and fame, compared to the unquestioning love and admiration of his granddaughter?

The door chime pealed and his heart contracted. It shrank some more when he heard the low-voiced greeting of the butler and Hera's terse reply. When she found out he'd forgotten about dinner again there'd be Tartarus to pay!

"And where is Himself?" Hera bellowed from the hallway.

She swept into view, magnificent in the blood-red toga edged with rubies she'd adopted for business wear. Zeus couldn't help but admire her beauty, the mane of thick, silver hair that cascaded past her shoulders and her dark, flashing eyes. After their time in Seattle five years ago, when together they'd faced Veronica's rebellion and Ralph's near-destruction of the Alaskan Way Viaduct, their tired marriage of four-plus millennia had bloomed with new life. Hera's ability to meet and master the crisis had powerfully reminded Zeus of her vitality, her intelligence, her passion. It had all gone so well until…

"Greetings!" Hera shouted as she absently patted Aster's head. The noisy kiss she blew to Zeus smeared her palm with bright red lipstick.

Drunk again, thought Zeus with fresh agony.

"Tell me, Zeusy—" he winced at the use of a once-pet name, now a word of abuse "—what is Cook making us tonight that pairs nicely with Chardonnay?"

"Gam-Gam," cooed Aster. She pulled from Zeus' grasp and lifted her arms to Hera.

"Hebe's late again, I see," said Hera, looking down at Aster but not reaching for her.

Zeus shivered. Had the woman no affection for her adoring little granddaughter?

It hadn't always been like this. Before Zeus stepped down at Olympus, Inc., it was Hera who'd spent half-days looking after Aster when Hebe was busy. Aster and Gam-Gam had been the best of friends, but now Hera was uniformly cold to everyone. Had it started before he'd retired, when she'd had a mini-bar installed in her office, insisting it was necessary for entertaining visitors in connection with Marriage and the Media? He should have questioned the requisition order when she'd submitted it, but he'd been so busy getting Ronnie up to speed to take over as CEO he'd authorized the request without looking deeper.

Hera swung an arm toward Zeus and lifted his hand for inspection.

"So." The word reeked of wine. She regarded the red string tied to his index finger. "What's for dinner?"

"My dear," Zeus said. He looked up, into her eyes. Hera had taken to wearing platform sandals and stood half a head taller than he. "My dear, I'm afraid once more I've—"

"Heaven and Earth!" Hera swore, her cheeks flushed with rage. "Don't tell me you've forgotten to do that one simple thing again! It's not as if I've asked you to put the stars out at night and take them in in the morning!"

He didn't dare mention that the stars, Hera's responsibility, seemed to be appearing later and later every night.

"I should have known better," she muttered and stalked toward the kitchen. "If it was left to you, we'd starve to death!"

The doorbell rang again. This time the butler addressed his welcome to Miss Hebe. Zeus gathered Aster, whose eyes were welling with tears, into his arms and plucked her pink backpack from his Barcalounger.

Hebe stormed into the den and wrenched Aster away from him.

"I'm late!" she snapped, glaring at him as if it were his fault.

Without another word for Zeus she nodded to the butler to take the backpack. They bustled away. Though Hebe often behaved badly, Zeus felt as if he'd been punched in the stomach.

His head drooped. He shuffled toward the kitchen. From the corner of his eye he saw Hera dart through the kitchen archway and stride purposefully toward her private bedroom, a bottle of Chardonnay tucked under her arm.

Zeus sagged against the wall. If he hadn't been such a rotten husband for so many millennia—excepting the past five years—she wouldn't be acting like this. He'd been notoriously unfaithful, arrogant, swaggering. She'd cheated on him just once, a couple thousand years ago, and he hadn't even noticed. She'd told him herself, after being reunited with her bastard son, David.

He threw back his head and wailed, not caring what Cook or the butler heard or said to the other servants. It was his fault, all his fault. He'd stuck Hera with the most miserable jobs at Olympus, Inc., including the Department of Family Birthdays. She'd made her own success when she created Marriage and the Media. Building the program had given her confidence, but the increased work demands were overwhelming her and she was drinking more than ever. He should have paid more attention while he was still CEO, while he was still her boss.

Zeus carried his sorrows down the cold marble corridor to his private bedroom. For all the rich tapestries and gold fittings surrounding him, the only object he cherished was Aster's plush toy copy of Pegasus that she slept with at nap time. The Ex-Lord of the Universe sank onto the drapery-hung bed, curled around the stuffed winged horse and sobbed like a baby.

TUESDAY

Hera

Hera consulted the decorative chronometer on the wooden awning above the Club Dionysus bar. Adjusting back ten minutes to correct for "bar time," it was twelve minutes past twelve. Aphrodite was late, as usual.

The Goddess of Marriage signaled the sommelier.

"Your best Chardonnay, Ganymede."

"Yes, Madame," the youth said with a bow.

"And bring the bottle."

She unfurled the linen napkin, jauntily folded into a swan, which rested on the bread plate. Damn Leda and her kinky predilection for mating with waterfowl! Could Hera go nowhere without being reminded of Zeus' extra-marital caprices? Oh, he'd mended his ways and been a lot of fun for five fleeting years, but—

Hera flashed on the current incarnation of Zeus. She snorted in disgust. He was dowdy, housebound and dominated by the whims of a toddler. What had happened to the Big-G God she'd married, the Lord of the Universe who, even in his first job as Zeus the Thunderer, had charmed mortals and immortals alike?

And where was that damned Ganymede?

Hera drummed her fingertips on the linen-covered tabletop. The first goblet of the morning was wearing off. Her thoughts teeter-tottered between the former Zeus, the present Zeus, and her imminent meeting with Aphrodite, the Goddess of Love, Beauty and Sexuality.

The topics were intertwined as Aphrodite was one of Zeus' bastards, borne of the insufferable Dione, daughter of Atlas and self-appointed earth mother. It had been a youthful indiscretion, when Zeus was in his 14th century. Aphrodite was also Zeus and Hera's daughter-in-law through marriage to Hephaestus and mistress of their other son, Ares.

Ganymede's return freed Hera's thoughts from the tangled familial web. A deft twist of the corkscrew opened the gates to Dionysus' superior craftsmanship. Ganymede poured a quarter inch of pale, liquid gold into Hera's goblet and stood at attention as she swirled the wine, sniffed and sipped.

"That's fine," she said, and released him with a nod after he'd topped off the sample to a decent-sized pour. The first goblet went down easily. As she achieved a semi-relaxed state, Hera puzzled over why Aphrodite had insisted on meeting her for lunch today. They hadn't seen each other for almost a year, since the miserably dull family party in honor of Veronica's ascension to CEO. What in Tartarus did the bitch want? It's not as if either of them were Goddesses of leisure—Aphrodite ran her own business empire, entirely independent of Olympus, Inc.

Half the bottle was gone by the time Ms. Love Goddess crossed the threshold of Club Dionysus, half-an-hour late. The tart wore a miniscule hot-pink toga with a draped, plunging neckline. A few sections of her white-gold mane were gathered at the crown in a bejeweled clip but most of it fell helter-skelter around her shoulders. Earrings as long as pendulums with shining gold hearts weighting the ends swung back and forth on either side of her neck. Implausibly long, glittering lashes completed the *hetaera* look. There was a reason, Hera smugly surmised, why Aphrodite always looked as if she'd just tumbled out of bed.

"Sorry I'm late," Aphrodite purred while her hard, glittering eyes contradicted the apology. She reclined in the chair opposite Hera, her long legs arranged to luxuriant, curving advantage, easily viewed from all seats in the room. Elbow poised on the table to extend the diagonal line, Aphrodite yawned, rested her chin on her hand and said, "It's all I can do to keep up with my schedule without having to fight corporate sabotage."

"Sabotage?" Hera snapped her fingers to get Ganymede's attention as he passed and signaled him to bring another bottle. "Whatever do you mean, Aphrodite, dear?" she said in a biting tone.

"Marriage and the Media." Aphrodite yawned again. "Dull name, duller proposition."

The Goddess of Love and Skanky Ho-Dum thrust her chest forward and positioned her cleavage at an angle that drew the returning Ganymede's eyes into the rouged depths. He shook his head as if to clear it, removed the cork from the fresh bottle and bustled away as if pursued by Aphrodite's satisfied smile.

"You're a woman of the world, Hera," Aphrodite continued. "You know the story of marital infidelity is as old as Cronus and Rhea. Any fool can see it's the natural order of things." She blew on her overlong hot pink fingernails and polished the enamel on her shoulder. "Those books and seminars and talk-show interviews you're inflicting on the mortals are a complete waste of time. How in Tartarus do you expect your protégé, that small-g washed-up rain goddess Candy what's-her-name, to inspire mortals to embrace monotony—" she paused as if she'd not intended the malapropism, save for the vicious flash of gleaming white teeth "—I mean monogamy, instead of riding the thrill of forbidden passion? They'll be over it in a decade and you'll have wasted your time and talents, mother-in-law, dear."

Hera spared Aphrodite a modest pour of Chardonnay and topped off her own goblet. After witnessing millennia of Olympian intrigue, she knew a bluff when she heard one. Candy's Marriage and the Media interviews were topping the mortal television ratings and everybody in the City of Mount Olympus knew it. For the first time in history, Hera was making inroads on Aphrodite's turf. Revenues from the Love Goddess' "No-Tell" hotel chain and world-wide "Rent-A-Room" hot tub concession must be plummeting. Divorce specialty lawyers were going out of business. Lavish renewal of vows ceremonies and second honeymoons had become hot new mortal industries. Cheaters, at last, were not prospering, and Aphrodite, the manipulative slut, was running scared.

"Think of it as an experiment," Hera said. She set her goblet aside and looked unwaveringly into Aphrodite's combative violet eyes. "I put forth the proposition that if fidelity got as much air time in mortal media as adultery, keeping marital vows could become as exciting as breaking them. And though I'm not as experienced in propositions as are you," she added, the warmth of malice filling her veins, "it turns out I was right."

Hera grasped the wine bottle and poured amply into Aphrodite's suddenly drained goblet. "But it's insensitive of me to talk about business when you've invited me to lunch. Let's talk about you instead." Hera beamed a wicked smile. "Tell me, daughter-in-law, dear, how are my boys?"

Veronica

After gut-wrenching deliberation, Veronica had decided to hold her meeting with Hephaestus at the CEO office of Olympus, Inc. Her eldest full sibling had an antipathy for corporate headquarters. His discomfort would give her the advantage in the negotiation. No, negotiation wasn't the right word. She was in charge now.

Veronica leaned back from her desk, into the depths of the black leather armchair, and drew a deep breath. Though it violated her own sense of fairness, Hephaestus would have no voice in her decision. She'd been pushed too far. Evaluations had been given. Plans for improved performance had been discussed—and ignored.

She realized it wasn't entirely his fault; Dad had managed her elder siblings with what could generously be called benign neglect. Still, Hephaestus, Ares, Ilithyia and Hebe were two-plus millennia older than she. They should know better. It was time for the children of Zeus and Hera to grow up.

A buzz zapped her ears. Veronica pressed the intercom button. "Yes, Stella?"

"Miss Zeta, your two o'clock appointment is here," snarled the black box.

"Thank you, Stella."

Veronica released the button and counted to ten. How many times had she asked Stella to use "Ms." not "Miss"? She pushed the intercom button again.

"Please send him in, Stella."

The door from reception opened a slit, admitting the sound of bright, parting words. On Veronica's first day as CEO, Stella had told her Hephaestus should have succeeded Zeus, as he was eldest born—and male. "It's a man's universe," Stella had sneered, ignoring the change in corporate culture that was sweeping Olympus, Inc., from a stagnant past into the twenty-first century.

The door opened wider. Hephaestus advanced, his stride long and lopsided. Instead of a dress code-compliant toga he wore the leathers of a motorcyclist, studded with silver outlines of a hammer and anvil over his heart. A single eyebrow crested his eyes. Centuries of bitterness were etched on his square, grimy brow. His appearance had startled Veronica ever since she was a child. Knowledge of the volcanic temper lurking underneath sent a shiver through her bones. Veronica shifted her focus away from fear, toward the tool she'd deploy for the first time since Dad had entrusted it to her.

Hephaestus sauntered insolently to the one available chair (she'd had the other seats in the office removed to give him no choice) and threw himself into it, his shorter leg draped over the stainless steel arm.

"Thank you for being prompt, Hef."

She loathed his self-chosen diminutive, as much a part of his protective armor as his overall bearing of male entitlement.

"Just trying to cooperate," Hef said, his narrowed eyes inferring the opposite.

Her expectation he would make the interview as difficult as possible fulfilled, Veronica leaned forward, rested her elbows on the desk and tightly laced her fingers in an effort to control her rage.

"The change we discussed six months ago, to put volcanic activity on hold until the mortal world economy is out of recession, hasn't been implemented. You haven't responded to my memos—"

"Little sister, you don't understand the situation." He yawned and stretched his arms. "Dad knows better than to—"

"This is not about what Dad would do, this is about what's best for the world. Today's world, Hephaestus," she said, using his name like a dagger. "I gave you a chance to keep your authority but you've ignored the goals we set." Her stomach barely knotted as she cut to the bottom line. "You will no longer work autonomously."

Hef clenched his fists and started to speak but she cut him off.

"You will report to Hermes," she said, her voice harsh. "You will work on robotics. Only robotics. No more volcanoes."

Hef half-rose and slammed his palms on her desk. "What in Tartarus—"

Veronica unlaced her fingers, cold as ice, and waved her right hand in an arc. Hephaestus jerked back into his chair. His boot soles slammed to the floor as if nailed there.

"You vibed me, Ronnie!" he said in a stunned whisper. "Dad gave you The Power!"

"Where've you been all these years, Hef?" The hard-edged joy of controlling him flooded through her. "Did you really think he'd retire without leaving me totally and completely in charge?"

She snapped her fingers, releasing him.

"This isn't right!" Hephaestus jumped to his feet, fists raised. "You think you can run Olympus, Inc., but you're just a whelp, wet behind the ears. When I talk to Ares about this—"

Veronica smiled. Everyone knew her brothers hadn't talked to each other since Hef's wife had become Ares' mistress.

"Effective immediately, there will be a decrease in your salary, commensurate with your decreased responsibilities."

"Castrating bitch," he said under his breath.

"Don't tempt me," she growled back. "You'll find Hermes in the lab, fourth floor."

Hephaestus tried to stare her down but he could no longer intimidate her. She rose from her chair, chin high, shoulders back.

"That is all," she said evenly. "You may go."

Jitters of amazement quaked through her when the door slammed behind Hef's stony shoulders. She dropped into her chair, trembling. Veronica's head throbbed. She closed her eyes and willed herself to draw slow, deep breaths to flush out the toxins—the price Dad had warned her came with using The Power.

"One down, three to go," she said, with a brief, mirthless laugh.

wednesday

David

David Bernstein's heart raced as he looked down from his window seat at the Atlantic Ocean. At last he was on his way to the City of Mount Olympus, via Athens.

Veronica had sent the one-way ticket, for which he was grateful, as he was a recent college graduate and low on funds. Though he'd often soared on his own power between Salt Lake City and Seattle for visits with his foster parents, the Bernsteins, David had yet to acquire the chops for a transoceanic trip. He'd only learned to fly in the last five years, since he'd discovered he was the son of Hera, Goddess of Marriage, and some guy who'd lived in Jerusalem a couple millennia ago.

David shifted in his seat, trying to find a comfortable position. He'd been traveling ten-plus hours and was feeling it, especially in his butt. The flight for Athens had departed from Seattle-Tacoma International Airport a couple of hours late due to security concerns, which culminated with a burly pair of Federal marshals extricating a grandmotherly-looking woman from the seat behind David.

"Such a crazy world," the man across the aisle had remarked. David had nodded in agreement, thinking *and he doesn't know the half of it.*

Watching the Atlantic was making him nauseous. David looked away from the window and rummaged for the airsick bag in the pocket on the seat in front of him. *This is nuts* he thought for about the thousandth time. He'd sold his bike, his computer, everything he owned that wouldn't fit into his backpack and was bound for a behind-the-scenes city the mortal world didn't know existed. For two hundred years he'd study for a masters' degree. If his talents proved satisfactory, he'd become an entry-level manager at Olympus, Inc. The whole adventure was insane, but what other choice did he have? He didn't have the education or training to apply for the openings Olympus, Inc., had in the Seattle area, and he couldn't stay there working in a mortal job, aging one year for every hundred.

These sober reflections replaced his nausea with anxiety. He glanced at his seat-mate, a heavy, middle-aged man who needed deodorant and was dozing, his head lolling on his thick neck. David sighed, unzipped the middle compartment of his backpack and pulled out his dog-eared copy of *Mythology*. It was difficult enough, absorbing the fact of his own immortality even after the Bernsteins had lifted the forgetfulness charm he'd been under since he was a baby and allowed him to remember events of his earlier life. Now he'd be meeting Big-G Gods and Goddesses of legend, and they were all family! Veronica had advised him to brush up on names, how individuals were related to each other and what duties they performed. David flipped through the pages, quizzing himself. Aphrodite, Apollo, Ares, Athena—why did so many of them have to have names starting with "A"?

After a few minutes of study David's eyelids drooped. He stowed the book, leaned back and tried to focus on the complete bonus of seeing one of the world's most famous ruins—the Acropolis. Instead, he thought about the weird instructions he'd received for finding the portal to the City of Mount Olympus. A print-out of Veronica's e-mail was in his backpack, something about blurring his eyes a little bit, until they caught a sliver of golden light…

David's stomach rumbled. The in-flight meal had been flavorless and smaller than a mouse's doggie bag. He thought of the two remaining energy bars in the outer pocket of his backpack but fell asleep before he could reach for them.

THURSDAY

Clifford

Clifford gripped the clipboard propped in his lap so hard his knuckles ached. He didn't mind meetings in general and usually enjoyed strategic planning sessions but when it was just the three of them—suffice it to say, Hermes was not his favorite person.

He glanced around the dark corners of the CEO office in quest of—what, exactly? Something to focus on so he could avoid the warm smiles Veronica showered on Hermes. Clifford knew he should not react to this seeming favoritism. It was not appropriate to take Veronica's behavior toward another department head personally. Besides, there was work to be done.

"And that's your recommendation on the Seattle situation, Clifford?"

Clifford snapped back from his jealous musings to the business at hand. He cleared his throat and glanced down at his clipboard as if he needed to refresh his memory. "To discourage our intervention at this juncture? Yes, Ms. Zeta, that's my advice."

His face warmed. He sounded as prim as a boiled shirt. Why did he always talk like a git?

"I still say my robotics crew should have a look at Bertha," Hermes said in a pleasant tone, though Clifford sensed a challenge. "Should be easy to charm the project engineers into believing we're from the Japanese company that made her."

Hermes beamed a perfect, white smile at the boss. Of course his teeth were perfect, being a son of Zeus, which made him Veronica's half-brother. Not that incest was a barrier to Big-G romance, Clifford thought bitterly.

"That's a possibility, Hermes," Veronica said, smiling again at her favorite.

Clifford acknowledged, silently and grudgingly, that Hermes could indeed solve this sticky mortal mechanical and engineering problem. Under his surfer-dude build and shaggy gray-blonde hair lurked the mind of a genius and the curiosity of a cat.

"If the tunnel project is stalled longer than expected," Veronica continued, "I may take you up on it. But now," she turned toward Clifford, "we have a more pressing matter to address. What can you tell me, Clifford, about the cost of war?"

Clifford permitted himself a close-mouthed smile. At least Veronica respected his intelligence and entrusted him with sensitive projects. This was the second time she'd tapped him to analyze data from the Finance Department, though his own department was Architectural and Computer Services. He flipped the pages on his clipboard to the second tab and cleared his throat.

"The cost of war," he began, in an authoritative voice he hoped sounded like a BBC announcer, "increased significantly as a percentage of the Olympus, Inc., budget with the introduction of firearms. This increase has grown exponentially since the introduction of aircraft, which endowed mortals with long-range fighting capabilities."

Clifford paused and narrowed his eyes at Hermes. It was a well-churned rumor the former Winged Messenger had boosted the efforts of the Wright Brothers and other mortal inventors in their flying endeavors. Hermes smiled and shrugged his shoulders as if to say, "So what?" Veronica's lips twitched slightly upward.

Had this been a tennis match, Clifford was certain he'd just lost a point. He fingered the hem of his dress-code mandated toga, longing for the security of his tweed jacket and trousers.

"I've prepared two graphs," he said, rallying.

He pulled two sets of stapled sheets from his clipboard and handed them to Veronica and Hermes. Veronica scanned the first sheet from top to bottom, flipped the page and repeated the drill on the second sheet. Hermes set the report in his lap, unread.

"The first graph illustrates war as a percentage of budget for the past two millennia. The second graph," Clifford said, flipping to the second page, "shows current war expenditures by continent. The red bar represents Olympus, Inc., expenditures and the blue bar shows mortal expenditures."

"Interesting." Veronica held up the second graph and pointed to the third continent from the right. "Do you have information for this continent by country?"

Clifford's heart beat triumphantly. It felt magnificent to please her in some way. He riffled through the remainder of his stack and handed her another set of papers.

"I've taken the liberty of creating an additional report, highlighting social, religious and economic factors that may be important in interpreting the data."

His reluctant smile (he was painfully aware of his slightly crooked and discolored teeth) was returned by her gleaming approval. She pointed to the leftmost continent.

"And how about this one?"

Again he handed her the requested report.

She nodded as if to say thanks and pored over the documents.

"This is extremely interesting, Clifford, extremely interesting," she said after a few minutes of study. Veronica rose and extended her hand. "Thank you so much."

Clifford's jaw tightened as he stood and shook her hand. He was being dismissed! Dratted Hermes smiled up at him with eyebrows raised but made no movement to leave. Clifford held his head high and hoped he didn't look as foolish as he felt. Being admired for his brain was not enough. It had never been enough since the first moment he'd seen Veronica. At the time he'd been trapped inside Seattle's Space Needle, his molecules dispersed to reinforce the structure and make it safe for mortal use. It was no better now, trapped as he was by being himself instead of handsome, exciting Hermes.

He tempered his pace so as not to appear to be running away and passed the reception desk, bidding old Stella good day. There was much to do before his vacation. He should be glad he'd been released from the meeting at the earliest possible moment.

Clifford's mood ebbed lower as the elevator descended to his fifth-floor office suite. Mum and Ralph were visiting next week. They had recently rekindled their romance from college days, the romance that had led to Clifford's creation, and were absolutely wallowing in it. He dreaded seeing them. How long could he tolerate their lovey-dovey presence when his own romance had yet to take wings?

Zeus

The Ex-Lord of the Universe stood back, viewed his creation, and found it good.

It was a bold move—Zeus had given Cook the night off.

He'd shrunk the vast, carved dining table to a cozy table-for-two, illuminated by ever-burning candles and imitation moonlight through a conjured window. The air was filled with music—soft, sweet folk songs from the early days of their marriage—and scented with honeysuckle that twined gracefully up a golden lattice. Dinner waited in the kitchen, suspended at the perfect temperature as charmed by the caterer, ready-to-serve from a golden cart.

Zeus was off from babysitting as Thursday was Aster's play group day. He'd been working on dinner since Hera left for the office. First he'd called Club Dionysus to order all her favorites—

dolmades, moussaka, spanakopita and tacos, with ambrosia gelato for dessert. Dionysus himself took the order and suggested appropriate wine pairings for each dish, which Zeus accepted with a twinge of guilt. Hera had been bleary-eyed when she'd gone out the door this morning.

But how else was he supposed to get Hera, as she was now, to pay attention without wine on offer? It was an integral tool in the romantic battle he would pitch this evening. Tuesday's unpleasantness—when he'd forgotten once again to tell Cook what to make for dinner and had become the object of Hera's well-deserved rage—had given him pause. All day Wednesday, even during his hours of play with Aster, he'd pondered how everything had gone so wrong. Reviewing the past year with honesty, he'd concluded he was depressed. Since he'd stepped down as CEO of Olympus, Inc., he'd cut himself off from everything and everyone, except Aster.

After absorbing the shock of his realization Zeus had formed a resolution to reach beyond his own introspective world, to set his disturbingly diminished life on a larger stage, to impress Hera as he had in the old days.

Tonight was the night! Zeus glanced once more at his masterfully set table, plates nested atop each other for every course, golden eating utensils flanking the plates, goblets in shapes and sizes appropriate for each variety of wine lined up like soldiers at attention.

And now, to dress for the occasion! In his private bedroom, Zeus traded his dowdy house toga for one of snow-white linen. He placed a silver laurel wreath atop his still-thick white curls to look the part of the victor and opened the connecting door to the marital suite. Stale air tickled his nostrils. He strode into the suite and opened the windows wide.

Zeus felt a pang of anxiety. He'd worked so hard, planned the evening so carefully, but what if Hera's interest couldn't be aroused?

The doorbell chimed. He'd given the butler the night off, too. Zeus exited the marital suite, trotted through his bedroom and down the marble-floored hallway. A second volley of chimes pealed as he arrived. Zeus took a deep breath, grasped the knob and opened the door.

"My dear!" he said, throwing his arms wide to greet his wife.

Instead of leaping into his embrace, Hera stepped back and viewed him with suspicion.

"Where's Hughes?" she demanded, eyes narrowing. "You didn't irritate him so much he quit, did you?"

Her words stung but Zeus mastered himself and didn't let it show. His laurel wreath had been premature—the battle was just beginning.

"My dear," he repeated in a coaxing, gentle tone. He reached toward her, grasped her hand and drew her over the threshold. "I've given good old Hughes the night off."

Zeus led Hera to the den from which he'd banished the big-screen television, recliners and Aster's toys. In their place was a well-cushioned love seat and a low, candle-lit table, topped with chilled champagne and caviar.

"You've been working so hard lately," he said as he gestured for her to sit. She pulled her hand from his and continued to stand, glaring at him.

"What are you up to?" she growled. "What are you trying to hide?"

Tartarus. How could he have forgotten! In the first millennium AD he'd twice employed champagne and caviar to soothe Hera's rage when she'd caught him cheating.

The searing need to be in Hera's good graces nearly overwhelmed Zeus but the Big-G in him rallied. He would not, could not let his remorse spoil this evening. It would only make things worse between them.

"Nothing to hide, my dear," he drawled. He grasped her hand again, hard enough to tip her off her platform sandals and on to the love seat. Zeus sat alongside her and lifted a champagne flute. "A little bubbly?"

Hera raised an eyebrow. He looked back at her with unblinking innocence. When at last she muttered, "Whatever," he could smell the wine on her breath.

Zeus filled a flute and passed it to her. The look of longing she spared the bubbles pummeled his self-esteem, but he merely smiled—this was war.

She held the flute by the stem, waiting. At least she still had the self-control to remember her manners. He filled his own glass and raised it.

"To us," he said, clinking his flute lightly against hers.

"Whatever." She downed her champagne in a single gulp.

Zeus took two sips while he recovered from her sarcasm.

"You've been working so hard lately," Zeus said again, laboring to get his plan back on track. "Your new program's caught on so quickly with the mortals. I'm probably way out of date on what's new with Marriage and the Media."

Mention of her pet project hit the mark. Hera leaned back and smiled a little. She'd missed with her lipstick and left a slash of crimson on her teeth. Zeus quickly looked at her eyes to avoid telegraphing this blunder.

"At last." She held out her flute for a refill. Her smile deepened as the bubbles rose. "After all these millennia I'm finally doing something interesting. It makes me feel…"

She stopped talking, shook her head and downed half of her champagne.

Zeus leaned toward her and took her free hand.

"Something's troubling you, my dear. What is it?"

"Everything's been so damned perfect until now," Hera muttered, "but there've been rumors circulating. The mortals, of course," she said with a snort of disgust. "They're so suspicious, always looking for a reason to tear somebody down. Makes me ten kinds of furious just to think about it."

She polished off her drink, set her flute on the table and folded her arms defensively over her stomach.

For a sickening moment Zeus wondered if the rumors involved Hera. Had he been so inattentive that she, at sixty-six hundred years of age, had taken a lover? But no. Mortals, for the most part, didn't know Hera existed.

"Candy," Hera grunted.

Zeus reached for the plate of caviar and blinis. "I'm afraid I opted for something savory to go with the—"

"Not to eat!" she snapped, regarding him as if he were the village idiot. "I'm talking about Candy Smith. One of the mortal tabloids ran a piece on her today. They claim Candy's marriage is in a shambles."

Candy Smith. Zeus recalled the gorgeous but volatile former small-g rain goddess. She was the Marriage and the Media spokesperson, the immortal who was the face of the Marvelous Marriage books and seminars designed and developed for mortals.

"I can't have it, Zeus!" She clenched her fists and looked up at the ceiling. "It will destroy everything I've worked for. I'll—" she looked at him, tears welling in her bloodshot eyes. "I'll look like a complete and utter fool!"

Zeus set down his glass. "There, there," he said, easing his arms around her shaking shoulders and patting her back.

"Oh, Zeusy."

Hera sobbed, tears and mascara smudging the shoulder of Zeus' pristine toga. He smiled. She still needed him to be strong for her. In a few minutes she quieted, drew back from him and blotted her tear-stained cheeks with her fingertips.

"I'm sorry," she said, her voice choked. She leaned forward, picked up a blini and smothered it with sour cream and caviar. "Mmmm, tastes so good," she said after the first bite. "It was so hectic at the office today I missed lunch."

He watched her eat, noticed her cheeks were hollow. Had he been so caught up in his own depression he'd missed her growing thin?

"You're an intelligent woman, Hera. You'll find a way to combat the rumors."

"She's coming to corporate next week." Hera helped herself to another blini. "I've insisted she bring her husband and their little boy, too. I won't have those damn, snoopy mortals saying they take separate vacations. And believe me," she said, raising a cocktail napkin to her lips to remove an errant splotch of sour cream, "I'll grill her royally to find out if the rumors have substance."

Zeus smiled ruefully. Hera had proven an excellent detective in ferreting out his indiscretions over the millennia. If there was dirt to be dug, poor Candy Smith didn't stand a chance of keeping her secrets.

"So glad you've found your appetite," Zeus said. He took Hera's elbow and prompted her to stand. "I've laid in a bit of a feast—"

"You remembered!" Hera said, clapping her palms together. "You remembered to tell Cook what to make for dinner!"

"On the contrary, I've given Cook the night off."

"But?"

His smiled. "Come along, wife."

As they passed through the dining room archway Hera gasped.

"Oh, Zeusy, it's lovely!"

She circled the table to study the elegant settings, raised her head appreciatively to listen to the music, gazed at the conjured moon beaming through the enchanted window.

Zeus seized a napkin and draped it over his arm.

"Tonight's menu will feature dolmades, moussaka, spanakopita and tacos," he said playfully, "each dish paired with—"

A shriek cut his presentation short.

"Honeysuckle?!"

It was not a shriek of delight. Zeus winced and waited for the other sandal to drop, his mind racing to figure out what was so offensive about decorating the lattice with her favorite flower.

There was a long silence.

"Something wrong, my love?" he asked, watching her expression build to rage.

Hera's fists balled at her sides.

"They're Demeter's favorite!"

She grabbed a bottle from the nearest ice bucket and stormed from the dining room.

Zeus heard the furious slap of platform sandals against marble, the slam of Hera's bedroom door as the fatal mistake registered in his brain. Honeysuckle had been his *first* wife's favorite flower.

FRiday

Veronica

Veronica Zeta had bent her personal code of ethics. She'd told Stella she'd be away from the office Friday afternoon for a dental appointment but the story was pure fiction. Clifford's cost of war analysis had provided the details necessary to complete her plan for ousting Ares. Today, she'd set the plan in motion.

Instead of reclining in a dentist's chair, Veronica was in her condo kitchen fussing with take-out boxes she'd picked up at the to-go window in the rear of Club Dionysus. Should she transfer the cucumber salad, pita bread and salami onto serving plates or leave them in the cardboard containers? Would Athena care, one way or the other?

She took a deep breath and willed the anxious twists out of her stomach. Athena had been Dad's favorite before Veronica came along, and Dad hadn't bothered to hide his feelings about his children. Both of them were resented by their other siblings.

Veronica admired and envied her half-sister's achievements. Athena had championed heroes, negotiated treaties, inspired a cult of worship that produced not only monuments but cities. The Goddess of War and Wisdom was one of few Big-Gs who worked independently of the family corporation. Veronica needed Athena much more than Athena needed Olympus, Inc.

"Serving plates," Veronica decided. As she reached up into a kitchen cupboard soft fur brushed her calves.

"Meow!"

Veronica sighed.

"What do you want, Bill?" she said without looking down.

She felt as guilty as Tartarus she'd left her cat alone so much lately, but work had been crazy busy. She never seemed to have the time or energy to appease him.

"Meow! Meow!" Bill Gates, Jr., persisted, butting his square head against her shin.

He'd crapped in her favorite sandals this week, probably in retaliation for her mistakenly buying dog kibble instead of cat kibble when his automatic feeder had gone empty last Sunday. Busy as she was, she'd corrected her error the same day.

Veronica set three small oval platters on the counter and

reached down to scratch the cat behind the ears.

"Cut me some slack, will you?" she said, wondering what he would crap in when he learned she'd invited an owl to lunch.

Veronica's stomach clenched. Athena was the most gifted Big-G of her generation. Who did she think she was, trying to persuade Athena to go corporate? Athena was a rock star in the Pantheon. She'd done everything worth doing. All Veronica had to show for her twenty-six hundred years, besides being CEO, was the completion of her PhD in Business and Organizational Theory at Athens U. She shivered. Even her alma mater was named for her extraordinary half-sibling! You couldn't swing a lynx in Athens or Paris or even Nashville, Tennessee, without hitting a monument to Athena.

She took another deep breath and commanded herself to calm down. Athena was brilliant, wasn't that the point? The very qualities Veronica envied made Athena the perfect ally in removing Ares. As a bonus, she was female. Clifford's analysis had suggested a solution to war, elegant in its simplicity: as war activity and cost was highest in countries dominated by male leadership, increasing the number of female leaders should curb those activities and costs. Where better to initiate war reform than to make a change in management at Olympus, Inc.?

That horrible phrase, "It's a man's universe," roiled in Veronica's brain. Ares had made a career of perpetuating his own cruel, cowardly nature through inciting mortals, predominantly male mortals, to solve their problems through killing and other forms of destruction. His big, brash mouth had shouted down Athena's efforts in settling mortal disputes. First she'd tried to counter his violent methods by aiding heroes in battle. As mortal civilization grew more sophisticated, she'd nurtured the seeds of diplomacy in great thinkers. They were both Gods of War but over the millennia Ares, a devoted gear-head, had gained control of the weapons. Unable to make meaningful headway in pitting her diplomatic efforts against Ares' bloody-minded dominance, Athena had shifted focus to the Wisdom aspect of her nature. She now served as provost of both Athens U and Athens Tech.

Veronica speared a stack of paper-thin salami with a serving fork and slapped it on a platter. Now was the time for a true revolution. Now was the age of Athena and a women's army!

She finished plating the food, consulted the kitchen chronometer and took the chilled bottle of Pinot Grigio from the refrigerator. Nearly time. Bill Gates, Jr., yowled in protest when she picked him up and hustled him into his kitty habitat, the guest bedroom featuring a floor-to-ceiling scratching post. It would ruin everything if the cat and Athena's owl had a set-to.

The two-tone doorbell chimed in chorus with Bill Gates, Jr.'s, muffled howls. Veronica smiled her best business smile, gripped the doorknob and opened the door to greet—

"Ares?!"

He stood on her welcome mat, grinning, dozens of medals (all of which he'd awarded himself) gleaming on his forward-thrust chest. Ares had the same flowing curls as Dad but his locks were unnaturally blackened by one of his few inventions, what the mortals called *Grecian Formula*.

"Yo, Ronnie." He pushed his way past her without invitation, scanned the entryway and peered toward the living room. "Nice place."

"*I* like it," she said, for once distressed that she'd decided against Hermes' recommendation to install a face recognition electronic security system. She squelched the instinct to peek out the door. Where in Tartarus was Athena, anyway? But her arrival now would only complicate things.

"I'm busy, Ares," she said, moving directly in front of him to block him from pushing his way farther in. "What do you want?"

From his lesser height he stared up his aquiline nose at her.

"That's what I like about you, Sis, nice and polite." He draped his arm around a bust of Queen Elizabeth I perched atop a pedestal, a prized piece of art Veronica had bought when she'd first taken the condo. "I was just talking to Dad about appropriations for the new front I got NATO into. He was playing with the damned baby again, can you believe it?"

Veronica crossed her arms. Zeus had never been interested in babies before, not even his own, which made it doubly weird. Was there ever a day when he didn't spend time with Aster? Veronica hadn't talked to Dad for so long she honestly couldn't say.

"Dad says you're in charge of the budget," Ares said. "This new operation is really strapping me. Do you have any idea how much it costs to keep jets in the air?"

Veronica raised an eyebrow. She had an excellent idea of what Ares' military exploits cost since reading Clifford's report. But Ares would have his usual blood-letting fit if he knew what she planned to do about him and his jets. The best course was to stall.

"Budget needs to be discussed at the office, Ares, not here. Call Stella and make an appointment."

Ares retracted his arm from the bust and straightened himself to his full five-foot-six.

"Honestly, Ronnie." He stamped his sandaled foot. "I'm broke, I tell you, and the member governments won't cough up another dime! All they do is whine about the global recession."

Veronica, too, straightened to her full height and peered down. She gripped the edge of the front door. The cold, satisfied feeling she'd had when she'd demoted Hephaestus earlier this week tingled in her chest. Only the need to keep her possession of The Power hidden from Ares until a later time prevented her from vibing him now.

"I'm busy, Ares." She tilted her head curtly toward the door. "Make an appointment."

The God of War scowled darkly.

"If you think you can get high-handed with me, Ronnie, you're sadly mistaken. And if I were you," a malicious grin spread across his lips, "I wouldn't let that cat of yours outside. Accidents happen to small animals all the time."

He paused and leered significantly before storming out of the condo.

Veronica slammed the door behind him. Her heart hammered. How dare he threaten Bill Gates, Jr.! She sagged against the door, her nerves raw.

She'd just started to breathe again when the doorbell chimed. This time she looked out the peek-hole. A vast, golden eye peered back and a hoot sounded on the other side of the door. She rallied the same, forced smile she'd pasted on earlier and opened the door to Athena.

Veronica read the look of a sagacious warrior in Athena's gleaming, silver eyes. Her luxuriant, fair hair was pulled back and fastened with a golden cord, accenting high cheekbones and a determined, square jaw.

"Thank you for coming, Athena." She extended her hand.

Athena returned a firm handshake while Tim, her pet owl, rotated his head as if assessing the security of the condo.

"We saw Ares on the way here," Athena said, her voice deep and calm. "Thank Zeus I was able to cloak before he saw us."

Jealousy kindled in Veronica's stomach. So Dad had taught Athena the secret of Biggest of Big-G cloaking, something she, herself had had to learn by stealth! What other powers had he entrusted to Athena?

Veronica, thirsting for a sip of Pinot Grigio, waved Athena toward the kitchen.

"Ares is the last person I'd hoped to see this afternoon," Veronica said as she removed the cork from the bottle. She poured two stemmed glasses half-full and handed one to Athena, who raised it to the light and studied the liquid with apparent skepticism.

"I'm not one for tricks, Athena, there's nothing in the wine but wine." Veronica clinked her glass against Athena's. "Cheers."

Athena and the owl swiveled their heads toward each other, seeming to form a tacit agreement.

"Cheers," Athena replied.

The owl hooted softly. The half-sisters raised the wine to their lips and sipped.

"I have a proposal for you," Veronica said, her tone grave. "If you accept," she motioned Athena to a chair in the dining alcove, "I'm reasonably certain the mortal world will soon be untroubled by Ares."

David

David bounced and jostled through the crowded streets of Athens, nearing the end of an hour-plus bus ride from Athens International Airport. He was bound for the Acropolis, what his undergrad history of architecture text called "the city on the hill." Modern structures blurred by in his periphery, pale facades with red-tiled roofs interspersed with multi-storied apartment buildings. One more stop and he'd be at the portal to the hidden City of Mount Olympus.

The bus rattled to a halt on Theorias Street, disgorged David and lurched away, leaving a thick trail of black smoke. David slung his backpack over his shoulders, walked on travel-stiffened legs to the ticket kiosk and paid twelve Euros to the young woman working there in exchange for a ticket and a brochure.

It was mid-afternoon. White sun beat down, compounding his fatigue. David walked to the nearest spot of shade and opened the brochure to study the map. If he wasn't so worn out he'd visit all the sights—would linger to study the Propylaea, the great entryway standing before him, and venture to the south side to see the Theatre of Dionysus. Instead, he touched his finger to the map and traced the most direct path to the Parthenon.

David joined the crowds and climbed the broad marble steps of the Propylaea, admiring the fluted columns at the top of the structure as he passed between them. Ahead and to his right sat the Parthenon. He stopped and closed his eyes for a moment, feeling the weight of history and the wisdom of Athena (who was, by his figuring, his cousin through Hera). The Parthenon was her temple, and within lay the portal to Mount Olympus.

The most famous ruin in the world was crawling with tourists, many of them approximately his mortal age of twenty and similarly outfitted in jeans, tee-shirts and backpacks. He'd have to be careful no one noticed when he vanished from this world into another.

David sat on a rock outside the temple. He rifled through his backpack, through the clean underwear, extra socks and toothbrush to find his last energy bar. Removing the wrapper and tucking it in to his jeans pocket, David chewed thoughtfully. When he'd consumed the bar and licked the sticky traces from his fingers he searched the backpack again for the printout of Veronica's instructions.

She'd given him the option of entering through the Parthenon or catching a special express from the airport to the City of Mount Olympus. A lover of architecture, David had opted for the Parthenon, though she'd warned him this route had complications.

Her e-mail was brief. He was to go to the west end of the temple, locate the third column from the left, let his eyes blur until he saw golden light, then close his eyes and walk toward the light.

It wasn't much to go on. Anxious, he shouldered his backpack and entered the temple.

The tourists were packed into the east end of the Parthenon, caught in the spell of an animated tour guide delivering his patter. David walked to the west end, the guide's description of the statue of Athena that had once dominated the cella echoing behind him. He passed along the south frieze until he reached the corner, counted from the corner to the third column, took a deep breath and blurred his eyes. All he saw was a fuzzy column.

David released a frustrated breath. Had he come this far for nothing? An inner voice coached him to think. Had Veronica missed a critical nuance in her instructions? On impulse, he took several steps back until he could easily view the designated column as well as those to its right and left. He tried again.

"Wow!"

Slivers of golden light danced around the column. All he had to do now was close his eyes and walk toward the light. David measured the path in his mind, dropped his eyelids and paced toward his goal.

"Hell," he muttered after his third attempt. No matter what he tried, his kept drifting several yards to the right. David stomped toward the impassible column as if he meant to argue with it, stared up the tall expanse of marble and the white-blue sky above.

"Hell and damnation!"

"Strong words there, youngster," crackled an ancient voice.

David jumped. An elderly man, bent with age and dressed in a toga, stood beside him.

"Whoo-hoo, you should see the look on your face!" The man chuckled and slapped his ancient knee. "Ms. Zeta told me to keep a look-out for you, in case you had trouble getting through. Good thing!" He extended a gnarled hand. "Name's Myclops. Brother of Cyclops. I'm a lot shorter than he was but at least I have two eyes, thank Zeus!"

Myclops' sky-blue eyes crinkled until they almost squeezed shut.

"David Bernstein," said David, taking the man's hand and receiving a jolt. "Yiii!"

"Whoo-hoo! Gotcha!" Myclops raised his right hand. A joy buzzer was strapped to his palm. "Just a little something Hermes brought me from his last trip out. What a riot that boy is."

Myclops stopped laughing and held out his other hand, palm up.

"I can let you in as soon as you make your offering."

"Offering?" David blinked behind his Coke-bottle lenses. The instructions hadn't mentioned an offering. He looked around, relieved to see the other tourists were still at the east end, entranced by the tour guide.

"Nothing bloody, that's my only rule," Myclops said in a lowered voice. He shoved his hand farther forward. "Just a little something, a token of appreciation for my services."

David opened his backpack and reviewed the contents. He handed Myclops an unused disposable razor.

"Hmm." Myclops took the razor by the handle and stared at it. "Won't do much good on the sheep, but thanks for the thought." He tucked the razor somewhere in the folds of his toga and raised an elbow. "Take my arm, sonny, and we'll be off."

The old man's arm felt like parchment wrapped around a piece of dowel. Myclops drew David a few yards back from the column and approached it straight on. "Close your eyes, now," he coached.

David shut his eyes and Myclops propelled him forward. For an instant the tip of his nose seared. Before he had time to finish saying "Ouch!" they were standing on a green hillside with a gentle grade. Leafy trees grew here and there and birdsong wafted through the air.

Myclops glanced at David apologetically.

"Forgot to mention the side-effect folks have their first time through," the old man said, tapping the tip of his blue-veined nose. "It's been a while since I've had a new visitor. They'll have something for the burn at Corporate." Myclops took David by the shoulder, turned him half-way around and pointed. "Just over the next hill and down and up and down again."

He thanked Myclops, who bowed and disappeared. David shrugged and started up the first hill, hoping Myclops' instructions were more complete than Veronica's.

Just past the crest of the second hill David looked down on a vast, flat roof. As he walked down the slope a white marble wall seemed to grow alongside him, resolving in a multi-story building that overlooked a dense city below. The front of the building featured a wide entryway, adorned with Ionic columns. David counted ten, maybe eleven floors—somehow the number kept changing on him. Six white marble stairs stretched the length of the façade.

Toga-wearing persons of both genders moved in and out of the building, probably coming and going from an afternoon break according to the time shown on his watch. David ascended the stairs, feeling underdressed in jeans and tee-shirt.

The quality of the marble used for the columns was a better grade than any he'd seen in the mortal world. He passed underneath the pediment, the carved eyes of the figure of Zeus staring down at him from the center. David shivered, though he realized there was nothing he, himself, could have done to stop Hera from cuckolding her husband two thousand years ago. Hopefully Zeus, the Ex-CEO, wouldn't be anywhere near the corporate office today.

The lobby of Olympus, Inc., was constructed of the same excellent marble as the columns. Broad staircases with gold railings swept to the left and the right, with an atrium in between. In front of the atrium stood a directory. Veronica's office was on the sixth floor. Elevators, the directory indicated, were on the mezzanine.

David ascended the nearest staircase, smiling at the people he passed. Some smiled back, others looked away after taking in his attire. On the mezzanine he stood between two banks of elevator doors and pushed the up arrow button. The first pair of doors that rolled open expelled a trio of young women who giggled as they passed.

David's heart stuttered. Girls! He'd been so absorbed in his travel plans it had never occurred to him there'd be girls working at Olympus, Inc., headquarters! David selected the button marked VI and jabbed it, grinning. Two hundred years might not be so long after all.

He'd toured most of the sixth floor before he found Veronica's office, prestigiously located on a corner. "Veronica Zeta, Assistant CEO" read the gold plaque on the half-open door. David knocked tentatively.

"Uh, hi?"

"Come in," said a female voice—not Veronica's.

He opened the door wider and stepped in. Behind a sleek desk with gold legs and a glass top sat the prettiest girl he'd seen today, or possibly ever. Her sapphire blue eyes were large and tilted up at the corners, like a cat's. Her face was heart-shaped, her hair jet black and chin-length with bangs. And from what he could see of her figure without being obvious—wow!

"Can I help you?"

David closed his mouth after belatedly realizing his jaw had dropped.

"Do I have the wrong office?" he blundered, feeling like an idiot. "I mean, I'm here to see Veronica. Uhm, I mean, Ms. Zeta."

The girl looked him over, stopping at the tip of his nose. Her smile broadened.

"You must be David. Let me get you something for that burn."

The girl stood up and turned toward one of two doors on the back wall. David gasped, impressed by both her perfect curves and her height—six feet tall, at least! When she entered what he assumed was some kind of supply room he glanced at the placard on her desk.

Her name was Cleo Petra.

She reappeared, brandishing a small white tube.

"Just the thing," she said. She squeezed a ribbon of ointment from the tube onto her index finger and moved in on him. He tried not to look down, his eyes level with her chin. When she dabbed the unguent on his nose it made his knees wobble.

"It'll be better in no time." She re-capped the tube and said, "Back in a sec," as she returned to the supply room. He heard the sound of running water, the crackle of a stiff paper towel.

When she returned she motioned him to sit on a couch for visitors and resumed her seat.

"I'm Veronica's assistant, Cleo Petra."

Her expression was friendly but held a trace of mirth that made David uneasy. Had Veronica told this beauty to keep an eye out for her idiotic pup of a half-brother? The thought made his face burn.

"I guess I should have made an appointment," David said, brazening through his embarrassment. "I take it she's out?"

"Oh no, she's in. She's definitely in."

Cleo rolled her eyes and shook her head as if she disapproved of something.

David looked toward the second door, the one he assumed led to Veronica's office.

"She spends most of her time in the CEO suite these days." Cleo reached for a digital pad that lay on her desk. "I'll send a message and let her know you're here. So," she said as she tapped the screen, "how was your trip?"

"Great," he said, incapable of a more detailed response as he'd grown mesmerized by the graceful movement of her hands.

"Good," she said. "That's what we like to hear."

A soft bell chimed.

"David, you're in luck," said Cleo, looking up from her pad. "Veronica's just come back from a dental appointment. You can see her now, if you hurry."

David thanked Cleo and strode to the elevators. A car stood waiting, doors open. He entered and pressed a button on the top of the panel marked "CEO" that he hadn't noticed before. The ride was mere seconds, the elevator lifting so quickly his knees buckled. The doors opened onto a reception area with walls of polished onyx and twenty-foot ceilings. It reminded him of a mausoleum he'd seen on a tour with his foster parents when he was a kid, a place where kings and queens had been interred, but he couldn't remember exactly where or when. Slightly nauseated, David touched the tip of his scorched nose, ran a hand over his unruly black curls and drew a shallow breath, anticipating the smell of formaldehyde.

But a different scent curled in his nostrils, something cold and stern, like a costly and subtle aftershave: the smell of power. On the far side of the reception area, a single chair sat before a desk the color of bronze. Behind the desk, sitting very straight with her mouth twisted sourly downward, was a woman who made David think of Medusa, but with steel gray helmet-hair instead of snakes.

She wasn't Medusa, he realized, when his flesh remained flesh instead of turning to stone. David tentatively approached the woman, feeling small and vulnerable in the heavy, dark surroundings. When he was close enough to read the name plate on the desk he screwed up his nerve and introduced himself.

"Hi, Stella, I'm—"

"I *know* who you are," she barked, her copper-colored eyes blazing with annoyance. "This is the executive office, young man, and we *rarely* tolerate walk-ins. As if we didn't have enough to do," she muttered. "Miss Zeta is running herself ragged with new programs and me along with her, thoughtless child."

David drew back a step.

"Don't look so shocked, hatchling," Stella snapped. "I have enough seniority to speak my mind. Zeus knows I've done plenty for Himself over the centuries to earn the right. Close your gaping yaw and have a seat!"

She gestured forcefully at the chair in front of her desk. When

David was seated he noticed the front legs were shorter than the back ones and pitched the chair uncomfortably forward. Stella jabbed her index fingertip on an intercom button and announced, "Another of your *half*-siblings to see you, Miss Zeta."

David winced. He knew it was childish to feel the sting of being called a bastard (especially as his birth mother was Hera) but he'd grown up in the mortal world with mortal conventions.

"Send him in, Stella."

The voice issuing from the intercom was familiar, but impatient. Acid reflux rose in David's throat. Maybe Veronica didn't want him here after all? Stella jerked her head toward a door in the wall behind her. The door opened soundlessly, revealing another vast room.

David's eyes adjusted to the increased darkness. He squinted to make out Veronica's face, floating above a hulking black desk edged with gold. As he gained focus he could see her lips were tight.

"David," she said, with the barest hint of warmth.

He advanced to the comfortable-looking black armchair she pointed to, shifted his backpack off his shoulders and sat.

"Hi. Did I come at a bad time?" Maybe her mouth hurt after being at the dentist? "I—I guess I should have e-mailed you before I left Seattle?"

"No. No, every day is the same. Welcome to Mount Olympus," she said with scant enthusiasm. "Unfortunately, I don't have time to show you around myself. So much to do."

Veronica looked at a digital pad on her desk. She pulled up some sort of list and scrolled down and down and down some more.

"Heaven and Earth!" she said under her breath. "No one available with the right credentials except Pan. I guess he'll have to do."

Pan. When David heard the name, a snippet of raucous flute music scrambled his brain.

"You mean, *the* Pan?"

"Oh, David." Veronica flopped back in her chair. "Try not to sound like a tourist! Everyone in the Greek Pantheon actually exists and most of us live and work on Mount Olympus. Please don't make a fool of yourself."

"Sorry, I—"

Her expression softened.

"I don't mean to be short with you," she said, "it's just that I'm out-of-my-mind busy and every project has a miniscule timeline." She tapped out a line or two and hit enter. "There," she said. "I've asked him to meet you at the Campus Pub tomorrow at five. Stella can give you directions. Oh, and you'll be staying at the Athenian

Hotel until classes start. Any chariot driver will know where that is."

Veronica stood and so did he. She reached across the desk and took his hand, her grip strong but her fingers cold.

"I *am* glad to see you," she said with the trace of a smile. "We'll have coffee when you get settled."

David passed back into reception where Stella grudgingly handed him a map of greater Mount Olympus. In the elevator he braced himself for a blindingly fast descent but the car floated gently down to the mezzanine level. By the time he reached the street in front of Olympus, Inc., corporate offices and waved down a passing chariot, David was humming the raucous tune that had recently scrambled his brain, the tune that meant Pan.

SaTURDaY

David

David Bernstein rose early his first morning in the City of Mount Olympus. He quickly showered, pulled on his jeans and tee-shirt, snagged a couple of pastries and a paper cup of thick, sweet coffee from the dining room and dashed out the front door of the Athenian Hotel. The sun was barely above the horizon and the streets were quiet. He turned west, bound for Athens U.

A kiosk at the campus entrance was well-stocked with brochures. David dumped his empty cup in a nearby garbage can, scanned the brochure rack and selected a map.

He strolled the vacant halls of the Architecture and Engineering Building, peered into silent classrooms, imagined himself seated amongst other students. What would they be like, he wondered, these young immortals who'd grown up fully aware of their infinite longevity? Would they know he was Hera's son?

The question evaporated—there was so much to see! He headed to the end of the corridor. There was no door; he simply passed through columns to the outside, his nose buried in the map. He paused and looked across an expanse of lawn at a long building the map identified as "dormitories." The dorms, like the rest of the buildings, were of the Doric Order of Greek architecture, the same style as the Parthenon, which was his next stop. To his delight, on the other side of campus was a common area shared by Athens U and Athens Tech with a full-scale model of the Acropolis!

David climbed the fully intact stairs of the Propylaea, passed through the gateway and gazed upon a pristine copy of the Parthenon. His heart beat in his throat as he approached the temple dedicated to Athena. He entered the cella. The huge statue of the Goddess of Wisdom towered above him, leaving him in open-mouthed awe. If the real Athena, provost of Athens U and Athens Tech, was this formidable, he'd probably pass out when he met her.

Blown away by his encounter with the statue, David left the campus and wandered onto a nearby street. He found a bookstore and lost himself in the huge selection of titles, in both regular book format and large-print scrolls for older readers. Wheeled ladders stood at intervals along the floor-to-ceiling shelves, and shoppers were free to climb up and down to examine the inventory. David launched himself up the ladder in a section marked "biography" and descended with a paperback copy of *The Gods of Today: Contemporary Lives of Zeus, Hera and Their Offspring* by Herodotus Jones. He didn't understand the price marked on the back but handed a prim-looking male clerk a twenty-dollar bill, hoping it was enough. The man surveyed David from head to toe.

"Interesting costume," he sneered as he rang up the sale. He handed David the book and three flat copper coins.

"Thanks a lot," said David, just to make the guy wonder.

He left the bookstore and looked for familiar landmarks, something to lead him back to his hotel where he could change into a less conspicuous get-up. This morning he'd laughed at the idea of wearing a toga, though he'd found three such garments and a pair of sandals in his closet.

At five minutes to five he stood on the sidewalk above the Campus Pub, his fingers pinching the toga's mid-thigh hem. It was a lot to get used to, the breezy feeling underneath. He loped down the stairs, anticipating the next excellent prospect of the day—getting into a bar and meeting Pan!

The stairs terminated at the pub entrance; a bright green door, the portal to a windowless basement. The interior was a disappointment. Far from appearing foreign and exotic, the Campus Pub looked a lot like what he'd seen through the doorway of Seattle's most popular U-District tavern—grubby wooden booths filled with college-aged people, though they wore togas instead of jeans.

David's stomach rumbled like Mount Vesuvius. He hadn't eaten much since morning. Cooking aromas wafted in the air. Would there be moussaka? Spanakopita? Dolmades? His mouth watered so hard he had to suck in the saliva before he drooled.

A hearty slap on the back nearly made him choke.

"Hey, stranger!" nickered an earthy voice.

David turned toward a guy approximately his age who was disturbingly bare-chested and sported a goatee.

"I'm Pan," the guy said. "Pan by name, pan by nature." He clamped his hands to his ribs and laughed uproariously at his own joke, one that David didn't quite get. "Here to show you around, cousin." The God of Shepherds and Flocks laughed again. "Can't swing a stoat without hitting family in this place."

"David Bernstein," David said, grinning nervously.

Pan's hair echoed the wild light in his eyes, his deranged curls standing up in twists and tufts that resembled horns.

"Happy hour, the best time of day," Pan announced to the room, though no one seemed to notice. He swaggered toward a vacant booth. His legs, sprouting from beneath a sort of loin cloth, were so hairy they looked thatched. David saw with relief that his companion's legs ended in sandal-clad feet instead of hooves. He followed in Pan's wake and wondered out loud about the legal drinking age.

"If you have enough vocabulary to place an order, you qualify," Pan assured as he sprawled on a high-backed bench joined to a table. David slid onto the bench opposite, his eyes flitting over the riot of initials and hearts carved into the heavy wooden table top.

Pan let loose a whistle and signaled a barmaid across the crowded, noisy cavern. He held up two fingers, gave a "thumbs up" and fired off a lewd wink. The barmaid, a plain-faced girl with a large chest, shot back a look of annoyance and a quick nod.

"She's crazy about me," Pan said, his head tilted at a rakish angle.

David, though stunned by Pan's behavior, tried to stay in the spirit of things.

"Quite a looker," he said.

"If you're up for a tumble," Pan said with a horny leer, "tell me what kind of girl you like and I'll line one up."

David pictured Veronica's assistant, Cleo Petra, but immediately banished the image. Though he'd just met Pan, he was confident no woman in her right mind would have anything to do with this creepily lusty god.

A trio of young women entered the pub. They headed toward the vacant booth across from Pan and David's but quickly changed course when Pan shouted, "Yo! Babes!" and favored them with a shoulder shimmy.

"They're all crazy about me, every one of 'em."

David sighed. Pan was a lot like his former University of Washington roommate, Michael. Whenever David had gone somewhere with Michael, girls had treated them both like social pariahs. He had to get free of this jerk if he hoped to have any kind of social life.

"What do you do at Olympus, Inc.?" asked David, partly to change the subject but mostly because he wondered what sort of work Veronica would assign to someone like Pan.

"Hah! They'd be up a creek without me!" Pan boasted. "I'm the liaison between the herdsmen and the factories. There'd be no commercially available goat cheese without me!"

David knew nothing about the cheese industry. He groped for what he could remember from *Mythology*.

"And Hermes is your dad?" he ventured.

"That's his story and he's sticking to it," Pan returned with a wink. "Not so sure about my mom's identity. Rumor has it she's one of the Pleiades, but none of the silly cows will claim me." For a nanosecond Pan's expression turned wistful. "Jealous of each other, that's my guess," he said with an over-bright grin.

"At least you have some idea who both your parents are," David said, mostly to himself.

"Ho-ho, that's right, you're Hera's dirty little secret!"

David looked away, pretending he could see far enough to read the chalk-on-blackboard menu hanging behind the bar.

"Don't let it get you down, cousin." Pan's softened tone drew David back. "Honestly, dude, most of us here are bastards, so welcome to the club. Ah, here she is," he said, his tone recovering its loathsome, lecherous quality as the barmaid arrived with two tankards and a covered dish on a tray. "Thank you, dearest nymph, from the bottom of my heart," Pan said. He reached under the table as if to grab his crotch.

"Stuff it!" She slammed their order on the tabletop. Ale sloshed from the tankards.

"Ooooh! Is that an offer?" Pan taunted.

"You can pay the cashier," the barmaid shouted over her shoulder.

"Absolutely crazy about me," Pan cackled. "And now, for today's special."

David's stomach growled. What exotic treat lay under the dome?

"Our drink, Ganymede's Pale Ale. Our appetizer," Pan said, raising his shaggy eyebrows for added drama, "a delicacy discovered by Zeus himself as he traveled world-wide."

He whisked away the dome and revealed a steaming mound of beans and cheese atop tortilla chips.

"Nachos!"

SUNOAY

Zeus

The gods slept in on Sunday, except for Zeus.

He'd slept poorly ever since the disastrous Thursday night dinner. What a fool he'd been, thinking honeysuckle was Hera's favorite flower! After tossing and turning three nights it had come to him. It was jasmine she adored!

Another realization had dawned as he lay, night after night, fretting over what had happened. Examining the evening objectively, he recalled feeling flickers of hope their marriage could be resuscitated.

Zeus plumped two extra pillows under his head and looked out the open eastern window of his private bedroom. He waited like a child anticipating the start of a holiday and leapt from his bed the instant the sun glinted over the horizon.

"Ouch!" He'd forgotten about the nagging lower back pain he experienced most mornings when he first arose. But the picture in his mind compelled him to also shout, "Yes!"

He donned a toga, stepped onto the window ledge, paused to position his arms in good flying form and leapt into the air.

"Aaaaaah!" he screamed as he plummeted past five of twelve floors. Zeus furiously flapped his arms and bellowed a spell for weightlessness. He was hovering in front of a second-floor window by the time he recovered himself and started to ascend. His heart hammered against his ribs.

"Rusty," he panted. Zeus couldn't remember the last time he'd flown. The muscles in his arms, legs and torso protested as he sluggishly rose up, up, up and turned west, bound for Athens U. There, jasmine bloomed year 'round.

Zeus flew at a leisurely pace, admiring the City of Mount Olympus, below. The downtown area featured luxury hotels, an opera house and a host of fine eateries, the marble sidewalks lined with shade-giving deciduous trees. A large plaza with a magnificent fountain in the center anchored the district. Even at this early hour a few people strolled there, pausing to watch the play of water.

Athens U lay west of downtown, as did Athens Tech. It had been his own good idea to locate the institutions side-by-side, with shared facilities (including the Great Library, the Nike Sports

Coliseum and a full-scale model of the Acropolis) in between. Pride swelled in Zeus' chest. It quelled abruptly when he remembered he'd built these wonders thousands of years ago.

He made a respectable two-point landing on the administration building lawn. Dew-dampened blades of grass tickled through his sandals. He'd long known that, in spite of being immortal, life would change as he grew older; until this moment, it hadn't felt personal. Zeus, Ex-Lord of the Universe, was someone he no longer recognized.

Zeus, Whoever He Was, strolled up a trellis-covered walkway. The subdued fragrance of slumbering jasmine surrounded him, conjuring memories of happier times. Yes, he'd been greatly feared and admired, the one immortal being everyone had revered and obeyed. But his happiness existed elsewhere. He was happiest when he felt loved.

He stopped, reached up, plucked a handful of the closed, delicate blossoms that opened only at night. Tonight he would steal into Hera's bedroom and place them on her pillow, a token to show her she, too, was loved.

week two - monday

Veronica

Veronica Zeta sat on a marble bench in the Athens U Rose Garden. Her fingertips drummed against stone. It was mid-morning. A blooming hedge of roses encircled the benches. Their fragrance made her nose itch. Fittingly, she'd told Stella she was seeing an allergist, a cover story for today's meeting with Athena.

She had arrived five minutes ahead of time, in case Athena could make an early escape from her weekly meeting with Dean Phineas. Veronica struggled to overcome her jealousy of Provost Athena of Athens U and Athens Tech. Would there ever be a place of higher learning dedicated to Veronica Zeta? She discarded the question; contemplating her legacy at twenty-six hundred was too morbid.

"Good morning."

The calm, deep voice, followed by a sleepy hoot, broke her musings.

"Good morning, Athena."

Veronica rose and extended her hand. She fleetingly wondered if it was proper business etiquette to also greet the owl, Tim, perched on Athena's shoulder, but decided against it.

"Thank you for meeting me this morning. Please, sit."

Veronica indicated the twin of her own bench, opposite. Once they were seated she raised and rotated an index finger, casting a spell to muffle their conversation from passersby. Athena's silver eyes bored into hers. Veronica swallowed, unnerved but unwilling to show it.

"So. You've considered my offer?"

"I have," said Athena. She reached up to stroke the owl, who'd shuttered his eyelids. "Your idea of creating a predominantly women's army is good."

Veronica waited, barely breathing. Was Athena saying yes or no to the newly-created position she'd been offered, Director of Armed Forces?

The Goddess of War and Wisdom ruffled Tim's head feathers. "It's the culture women have developed and passed down over hundreds of generations," Athena said, "the primary need to defend their children, their homes, even their men when necessary. The men, though they generally start wars to protect what they hold dear, are too often incited into conquest and mindless destruction by brother Ares." She paused and folded her hands in her lap. "I've outlined a possible solution to the problem."

"Go on," said Veronica.

"There are two phases to the solution. One challenge underlies them both. The first phase is securing female leadership in mortal diplomatic and military agencies. The mortals are already making slow progress in this direction, especially in the more developed countries. For the first phase, Olympus, Inc., would intervene with the mortals to accelerate this process."

Veronica nodded, holding her question of "How?" until she'd heard the rest of Athena's solution.

"The second phase," Athena continued, "is recruiting and training sufficient female soldiers to create a majority of women, including officers, in mortal armies. This will be a drastic cultural change, particularly in countries that are, as the mortals like to say it, traditional. The transition may take decades of political, social and religious realignment and could lead to wars in and of itself."

"The cost?" Veronica asked.

Athena raised an eyebrow. "In human life and treasure there's potential for great loss. But I believe over time the cost will be less than what the world spends today."

Was Athena's belief enough to go on? Veronica reserved this question for later contemplation.

"You mentioned Olympus, Inc., intervening with the mortals," she asked instead. "Can you tell me more at this point?"

"As you know, I'm well-experienced in diplomacy."

Veronica nodded.

"As a first step," Athena continued, "I would enter the mortal world, disguised as one of their number. I would promote the election or appointment of qualified women to military and diplomatic leadership roles and help create networks amongst these leaders."

Veronica bit her lip. To work directly with mortals for a prolonged period of time posed a security risk for the gods. Ares sometimes appeared to mortal armies, but only to incite rage; he disappeared once the spark of conflict had flamed.

"And the challenge that underlies your solution?" she asked, knowing the answer.

The Goddess of War and Wisdom squared her shoulders. "Ares."

"What do you propose?"

"It's imperative Ares doesn't know a transition is in progress. His cunning is great and he'll stop us if he can. The changes I propose will happen more quickly if his influence is—" Athena paused as if weighing her words "—removed."

Veronica shivered, wondering for a split second if Big-G Gods could die.

"Keeping him sufficiently off-guard would likely be impossible," Athena continued, her gaze stern. "The simplest solution is imprisonment."

Veronica's temples started to throb. She'd thought many times of exiling Ares to the planet named for his Roman counterpart as fitting punishment for all the horrors he'd caused in the mortal world, but suddenly felt a trickle of doubt. What toll would it take on him—and on herself? Using The Power when she'd demoted Hef, an infinitely simpler operation, had left her feeling sick for hours. But if imprisoning Ares would greatly reduce mortal warfare—

"He'll be difficult to capture," Athena said. "I recommend a special agent to deal with Ares, someone loyal to you but capable of undetectable duplicity. Is there anyone in your confidence who comes to mind?"

"Hermes," Veronica said after a thoughtful pause.

Athena's brow furrowed.

"Keep thinking. Hermes is a known trickster and too obviously on your side."

Veronica discarded the thought of Clifford as a special agent as soon as the idea occurred. She trusted him, but he barely knew Ares and was too straight-laced to take part in a sting.

"Keep your eyes and ears open," Athena advised. "Allies can come from surprising quarters. The sooner we find him or her, the sooner we can start."

"You'll do it then?" Veronica blurted, startled. "You'll be Director of Armed Forces?"

Athena and Tim swiveled their heads toward each other. The owl opened his eyes and winked. Athena smiled gravely.

"For four hundred years I've worked here," she said, spreading her arms to indicate campus. "I gave in to frustration and exiled myself from fighting Ares. Zeus never offered the support I needed to properly manage war, but this—" her gaze tilted skyward as if tacitly thanking Heaven, "—it's the chance I've hoped for, for a long, long time."

Something rustled in the roses. The owl screeched and turned his head 180 degrees. Athena sprang to her feet and strode toward the opening in the hedge, Veronica at her heels. She motioned to

Veronica to check the perimeter in one direction while she scouted the other. They met on the opposite side.

"No one?" Athena said.

"No one," Veronica concurred, though she definitely sensed a presence. Perhaps a small bird had been scrabbling in the rose hedge? She was confident her muffling spell would have held during their conference, unless—ice tickled Veronica's spine—unless someone as powerful as she was had wanted to eavesdrop. The thought of being spied on for real made her nauseous. This cloak-and-dagger stuff was definitely not her cup of mead.

Zeus

Zeus ducked into the jasmine-covered walkway and squeezed himself behind a blossom-covered vine to conceal himself. Aster struggled in his arms, her mouth moving in silent toddler cries. The Ex-Lord of the Universe trembled in his hiding place, stunned by what he'd overheard.

The weather had been so pleasant he'd decided to show Aster the best place to pick Gam-Gam's favorite flowers instead of playing indoors. A chariot had transported them to Athens U. They'd strolled the length of the jasmine walkway hand in hand, Zeus pointing at the closed blossoms and Aster burbling, "Pretty." When they'd reached the end of the walkway, he could see into the heart of the Athens U Rose Garden.

"—someone loyal to us but capable of undetectable duplicity. Is there anyone in your confidence who comes to mind?"

It was Athena who spoke, her words muffled as if they came from a television in another room, but Zeus had excellent hearing. He edged closer. Athena and Veronica stared at each other from twin marble benches.

"Hermes," Veronica said after a pause.

"Keep thinking," said Athena. "Hermes is a known trickster and too obviously on your side. Keep your eyes and ears open. Allies can come from surprising quarters. The sooner we find him or her, the sooner we can start."

"You'll do it then?" Veronica said, sounding mightily relieved.

That was all of their plot Zeus could bear to hear. He cast a mute spell on Aster and stepped backward as quietly as he could, but a corner of his toga caught on a thorn sticking out of the hedge. Athena's owl issued a blood-curdling screech, covering the sound of Zeus' footsteps as he'd scrambled to his present hiding-place in the jasmine. An instant later his daughters burst through the archway in the hedge. Athena signaled Veronica to go one direction around the circular hedge while she went opposite. Zeus cast a standard-level invisibility cloak over himself and Aster and prayed to Heaven and Earth the Goddesses wouldn't see through it. For months he'd been unable to activate one of his best inventions, Biggest of Big-G cloaking, the one thing that would conceal his presence from other Big-Gs.

Athena didn't return but soon Veronica strode down the jasmine path without noticing him. Did the two of them not want to be seen together? This question, coupled with the conversation he'd overheard, made his immortal blood run cold. It wasn't supposed to happen this way anymore. The guilt he'd carried since he'd killed and replaced his own father, Cronus, was what had prompted him to plan for his own succession by naming Veronica as CEO. But maybe that wasn't enough for her. Maybe she wanted him out of the way completely. Why else would she meet with Athena under the shroud of secrecy?

Zeus, heartsick, watched Veronica pass purposefully out the campus gate.

"Aster, my dear," he whispered to this granddaughter, "it seems you're the only one Ba-Pa can trust."

If only he had an adult to confide in! Zeus shivered when he replayed Athena's words, but they gave good advice—he must keep his eyes and ears open for an unexpected ally.

Jim

Traveling to the City of Mount Olympus had never been a favorite activity for James Ares Smith.

It was even worse with a toddler in tow.

Titus wasn't bad for his age, but he was in a special phase of life where he ran every time Jim set him down. Last week he'd started teething.

They'd just arrived at Athens International and Jim was dragging. Without thinking, he set Titus down in the terminal so he could search his pockets for his baggage claim ticket.

"Tartarus!" Jim swore. "Wait for me, big guy!" He sprinted after the knee-high figure who wove speedily through the other disembarked travelers. Luck favored Jim when Titus stopped, transfixed, in front of a brightly lit vending machine.

"Papa! Cookie!"

"I've got your zwieback right here, big guy."

Jim set his carry-on bag alongside Titus, rummaged through the toys and disposable toddler pants that had become hopelessly intermixed during the long, tedious flight and unearthed a package of hard baby cookies at the very bottom. Something didn't feel right. He shook the package tentatively—the contents, smashed to shards, rattled.

He crammed their travel detritus into the carry-on bag and pulled the zipper hard when the contents pushed back. Titus banged his tiny fists on the front of the vending machine screaming, "Cookie! Cookie!"

Jim nodded to acknowledge the sympathetic looks of passersby and slung the bag over his shoulder. He scooped scarlet-faced Titus into one arm and followed the overhead directional signs to Mount Olympus Transport.

The signs had a faint purple aura, an indication they were invisible to mortals. Jim counted six signs, the last of which pointed to what appeared to be a broom closet. He opened the door and shouldered his way through, there to find a counter staffed by a stern-faced, toga-wearing matron.

"Ticket?" she barked.

Jim shifted Titus to his left hip and poked around in the right pocket of his chinos. He handed the woman a rumpled piece of faintly glowing purple paper.

"Nice outfit," she snarled, eyeing his short-sleeved plaid shirt.

One of the things Jim hated most about Mount Olympus was the pressure to dress traditionally. In a gesture of defiance, he'd unpacked all but one toga Candy had packed for him and replaced them with mortal wear. The trip certainly wasn't his idea. He and Titus had been more-or-less ordered here by Hera so Candy could be seen with her family. Since Marriage and the Media had soared into mortal popular culture with Candy as its spokesperson, Jim's world had turned upside-down.

The woman thrust his ticket back at him. "Luggage?"

"Two suitcases and my carry-on."

"Hah!"

Her laugh, delivered with a scowl, made him wonder if his baggage would arrive any time during their three-week stay. On the positive side, taking the Mount Olympus shuttle relieved him of having to go through customs with a fussy toddler.

"Next shuttle departs in twenty minutes," she said and inclined her head to the right. "You can wait over there."

Jim turned toward a grouping of well-worn chairs, two of which were taken by a tall, muscular man and a handsome woman alongside him.

"Ralph!"

"Jim!"

The carry-on bag slid to the ground as Jim and Ralph, a former client of Jim's, met in a hearty half-hug. Titus reached for Ralph's bushy gray beard.

"Don't touch, big guy," Jim said as he untangled Titus' fingers from Ralph's facial hair.

"No harm done," said Ralph, chuckling. The woman who'd been sitting beside him rose, smiling. "Brie," Ralph said to her, "this is Jim Smith, the one who helped me keep my wits when I was holding up the Alaskan Way Viaduct. He's still at it, counseling the old-timers who've made the switch from molecular disbursement to computers."

"Charmed." The woman had a British accent. She extended her hand to Jim and made a funny face at Titus, who giggled. "Who's the little bloke?"

Jim introduced Titus to Briana, another structureling and the love of Ralph's life. Briana, as well as Ralph, wore a toga like a regular Olympian. She, too, was well-muscled and tall, what used to be necessary qualifications for the work they'd both retired from.

"It's been—"

Jim paused, trying to remember when he'd last seen Ralph.

"Two years, anyway," Ralph supplied. "Retirement party, the Irish pub on Second Avenue. We nearly drank the place dry with a little help from Cliffie."

Only two years. It seemed an age since Jim had had a drink and talked things over with Ralph—or with anybody. And as for Cliffie—

"That's why we're going to Mount Olympus," Briana said, beaming, "to see our Cliffie before we take a little vacation."

Jim groaned inwardly. Briana and Ralph's Cliffie was Clifford Essex. The young former structureling had, like Ralph, been Jim's client when his molecules had been dispersed to reinforce the Seattle Space Needle. Through a recent corporate restructure, Clifford was now Jim's boss.

"I don't suppose you have time for a beer this evening?" Jim said. A sudden desperation to confide in a contemporary added self-pity to his tone.

Briana's eyes twinkled with understanding.

"Ralphie," she said, smiling girlishly at Ralph and twining her fingers with his, "you know I need to visit some shops."

Ralph cleared his throat.

"Now, if you have other plans—" Jim said, realizing he'd made some sort of blunder.

"Oh no, nothing special," said Briana. "Ralph and I have barely been apart since I was rematerialized out of Big Ben." She slapped Ralph's buttocks and winked. "A little 'boy talk' will do him good."

A man in a navy-blue toga appeared through a door behind the shuttle counter and announced, "All aboard for the City of Mount Olympus!" They followed him outside. A marble sidewalk ran parallel to a tree-lined avenue, deserted but for a stretch chariot pulled by six pairs of white horses. There was no sign of Athens International Airport.

"Up you go," the man said, offering a hand to Briana as she climbed two steps attached to the back of the rig. Ralph, Jim and Titus followed. They sat on cushioned benches along both sides of the chariot, a configuration that reminded Jim of a sailboat cockpit. The man closed a low door at the rear of the chariot and took the driver position up front. He gathered a complicated arrangement of lines into his hands and shouted "Ha!" The team took a few paces, then the scenery blurred by as if fast-forwarded. In seconds, the chariot stopped in front of a luxurious-looking sky scraper in the heart of downtown Mount Olympus.

"Mountain High Plaza Hotel!" the driver announced. He tied off the lines, strode to the back of the chariot and unlatched the door.

"This is our stop, buddy," Jim said to Titus. "You, too?" he asked Ralph and Briana.

"Nope. Hotel Aphrodite," Briana said with a broad grin.

Ralph blushed and Jim's cheeks burned. The Hotel Aphrodite was a themed luxury accommodation, favored by honeymooners and the romantically adventurous.

"Campus Pub okay?" Jim asked the air alongside Ralph's head.

"Yeah, fine," Ralph mumbled.

"It'll take us a while to get settled," Jim said, bouncing Titus, who'd started to fret, on his hip. He glanced at his analog wristwatch. "Let's say five-thirty?" Four hours should certainly be enough time for the two of them to, well…

Briana bumped her shoulder against Ralph's. "I'll be good and ready to go shopping by five-thirty," she said with a naughty wink.

One of Jim's suitcases appeared from a storage bin under the seats.

"I believe I have two suitcases."

He handed his baggage claim ticket to the driver. The driver pulled a digital pad from a fold in his toga and tapped his fingers on the small screen.

"Delayed. Missed the connecting flight in Amsterdam," said the driver briskly. "Should show up in a day or two."

"Okay, thanks," said Jim, skeptical. The suitcases were a matched pair. He'd have to unpack to find out if his clothes or Titus' had been left in Amsterdam.

Jim cursed under his breath when he discovered stacks of neatly folded rompers in the suitcase. On the plus side, there was a reserve box of zwieback, unbroken after a long day of baggage handling. He settled Titus and a small stack of the teething cookies in the playpen that hotel services had provided and quickly showered. Jim's nose wrinkled when he put on his travel-saturated plaid shirt and chinos. They were on the edge of rank, but at least there were no obvious stains and he'd thought to pack a small shave kit, underwear and socks in his carry-on.

The two of them arrived at the tavern at five-thirty, looking as dapper as circumstances allowed. Jim felt like a time traveler as he descended the steps to the Campus Pub. He hadn't been here since he'd finished his PhD, the century he'd met Candy. She'd been moonlighting as a waitress, her day job working for Hestia in the Department of Home and Hearth both low-paying and dull. He smiled and gave Titus an extra squeeze, remembering how sexy Candy had looked in a scant red toga, a uniform the waitresses used to wear before female employees had picketed management for better working conditions. It had taken him years to get up the nerve to ask her out. Jim smiled, remembering the triumph he'd felt when she'd said yes.

He pushed open the green door and scanned the room, looking for Ralph. There was no sign of his middle-aged pal amongst the light assembly of young people. Guided by instinct, Jim veered to the booth he and Candy used to claim. The heart that enclosed their initials, the one he'd carved into the tabletop, was still there after all this time.

Jim slid into the side of the booth facing the door and settled Titus on his lap. A waitress—young, but nowhere near as beautiful as Candy had been and modestly dressed—had twice asked if he was ready to order by the time Ralph appeared in the doorway, disheveled-looking and twenty minutes late. He looked around for several seconds before he spotted Jim.

"Hey," said Jim. He reached across the table to shake hands as Ralph slid into the opposite side of the booth. The bench groaned under Ralph's bulk.

"Hey," said Ralph, his expression a dazed half-grin.

Jim tried not to think about what Ralph and Briana had been doing at the Hotel Aphrodite. He cleared his throat. "Thanks for taking the time to get together."

"Uh, yeah," said Ralph, his eyes slowly regaining focus.

Jim signaled the waitress to bring two beers, then reached into the bag of Titus' necessities for a tippy cup and a small can of apple juice. The waitress was back by the time Jim had filled the cup and handed it to Titus. Ralph drained the tankard set before him, wiped his mouth on the back of his hand and belched, looking somewhat restored.

"Thanks," Ralph said to Jim, then looked at Titus. "Drinking with the big boys, are you?" He wiggled his long, thick fingers in front of Titus' face, eliciting a peal of delighted laughter.

"So, you're going on a vacation?" Jim said to kick-start the conversation.

"Oh yeah," said Ralph with an indulgent grin. "Something Brie's wanted to do for years. We're flying to New Zealand, then on to Australia."

Jim winced before he could stop himself. He could never think of the island continent he used to manage without reliving his own pathetic demotion more than a century ago.

"She had a lot of tourists from Down Under when she was working in Big Ben," Ralph said, without seeming to notice Jim's discomfort. "Kind of piqued her curiosity. You on vacation too?"

Jim took a long pull from his tankard and signaled the waitress for another round.

"Business," he said as he set the empty vessel on the table.

Ralph looked perplexed. "Cliffie's supposed to be on vacation this week. His mum and I are meeting him for dinner tomorrow."

Jim struggled to keep his expression neutral. Clifford Essex, Jim's boss, had been in Seattle last week. Jim had seen Clifford and David Bernstein walking down Madison Street together in earnest conversation. Had they been talking about him? Why hadn't Clifford met with Jim or at least mentioned he was coming to Seattle?

"Candy's business," Jim clarified.

"Oh yeah, that," Ralph said, his smile returning. "She's doing the marriage and what-do-you-call-it thing now? Brie's a big fan of hers."

"Marriage and the Media," Jim said, trying to sound proud. Titus wriggled in his arms and started fussing. "She's flying in tomorrow, had a television interview today."

Jim thought about the damn digital pad he'd stored Candy's

flight number and ETA in. He'd powered it up at the hotel but couldn't get the scheduling app to work right. Should he just go to the airport first thing in the morning and wait it out?

"We kind of wondered why she wasn't with you," Ralph said. "Glad to hear everything's okay."

"You bet," Jim said. "Everything's ninety-nine percent okey-dokey."

Jim sucked in a sharp breath. He hadn't spoken that mantra in ages, one he'd invented five years ago when the world was crashing down around him—Candy hormonally insane for a baby, Ralph teetering on the verge of leaving his post in the Alaskan Way Viaduct and taking thousands of mortal lives with him. *Snap out of it*, he silently coached himself, *it's not as bad as all that*. Just because he rarely saw his wife, had the baby full-time and had a boss who couldn't utilize Jim's millennia of behavioral sciences expertise didn't mean life was hopeless.

Titus burst into a full-throated wail. Ralph made sympathetic noises while Jim held Titus against his chest and patted his back. A second pair of tankards arrived. Ralph showed the courtesy to down his beer in two gulps instead of one, made his excuses and paid the tab. As Ralph passed out the door, Jim, too, felt like wailing.

Tuesday

Jim

Jim stood up from the back-breaking vinyl seat he'd been occupying for far too long at Athens International Airport. He and Titus had arrived at 6:30 AM, victims of the digital pad thingy that wouldn't yield up his schedule no matter what he tried, only to learn that Candy's flight was due at 1:45 PM.

Nothing had gone right today. The air conditioning system at the terminal was on the fritz. The bouquet he'd purchased (for an exorbitant price at an airport gift shop) as a token of welcome had wilted into tired heaps of red petals drooping on long stems. Thank Zeus he'd brought Titus' teething ring and plenty of zwieback—if the wailing and fussing had been more than minimal, Jim was relatively sure he would have lost his mind.

The infinity of waiting ended at 2 PM. Candy, wearing her Marvelous Marriage face, emerged from the plane in a swarm of debarking passengers. She said goodbye to well-wishing fans and posed for two selfies before she reached Jim and Titus. Her expression held as if sprayed in place.

Jim feared the Marvelous Marriage face, the way Candy raised her cheek to him for a kiss when they greeted each other, how she pulled Titus away from him and into her arms. Titus, the traitor, beamed, drooled and chirped, "Ma-ma!"

The spray-on face held forcefully as Candy delivered polite remarks in riposte to Jim's bland questions. They made their way to the Mount Olympus Transport office, experienced the lightning-quick chariot ride to their hotel and tipped the driver.

Candy looked so happy, so fulfilled on the surface but Jim could read the signs. As soon as he tipped the bellhop (his services necessary as Candy's three large suitcases had arrived like clockwork) and closed their hotel suite door behind him, the volcano blew.

"Holy fricking Zeus, Jim!" Candy shouted. "What kind of outfit did you put on Titus? He looks like a fricking Christmas tree."

Psychological theory might argue Jim had paired the red and orange plaid overalls with a bright green shirt sporting big yellow stars deliberately, to offend Candy's sense of style. It had happened once before due to Jim's genuine fashion ignorance; a mistake he'd been careful not to repeat. Until today.

"It was dark when we left," he lamely offered.

Candy shook her head in disgust. "Oh, Jim." Her tone made him feel two feet tall.

Jim silently cursed the mysteriously unfriendly digital pad thingy that had forced him to arrive at the airport hours too early. Why did Veronica insist all management personnel use the unreliable pieces of junk?

Candy moodily bounced between organizing everyone's clothing and toiletries to her satisfaction and preparing for tomorrow's meeting with Hera. After a room-service dinner she announced she was exhausted, pulled an eyeshade over her face and fell into bed. She tossed in her sleep, muttering the words "seminar", "interview" and "oh fuck"—pretty normal for their time together lately, a "normal" Jim was starting to hate.

Clifford

Clifford averted his eyes from the constant interplay between Mum and Ralph. The romantic ambiance of Club Dionysus amplified the feeling he was a third-wheel at what was supposed to be a family dinner. It was the first such occasion he'd attended; Clifford had learned Ralph was his father just five years ago.

It was the family meal from Tartarus, the Olympian version of Hell. He didn't even feel comfortable with Mum anymore, not surprising, he guessed, as they hadn't seen each other for half a century. All three of them had worked as structurelings in the old days (roughly defined as the beginning of mortal architectural history through five years ago), when structurelings had reinforced unstable structures by dispersing their molecules *into* the structures. They lived in isolation, virtual prisoners as long as the structure stood, with one year of vacation per century. Mum, except for one vacation, had been in Big Ben since it was built. Clifford, after completing his doctoral degree, had occupied Seattle's then-new Space Needle. Ralph, due to some disagreement with Zeus of which Clifford had never learned the details, had also been placed in Seattle, sentenced to an ugly and unloved raised highway, the Alaskan Way Viaduct.

Mum reached across the candle-lit table and pinched Clifford's cheek. "You're awfully quiet tonight, love," she said, smiling her Mum smile that meant she knew something was bothering him.

"Just work," he countered. Clifford's duties directing the fastest growing department at Olympus, Inc., did at times overwhelm him. Structurelings now fell under Architectural and Computer Services as the work was now performed by computer. Two workers shared round-the-clock shifts for each relevant structure (except for the Burj Khalifa in Dubai, which required double the staff). As a result, the number of immortals needed for structureling work had exploded. Clifford was responsible for thousands of employees world-wide.

"How's it going with that girlfriend of yours?" Ralph asked with a wink.

"We're just friends," Clifford said testily. Would it were otherwise! He'd subjected himself to two sessions at Life's a Beach tanning salon this week. Hermes, the weasel, sported a healthy tan year 'round, in spite of working a desk job.

The waiter delivered a platter of oysters on the half-shell.

"At last!" said Ralph. "Famished, aren't we, Brie?" he said, his eyes glinting as he patted Mum's thigh.

In his role of fruit of their alliance, Clifford looked everywhere but directly at them. It was too much to bear—the twining of their fingers, the way Ralph nuzzled Mum's neck with the same nose genetics had passed on to him.

"You first, Cliffie," Mum said, pushing the platter toward him. "You need to keep up your strength."

Clifford slid a few oysters onto his plate and poked at them with a miniscule gold-plated seafood fork. His pleated trousers fit loosely these days, no sense in denying it. He'd lost both weight and muscle tone since he'd given up the grueling work of holding up the Space Needle. Yesterday he'd purchased a weight machine which had been delivered this morning and now decorated his living room. He'd taken the week off not to relax, but to implement a new fitness regimen with the hope of regaining Veronica's interest. The stakes had risen since he'd left Seattle for Mount Olympus—in Seattle, there was no Hermes to compete with.

"Bottoms up," boomed Ralph, toasting Briana with an oyster shell and sliding the bi-valve down his throat. He belched heartily. "Ah. Just the sustenance for a man in love."

Mum giggled. "Cheers," she said before slurping her shooter.

Clifford chewed on an oyster and thought of Veronica with fresh agony. Why had she stopped accepting his invitations to dinner and the theatre since he'd been transferred to Corporate? She'd said she was simply too busy but he wondered; was he simply too small-g?

He narrowed his eyes and scowled across the table at his parents who were again distracted in their love-play. Why did Ralph have to be his father? Why couldn't he have the same luck as that git Jim

Smith and turn out to be an illegitimate son of Poseidon? All he could do to further his credentials was return to Athens U and spend another three centuries in the Continental Manager doctoral program. Making level g-17 was as high as he could go. If Veronica still wouldn't have him, at least he could take the next Continental Manager vacancy and leave Mount Olympus for good!

Clifford donned a mask of nonchalance and tried to ignore his parents' interactions—small intimacies, stray touches, words tinged with innuendo—through the salad, the main course, the fruit and cheese and after-dinner drinks. He could be every bit as romantic if Veronica would give him a chance.

At last the agonizing meal ended. Ralph paid the bill and elicited a giggle from Mum when he murmured, "Time for beddy-bye."

The three of them rose. Ralph and Mum were leaving tomorrow; his obligation to visit with them had been discharged. Clifford scratched his left hip to address a sudden, prickling itch. Heat rash, he supposed, given the unseasonably warm day. He shook Ralph's hand, folded Mum into a hug and thought longingly of the bottle of calamine lotion in his medicine cabinet.

Wednesday

Veronica

Veronica Zeta toiled at her CEO desk before sunrise. The pile of routine paperwork was double the usual size. Stella wouldn't be in for two more hours so she could work in peace, free from the squawk of the intercom.

Yesterday she'd been closeted with Hermes, setting up an online presence for Athena without letting Hermes know about the Ares project. She would have recruited Clifford for the job, but Clifford was taking a well-deserved week off. Hermes had, characteristically, tried to wheedle information she didn't want to share. She'd navigated him through the process of setting up a website and several social media platforms for NGO WomanFront Strategies without blowing her cover story; that Athena was making a survey of mortal gender politics to update some Athens U psychology texts. The survey results would be shared with Olympus, Inc., Immortal Resources in exchange for building the website.

Veronica set down her pen and blinked. Heaven and Earth, it was gloomy in the CEO office. Dad had insisted the entire top floor be windowless for some long-forgotten security purpose. It was summer, but she may as well be working in a cave. There'd been no time for fun lately and she missed the relative freedom she'd experienced during the structureling Beta-tests in Seattle. There'd been plenty of work to do during her quarterly visits—intense meetings with Clifford regarding program refinements and with Jim Smith about personnel issues. But there'd always been time to treat David Bernstein to a brother-sister lunch and attend a play or the opera with Clifford.

She powered up her digital pad and started a message to David. Eternity was too short to forego the company of family and friends! She paused to proof her invitation for a quick coffee this afternoon. Satisfied, she was poised to send the message but her finger froze and hovered above the screen. Her hand, ice cold, pressed the delete option instead.

The taste of metal filled her mouth. Now was not the time for idle socializing. *You must focus* said an inner voice she pretended was her own. Veronica shivered. The only pledge Dad had required from her before he'd transferred The Power was that she wouldn't misuse it. Had she unknowingly entered into another pact with The Power itself?

Veronica slipped the digital pad into a desk drawer and picked up her pen, determined to immerse herself in mind-dulling paperwork and quiet the inner voice with sheer boredom.

Aphrodite

Aphrodite made no effort to suppress a wide, languid yawn. She'd been trapped in The Board Room (a re-purposed theme room that formerly catered to erotic fantasies in a corporate setting) for more than an hour with her CFO, Monique.

"I know this is tedious for you, but please try to stay with me," Monique admonished, her expression stern. "Every sector of your business has experienced a decline in revenue for three months straight."

Monique fingered the short strand of pearls around her neck as she always did when frustrated. Though distressed about business downturn Aphrodite smiled, unwilling to show her feelings. All her life she'd presented herself as bullet-proof (or as arrow-proof, before there'd been bullets), through haphazard propagation (Monique was one of her daughters, fathered by what's-his-name, the Frenchman), marital estrangement and the unrelenting jealousy of most other goddesses. Being the Goddess of Love was not for sissies!

"Rent-A-Room Hot Tubs was down another two percent in May," Monique droned.

Aphrodite wrinkled her nose. If only her daughter would wear something more interesting than a straight-cut, navy blue wool toga, she thought in an effort to distract herself from the bad financial news.

Monique tapped her pencil on a graph that lay between them on the conference table.

"Hotel Aphrodite bookings have plummeted to seventy percent of capacity. Two years ago it was at full capacity and booked solid, ten months out. You can't ignore that kind of trend, Mother."

Aphrodite removed her pink rhinestone readers and polished them on the hem of her mini-toga.

"What about the tabloid?"

"In the dumpster," Monique sneered.

"Even the latest issue?"

Monique puffed a harsh sigh. "Mother, you *know* how I feel about journalistic ethics."

A silvery laugh burst from Aphrodite's lips. How had she created such a serious child?

"I was just having a little fun."

"You won't be smiling if there's a lawsuit," Monique countered.

"It's a marketing strategy," Aphrodite said dismissively. "You know Auntie Hera's nasty old Marriage and the Media rubbish is killing mortal-sector revenue."

"I cannot believe you stooped to doctoring the cover photo," Monique said with distaste.

"It was just a suggestion to the editor," Aphrodite said innocently, "and I'm sure it boosted sales, hmmm?"

"The mortals can't keep it on the racks," Monique conceded. "But Mother, this is no way to run a business!"

Aphrodite reached across the table and patted Monique's hand. Poor, dull girl, with her short, clear-polished fingernails, her luxuriant brown hair pulled back in a severe bun. She was nearly three thousand years old but had yet to taste life, did not understand the long view of business ethics and the multi-millennial sparring that naturally arose between Aphrodite, the Goddess of Love, and Hera, the Goddess of Marriage.

"Let's go shopping," Aphrodite said, inspired with maternal feeling. "We'll find you something pretty for summer, a kicky little toga that will show off your—"

"Mother!" Monique drew her hand away and sat bolt upright. "I've been trying to tell you, you need to watch your money!" She jabbed an index finger at the graph. "Your adult novelties division is barely breaking even, and you've nearly put yourself out of the counseling business." She gestured at the conference table, the twelve matching chairs and the gilt-framed oil portrait of John D. Rockefeller that glowered down at them. "You've cut back from fifty themed rooms to just two."

"I got bored," Aphrodite said frankly. "Do you have any idea how tedious it is to enable other people's fantasies?" The wigs, makeup and costumes had especially gotten old—at the age of five millennia it was hard enough to look stunningly beautiful in her regular clothes.

Monique frowned.

"I've done what I can," Monique said. She rose and shuffled the graph and other papers into her briefcase. "Please try to take my report seriously, Mother, you need to reverse the trend."

Aphrodite walked down the sweeping staircase with Monique and saw her to the door. The child had no reason to worry; the Goddess of Love already had a plan in place for reclaiming her rightful market share from Hera.

Hera

In her spacious tenth-floor suite at Olympus, Inc., the Goddess of Marriage sat back in a sleek, padded armchair. Hera tried to look relaxed. Seated across from her, a low table between them, was Candy Smith, the mortal world's face for project Marriage and the Media.

"How was your flight?" Hera said through her best public relations smile.

She made an educated guess the trip from New York to Athens International had been sheer misery. Candy, though careful with her appearance and skilled in applying makeup, hadn't succeeded in concealing the dark circles under her eyes.

"It was—" the former rain goddess turned media star scowled with concentration as if searching for the right word "—long."

Candy had lost weight since the last time Hera had seen her. That was six months ago, when she'd traveled to Seattle to prep Candy for a book launch, the third title in the Marvelous Marriage series, *The Best Thing in Life is We*. The dimples in Candy's hollow cheeks had nearly vanished. Was the change hormonal? Metabolic? Stress-related? Or did it have something to do with the headline screaming from the cover of the mortal tabloid Hera had purposefully placed on the table between them?

"A pity you had to travel mortal-style," Hera said. "Such a nuisance, but when you're flocked by the press," she glanced at the tabloid, "you can't exactly cloak in front of them and go flying off on your own."

"All those hours of sitting," Candy murmured, not catching the hint. "It really took it out of me." She fluffed her strawberry blonde hair with her fingertips and leaned back in her chair as if all the air had been let out of her. "The schedule's been crazy lately, hasn't it? A network talk show, six book signings, a couples' seminar and an awards show last week alone. Absolutely crazy."

"Long days," Hera agreed, "and late nights, I'm sure." Tired of evasions, she pointed at the tabloid. "Care to tell me what this is about?"

"Hah," said Candy. "Don't tell me you believe that trash. It's complete and total bullshit."

"Language, Candy," Hera said reflexively, then laughed, remembering the first few months when Candy was training for the job. She'd progressed from sounding like a mortal truck driver to a talk-show host, a hard-won achievement.

Candy laughed, too. "Sorry," she said. "I'm so wiped I can't think straight. It's just a mortal photographic trick." She pointed to the picture of herself and a popular male movie actor standing side-by-side on a red carpet, smiles wide. The words "Marvelous Marriage Not So Marvelous?" appeared in blinding yellow block letters above their heads.

"The pictures are from the awards ceremony, the one last weekend?" Candy continued. "There were photographers at the theatre entrance taking everybody's picture when they arrived. You told me to go since I was in New York already, said it would be good publicity."

Hera nodded, half-heartedly reflecting on the mortal advertising maxim: there's no such thing as bad publicity.

"Dirk Sureguard was there, too," Candy said, nodding at the handsome man in the photo. "I only know because he went on stage to accept some kind of award. That picture is two pictures someone spliced together."

"I see," said Hera, conceding the likely truth of Candy's explanation. "Still, it doesn't look good. The next time you go to one of those things you'd better take your husband."

Candy looked as if she were about to cry. "That'd be wonderful," she said, quietly. "Can you tell me how I might manage that?"

So the problem—part of it, at least—lay with Candy's husband, Jim. Hera sighed, relieved.

"I don't know what to do," Candy said. "Jim was so supportive at first, but the busier I get the more stubborn he gets. He never wants to leave home anymore, won't even try to set up his work so he can do most of it digitally like his boss wants him to." Candy dabbed the corners of her eyes with her red-varnished fingernails. "I'm so glad he and Titus are here, but he wouldn't agree to come when I asked him. He only came to Mount Olympus because you asked him to."

Hera smiled grimly. She'd played the family trump card. Jim, it had recently been uncovered, was Zeus and Hera's nephew, an illegitimate son of Poseidon (they should form a club, there were so many).

"And it's not just being away from Jim so much," Candy said, sniffling. "I feel like I'm missing all those important moments with Titus."

Candy's sad little problems made Hera's head spin. What was

she, a boss or a marriage counselor? She looked longingly at the door in the wall behind Candy, a door that looked like a closet but opened on to a mini bar. A glass or two of Chardonnay would slow the mental merry-go-round, but it was too early in the day to be observed succumbing to this palliative.

"Being a working wife and a mother is not for the faint of heart," Hera said in an effort to bolster Candy's spirits. She longed to point out that Candy, in contrast to her own circumstances, had never had to worry about a straying husband. Half Big-G or no, Jim was too much a Beta-male to consider cheating. Probably the only thing he'd inherited from Poseidon was his height.

"When I'm home, I'm always so tired I end up yelling at Jim and then Titus starts fussing and…"

Candy's voice trailed off. Was she on the verge of a breakdown? Maybe she should go to a spa for the next two weeks instead of spending hours in meetings, helping Hera map out the next steps for Marriage and the Media.

"Look," said Hera, thirsty frustration prodding her to wrap up today's meeting, "let's reschedule the rest of this week's meetings for next week."

Candy made a noise that sounded as if she'd argue but Hera raised a hand to stop her.

"You need to take some time off, Candy. We won't get anything done if you're exhausted and upset. So go back to your hotel—" Candy's steel blue eyes startled but Hera drove on "—no, don't argue with me, I'm the Goddess of Marriage, remember? Go back to your hotel and pamper yourself. Have a massage, have a body-wrap, get a hotel nanny to watch your little boy and have a romantic dinner with your husband. The rest of it can wait until Monday."

Hera stood to signal the meeting was over. Though she loathed workplace intimacies she hugged Candy, who looked more worried than grateful, before she sent her away.

The small hand of the chronometer above the mini-bar door pointed just below the numeral X. Certainly the sun was over the yard arm—somewhere. Hera allowed herself to inhabit the unspecified somewhere as she paced toward the certainty of wine, telling herself it would be easier tomorrow, promising herself she wouldn't have her first drink tomorrow until lunch time.

Zeus

The Plaza Fountain in downtown Mount Olympus shot graceful

curves of water that arced and fell in shimmering rainbows.

"Ba-Pa! Pretty!" cried Aster. She wriggled from Zeus' arms and ran toward the fountain.

The sun, crawling toward its zenith, warmed Zeus' aching shoulders. He hadn't fully recovered from his Sunday morning cross-town flight. The loss of muscle tone and stamina alarmed him. How could it fade so quickly after one year of retirement? He'd resolved to be more active, and today had shunned his chariot in favor of walking the half-mile from the penthouse condo to the fountain—not as easy as it sounded when packing a toddler.

Aster splashed her hands over the pool's edge.

"Stay out of the water!" he shouted. Zeus chose a sunny bench nearby and sat, poised to intervene if necessary. It pleased him to watch people linger as they passed, admiring the interplay of light and water. Classical music issued from the center of the fountain at this hour of day, between ten and eleven AM. Beethoven's *Fidelio* played, urging a reluctant smile from Zeus.

Such an unhappy week this had been, with Ronnie and Athena plotting against him and Hera's troubles at work. At least she could confront Candy Smith, who'd arrived yesterday, about the gossip that threatened Marriage and the Media.

Looking beyond Aster to the other side of the fountain, Zeus watched a tall, pale man in mortal clothing retrieve a toddler who was crawling over the pool's edge. Virtually everyone in the City of Mount Olympus wore togas. The man was probably a tourist, some visitor who worked in the mortal world.

"Well of course," Zeus said to himself.

It was Candy Smith's husband, Jim, and their son who looked the same age as Aster. Jim had worked for Olympus, Inc., for millennia, and was currently stationed in Seattle. There was some sort of issue with Jim, Zeus now recalled though he couldn't remember what, exactly. Something to do with digital technology, of which Zeus was not a fan. Jim was a counselor, one who'd provided psychological and emotional support to structurelings before structureling work was computerized. Might Jim be someone he could talk to about his fear of being eliminated by his two favorite daughters?

He half-rose, prepared to collect Aster and make himself known to Jim, when a familiar figure appeared to the east, in the street between the Mountain High Plaza Hotel and the Olympus Times building. Athena! Owl perched on her shoulder, she strode with determination.

Zeus scurried behind his bench and peered over the back.

Athena carried a large shopping bag, stamped with the Mortal Wear House logo. What in Tartarus would the provost of Athens U and Athens Tech want with mortal clothing? His heart froze. What if she was looking for him? Was Jim Smith shadowing him, in league with Athena and Ronnie?

But no, Jim was absorbed with his son, who'd started screaming. He had his back to Athena when she passed. Zeus returned his attention to Athena. She stared straight ahead and continued in a straight line west, the shortest route to campus. By the time he looked back toward Jim and his son, they were gone.

Zeus gathered up Aster and hailed a chariot. He'd get them back to the security of the penthouse as quickly as possible, try to weigh the meaning of what he'd just seen, and figure out what to do next.

Jim

Candy was a nervous wreck Wednesday morning, rifling through a selection of red togas and different styles of sandals in quest of the right corporate look. Jim wondered, as all the togas were red, what difference it would make but he kept mum. She fussed with her hair and makeup for nearly an hour before throwing a tube of under-eye concealer cream at the mirror and wailing, "They don't make this fricking junk the right way anymore!" He tried not to look too relieved when the front desk called to say her chariot was waiting. At last, she was out the door.

"C'mon, buddy." He gathered up Titus, who hadn't slept well— teething pain again. Titus dozed in Jim's arms, stirring only when they stopped at the hotel coffee shop for a bottle of apple juice, an espresso and two scones. They breakfasted on a sunny bench in front of the fountain at the downtown plaza. Titus watched the fountain in fascination but when Jim stopped him from crawling into the pool he got fussy. They returned to the hotel, primed for a nap.

When he set Titus on the bed Jim saw a note on his own pillow. It was Candy's scrawl: *Gone to the hotel spa. Where are YOU?*

Puzzled, Jim looked at his watch. It was just shy of 11 AM and she was already back from her all-morning meeting with Hera. He phoned the spa and was told Mrs. Smith was with the masseuse. She would be finished with her complete relaxation package by 3 PM. Jim left a message to let Candy know he was back and wondered how much this wellness spree would cost. The phone rang a few minutes later, a call from the front desk to confirm Mrs. Smith's reservation of a hotel nanny for the evening.

"I guess so," Jim said, baffled.

Candy returned shortly after 3 PM, so relaxed her face was void of expression.

"Hera's treat," she said with the faintest trace of a smile when Jim asked her how much her spa day had cost. "But you're on the hook for dinner."

The nanny, a bright-eyed young woman in a standard Mountain High Plaza Hotel toga (blue, trimmed with pale green) arrived for Titus at 5:30. Titus regarded Jim and Candy with wide, questioning eyes but after the nanny, who had a kind smile, introduced herself to him and took charge of his bear-shaped day pack he toddled off happily beside her.

"Jim, will you please change into a toga?" Candy asked as soon as they were alone.

He stifled a groan. An hour earlier his suitcase had returned from its unscheduled jaunt from Amsterdam to Beijing. He grudgingly changed into the one toga he'd packed, the beige one in a heavy fabric that Candy had bought him for formal occasions. She laughed when he reappeared and sent him back to change his Doc Martens and tube socks for sandals. Jim hated sandals. They made his size 18 feet look like furless animals clinging to the ends of his legs. It was worse since he and everyone else had found out he was a son of Poseidon—he'd heard "you must have gotten those boats from your old man" one time too many.

Candy approved his change in footwear and complimented him on how handsome he looked. She'd donned a red toga that even Jim realized stood out from the others—very low cut and quite short, which perfectly highlighted Candy's figure. For a moment he registered that she'd lost weight but he dared not mention the sensitive topic; she was still a bit rounded and quite lovely. They left their suite and rode the elevator to the hotel bar, an attractive reflection looking back at them from the mirrored doors.

The murmuring and pointing started seconds after they were seated at a table for two in a candlelit corner.

"It's her," said a hushed voice a few tables away. "I think that's her husband."

Candy turned down the first request for a selfie and winked at Jim. She asked him to surround their table with a privacy charm, kicked off her sandals and ran a bare foot up the inside of his calf.

"I'm so glad you're here," she said, her eyes soft and welcoming.

He lifted the privacy charm while the waiter delivered ambrosia martinis and escargot. Jim and Candy were suspended in a loving mood they hadn't shared for a long, long time. When the waiter arrived and they rose to be shown to their table, a squat, middle-aged woman in a double-wide toga wedged herself between them, brandishing a pen and some sort of magazine.

"Can I have your autograph, Candy?"

Candy's Marvelous Marriage face snapped into place but fell abruptly when the woman shoved a familiar mortal tabloid into her hands. Jim recognized the publication, one he and Candy had laughed at whenever they were stuck in a long line at the grocery store.

"I really can't," Candy said, her face frozen, her voice apologetic but edgy. "I'm sure you understand."

Candy took long strides to the restaurant entrance. Jim smiled and shrugged at the autograph-seeker before he followed her.

"What was that about?" he whispered en route to their table.

"It's stupid. It's nothing," she whispered back. "Please, Jim, let's just have a wonderful evening and not think about anything else."

And that's exactly what they did.

Thursday

Athena

Athena paced the length of her sitting room in a Washington D. C. hotel, her owl Nyctimene (called Tim, for short) perched on her right shoulder. The Goddess of Wisdom, Civilization, Warfare and a raft of other things was in a fix.

She'd flown in this morning (under her own power), disguised in a twenty-first century AD women's suit and low-heeled black pumps, to pitch her plan for reducing mortal warfare. Tim was transfigured into an owl-shaped broach and pinned to her breast pocket.

All day they'd haunted the halls of power. Athena had presented herself at every reception desk in every office of every female government leader or ambassador (both US and foreign) but had failed to persuade protective secretaries and executive assistants to let her meet with their bosses. She could read their suspicion from the scent of their perspiration, a faint but sharp odor she'd developed an awareness of over the millennia. Politely they accepted her business card (Athena Metis, CEO, WomanFront Strategies), professionally they assured her the contact information would be passed on to Madame President, Ms. Secretary of Defense, etc. She'd regularly checked the cell phone Hermes had provided her, had left explicit instructions at the hotel desk to put through any telephone calls regardless of the hour, yet no one had called.

She stopped pacing and looked at the grandfather clock against the wall opposite. It was nearly midnight. Chances of receiving a call were slim. Discouraged and flight-lagged, Athena changed from her suit to her usual chiton and silver belt of entwined snakes. A canker sore was building in the trench between her lower gums and her lip, the vulnerable spot she'd jokingly called her Achilles' heel in Trojan War days.

Athena sat in a high-backed armchair in front of the tiled fireplace. Tim, restless because she wouldn't let him out to hunt in a strange city, landed on the back of the chair and started preening. Usually the clicking of his beak irritated her, but now it sounded soothingly familiar.

Maybe this trip was a mistake. She hadn't exercised her mortal diplomatic skills for centuries, not since advising England's Queen

Elizabeth I and conjuring a little storm to help defeat the Spanish Armada. Maybe her own skills were out of date, or maybe—

"Is it just me, Tim, or have the mortals bureaucratized away all their common sense?"

The owl hooted once to concur.

Athena started pacing again. Where were the women warriors of old—Boudicca, Joan of Arc, Cleopatra—women who didn't need shielding from supplicants, who could make up their own minds without layer upon layer of toadies to peel through? How could the simple act of scheduling a meeting be so unZeusly difficult?

She passed the rolling table room service had wheeled in to deliver her dinner, picked up a scrap of Gorgonzola burger and pitched it to Tim. That old feeling she'd worked so hard to overcome was returning, the certainty she'd spend eternity banging her head against a figurative wall, unable to stop the mindless carnage wrought by Ares and his mortal followers.

A shrill ring made her jump. She vaulted to the secretary desk in the corner of the room and snatched up the telephone receiver.

"Yes?"

"I'm calling for Ms. Metis of WomanFront Strategies," said a low-pitched voice, monotone and female. "May I speak with her, please?"

"Speaking," Athena replied in a like tone.

"Ms. Metis, please stay on the line for Ms. Jocelyn Chadwick."

Jocelyn Chadwick! Athena's heart soared. The Secretary of Defense for the United States of America was returning her call!

Jim

Jim and Candy were dressed in complimentary terrycloth bathrobes and sipping dark coffee with cream when the hotel nanny delivered Titus Thursday morning. Titus ran to Candy and embraced her knees. The nanny laughed.

"He was a perfect little gentleman," she said, handing Titus' bear pack to Jim.

Titus turned and waved enthusiastically at his new friend. "Bye!"

Warmed with contentment, Jim excused himself to the shower. The hot, pulsing water felt divine, so good he started singing. By the time he was dressed (in khaki shorts and a Hawaiian shirt) breakfast had arrived. The three of them had just settled down to eat when the phone rang.

Jim and Candy looked at each other, eyebrows raised.

"Better get it," Candy said.

The spell was broken.

"Hello?"

Candy pursed her lips and shrugged her shoulders, indicating she didn't recognize the caller, then said, "Oh! Wow." She clamped her hand over the receiver as if she were going to say something to Jim but in a split second said to the caller, "Oh. Of course. Yes."

A brief, quiet conversation followed, Candy agreeing to things Jim couldn't hear while she nodded and shot him furtive glances. When the call ended Candy rifled through her purse for her digital pad thingy and typed a few quick strokes.

"Meeting tomorrow," she explained, a little too quickly with a smile a little too bright.

"Hera?"

"Yes. Uh, I mean, no."

"Well, who then?"

"Uh. Can't say. It's no big deal," she fudged. Her face turned red. "Shower!" she said and dashed into the bathroom, leaving Jim to wonder what in Heaven and Earth had just happened.

It came to him that afternoon when he was on a zwieback run. He was waiting in a long line at the corner convenience store, a box of the teething cookies tucked under his arm, when he saw it—this week's edition of *American Tattle*, splashed with the headline "Marvelous Marriage Not So Marvelous?" Jim closed his eyes. Nausea swept through him. He wished he'd never seen the picture of Candy, smiling her Marvelous Marriage smile, alongside some ruggedly handsome mortal actor.

Once the shock lifted he wondered what he should do. Buy a copy of the horrible rag and wave it in her face? Demand to know who she was meeting tomorrow? Hire a detective to follow her to her Friday rendezvous?

When he returned to the hotel he threw out a few lame questions that he hoped would spring a confession from her while berating himself for assuming she had anything to confess. Their marriage had never been perfect—as a couple they were prone to arguing and Candy could spew out verbal abuse like a pro—but never in two millennia had he suspected her of unfaithfulness. Was it naïve to assume her stardom and the increasing amount of time she spent away from home wouldn't provoke her into cheating out of sheer loneliness? Did she want a different sort of man, now that she was in the limelight?

In bed that night, Jim lay wide awake. He looked at Candy's sleeping face on the pillow alongside his. Was it a trick of the shadows, or was she smiling? If she would only talk in her sleep like she did when she was stressed, maybe he could figure it out. He kicked himself for failing to learn how to operate the scheduling app on the digital pad thingy, realized he could sneak a peek at her Friday schedule and figure out what she was up to when she was deep in the ritual of putting on her makeup in the morning. But he didn't know how to run the thing and it was his own damn fault.

Desperate for lack of options Jim resolved to call a detective agency tomorrow, when Candy was in the shower. "Everything is ninety-nine percent okey-dokey," he said, his lips moving silently as he tried, and failed, to lull himself to sleep.

FRIDAY

Athena

Athena landed and uncloaked at a Georgetown address in the small hours of Friday morning. Secretary Chadwick's home was a 19th century brownstone, complete with a groomed and fenced postage stamp-sized front yard.

The Goddess, wearing her mortal disguise with her transfigured owl affixed as a broach, touched index finger to doorbell. The chime was a brief passage from Beethoven's Fifth Symphony. When the tune stopped a trim, brisk woman in a blue blazer with brass buttons and matching pleated slacks opened the solid-looking front door.

"I'm with the Auxiliary Corp," Athena said, giving the pass phrase the Secretary had supplied.

"The Secretary is waiting for you." The woman tilted her head toward the hallway. Athena crossed the threshold. The door closed quickly behind her. Two tall, solidly built men wearing dark suits and electronic earpieces stood a few paces back from the woman, arms at their sides in a ready position. The woman apologized before completing a pat-down of Athena, then said, "This way, please."

Athena followed her down a narrow hallway hung with mirrors. They passed through an archway to a formal living room, decorated in rich beige fabrics with a fireplace at the far end and large pieces of abstract art on the walls. A door opened off the living room to a book-lined study with an antique hardwood desk. The woman stopped in front of a section of leather-bound books and pulled out a volume titled *The American Revolution*. A mechanical hum masked the creak of the bookcase as it swung open to reveal a conference room.

At the head of a long table flanked with straight-back chairs sat a woman in a black jacket and gleaming white blouse, open at the neck. A rope of pearls fell inside the blouse, the bottom of the loop hidden under the neckline. The woman's hair was soft brown and shoulder-length, as Athena had seen in a television newscast.

Secretary Chadwick rose and approached Athena, her hand extended.

"Thank you for making time to see me, Ms. Metis."

Jocelyn Chadwick's guarded smile was rimmed with a no-nonsense shade of red lipstick. A quizzical expression danced in her eyes.

"You can leave us, Margaret," said the Secretary.

The porter nodded and went through the secret entrance. The door hummed closed.

Secretary Chadwick returned to her chair and pointed Athena to the seat nearest hers. She rested her elbows on the table and laced her fingers together in a triangle.

"Ms. Metis, it's not my practice to meet with consultants who make cold calls, but I've had an opportunity to vet you and your organization. The evidence is good you're neither a terrorist nor a crackpot."

Athena silently thanked Hermes for planting biographical information about her alias on the Internet, also for his creation of a plausible-looking WomanFront Strategies website.

"The motto at your website is 'World peace through simple change.'" Jocelyn Chadwick leaned forward. Her grey eyes locked with Athena's. "Ms. Metis, can you tell me what, exactly, that simple change would be?"

They spoke intently, Athena relating the theory and method for converting the world's armies to a majority of female soldiers. Secretary Chadwick asked well-aimed questions. After several exchanges, the Secretary leaned back in her chair and cleared her throat.

"Your idea is full of intriguing possibilities, Ms. Metis," she said, frowning. "I agree that in many cases women would make superior soldiers for peace in terms of motivation and outlook. Cultural influences are, I believe, the major obstacle. In my nation, where women enjoy more equality with men than most places in the world, such a transition would likely take generations."

Jocelyn Chadwick fingered the string of pearls around her neck. "For more than two centuries my predecessors struggled with war as I do today, but none of us has found that special ingredient, that piece of magic to end the savagery, the needless waste of life and other resources." She raised the pearl rope, settled its full length outside her blouse and pointed to a medallion incorporated at the bottom of the loop.

"Your likeness doesn't do you justice, Athena," Secretary Chadwick said with shining eyes. "This medal was awarded to my grandmother for her service in the Women Army Corps during World War II, what they called WAC. Ever since I was a child I've been fascinated by the woman on Gran's medal. Metis is what caught my attention. It's been decades since I studied about you but I still remember your mother's name."

Athena stared, dumbfounded, at Jocelyn Chadwick. If she denied her true identity would the Secretary dismiss her proposal? Would taking a mortal into her confidence compromise the other Olympians and their behind-the-scenes world?

The Goddess of War, Wisdom and Civilization placed a damp palm on her owl broach and made a silent prayer to Heaven and Earth to help her frame an appropriate response.

Candy

A golden limousine swept soundlessly from the curb in front of the Mountain High Plaza Hotel. In the back seat was Candy Smith. She smoothed the hem of her best red toga, felt the weight of extra concealer under her eyes. She'd pretended to sleep well last night but hadn't. Jim was acting funny, ever since she'd taken the phone call from Aphrodite.

Aphrodite! The Goddess of Love had seemed glamorous and knowledgeable when a younger Candy had been desperate to figure out boys and dating, but as she progressed into her two thousands and married Jim, Aphrodite's importance had faded. Two millennia passed in marriage-as-usual, until middle age started making inroads into Candy's appearance. At first she'd despaired, but everything changed when her mother (Gymnastica, a retired goddess of physical fitness) sent her a piece clipped from a popular small-g health and beauty magazine.

It was an interview with Aphrodite. The questions and answers addressed almost every frustration Candy was experiencing, from repairing loss of skin elasticity to battling double chins. It hadn't hurt her Marvelous Marriage personae one bit to effectively reverse her appearance to that of a thirty-five-hundred-year-old and hold it there indefinitely, a feat owed solely to a few timely tips from the Goddess of Love.

Candy drummed her palms on her thighs in nervous excitement. She was going to meet her savior! She'd practically squealed into the phone Thursday morning when the caller identified herself as Aphrodite's personal assistant and named the time and place for their meeting. She'd nearly shouted the news to Jim but the assistant had cut her off just in time, saying the meeting must be kept secret on pain of cancellation. This was an excellent idea, she'd soon realized. If Hera learned her protégé was meeting with the Big-G Goddess who was her worst known enemy, Candy might get her nearly-perfect bottom kicked out of the Marriage and the Media department and be demoted back to Rain Goddess, Pacific Northwest Region.

Aside from Jim acting weird and the danger of Hera finding out what she was up to, Candy was thrilled about her once-in-eternity opportunity. The invitation was completely unexpected and, well— so exciting! The personal assistant had confessed she, herself, was a big fan of Candy's and intimated Aphrodite was, too. Candy was thrilled about seeing Aphrodite's mansion, to see if the fan magazine pictures did it justice. She'd read a lot about the "specialty" rooms the Goddess of Love used for her personal counseling practice. Would they meet in the Hollywood Room, or maybe the Marie Antoinette?

The chauffer (as buff as a mortal body-builder in his seemingly poured-on uniform, but she didn't go for muscular types) pulled the limo through a tall golden gate and up the circular drive to the front steps of a columned marble structure as big as a palace. Candy ascended the broad steps, passed through the open front double door and was greeted by a well-muscled butler wearing a golden thong, white cuffs with golden links, and nothing else. She studied his backside with a mixture of fascination and revulsion as he led her through the entry hall, a vast room of marble and gilt bathed in pink and amber light, and up the right side of a sweeping arc of stairs. Music, an instrumental arrangement of a tune by the 20th century mortal band the Beach Boys, wafted in the air. The stair landing opened onto a long, wide hallway. Gilt-framed mirrors hung between evenly spaced doors that stretched into infinity.

The butler opened the first door to the right and politely waved Candy in.

"Please make yourself comfortable, Mrs. Smith," he said in a melodious voice. "The Mistress will be with you shortly."

He closed the door behind him. Candy paced to the center of the large, circular room. Shimmering red and hot pink fabric hung from a center point in the ceiling, creating the impression of an exotic tent. The Romance Room—she'd seen a photo spread of it in the February issue of *Mount Olympus Lifestyles*. A gauzy curtain partitioned off a third of the space, behind which a large, round bed and bubbling Jacuzzi were visible. The remainder of the room was sparsely furnished with two fainting sofas, upholstered in red satin. A low marble table between them supported a golden tray loaded with graceful, stoppered bottles of rainbow-colored liquids and two gold goblets. A large box of Dilettante truffles lay open alongside the tray.

Candy's mouth watered. She sat on the sofa facing the door, folded her hands in her lap and tamped down the urge to nibble one of her favorite chocolates before her hostess arrived.

The Beach Boys tune switched to a symphonic rendition of Ravel's "Bolero." The chamber door opened slowly, admitting a ruby red light. Candy instinctively stood at attention.

The Goddess of Love glided in on jewel-encrusted platform sandals, her long, bronze-tan legs topped by a hot-pink mini-toga. Candy tried not to stare as she studied Aphrodite. She noted especially her violet eyes, the original of what the Goddess was rumored to have gifted to the mortal actress Elizabeth Taylor, simply for the pleasure of seeing them on the big screen. Diamonds glinted in her long, dark, lashes. Her gorgeous hair, a cascade of platinum blonde curls, was arranged loosely but effectively, pinned up in some places and caressing her broad, tan shoulders in others. Aphrodite's upper arms, encased in matching bracelets of golden, coiled snakes with diamond eyes, appeared extraordinarily firm for a Goddess of five thousand years. Candy wondered with envy if Aphrodite had a personal trainer, and if she could borrow the miracle-worker for a session or two.

The Goddess of Love extended her hand.

"Candy Smith," she cooed. "At last we meet!"

Candy grasped the Goddess' hand, startled by the sinuous quality of her handshake.

"I understand Hera's running you ragged," Aphrodite said with playful sympathy. "Please sit down, dear, and take some refreshment."

With a lilting laugh her hostess popped a truffle into her own mouth, pushed the box toward Candy and artfully reclined on the nearest sofa.

"What a charming frock," Aphrodite remarked as Candy reached for a chocolate.

Aware that her best red mini-toga and 22-carat gold hoop earrings looked frowsy next to Aphrodite's costume, Candy set the chocolate back on the table. When she'd fussed over her own hair and makeup this morning she'd been pleased with the result but, compared to her hostess, she felt as plain as a temple mouse. Aphrodite's steam-roller sexuality squashed her own television-approved hot looks flat.

Aphrodite knowingly eyed the chocolate Candy had set down. Her hot pink lips smiled.

"Surely with your lovely figure you don't need to worry about a little chocolate?" The Goddess helped herself to a second truffle, licking her lips coyly after the first bite. "You know what they say— when at Mount Olympus, do like the Olympians."

Feeling an odd chill, as if she were some type of prey, Candy wished she was safely back in their Seattle penthouse, even if the summer weather was cold and crappy as usual. But like all small-g gods she was chained to protocol—she couldn't leave until Aphrodite dismissed her. Warily, she picked up the truffle and nibbled the outer coating of dark chocolate.

Warmth flooded her as soon as the decadent richness passed her lips. Candy reclined on her sofa in the same artful posture as her hostess, wondering why she'd been so nervous. Silly, really. She should be honored someone as important as Aphrodite wanted to meet her. The Goddess of Love had never mentioned what they were meeting about, of course, but what did it matter, now that she was here?

"You poor child, it must be so difficult, traveling all the time from mortal city to mortal city, staying in their impossible hotels and being away from your darling baby."

Candy's head bobbed on her neck as if it were filled with lovely, lovely helium.

"And to be away from your husband. I understand he's quite brilliant, and a son of Poseidon," Aphrodite said with a sly wink. "God enough for any goddess, from what I know of his brothers."

Candy nodded in slack-jawed agreement. Yes, she needed more time, a lot more time, with Jim and the baby. She wanted that more than anything.

"Such a shame to have your lovely, meteoric career hampered by so much anxiety," Aphrodite said. "Wouldn't it be nicer if you could spend all your time working on your own marriage instead of helping the undeserving mortals?"

Aphrodite smiled, raised and hand and formed a circle with her thumb and forefinger. Candy's eyelids felt suddenly heavy. She rested her head on the sofa.

Candy dozed. Images of how busy she'd become, how much time she spent away from Jim and Titus since she'd started on the Marvelous Marriage seminar circuit, swamped her restless dreams. Yes, home would be much better. Surely Hera would understand.

She woke abruptly. Aphrodite was gone. The butler stood near the open door.

"The Mistress had another appointment but she thought it best to let you sleep, Mrs. Smith," he said smoothly. "The limousine is waiting, if you're ready to return to your hotel."

Candy's fuzzy thoughts snapped into focus. She jumped to her feet and strode to the door, longing to be back at the hotel with Jim and Titus.

Saturday

Veronica

The track shared by Athens U and Athens Tech was busy on Saturday morning. Both universities were holding chariot team pre-season tryouts. Freshman hopefuls, stars from their immortal high schools around the world, had been running elimination heats since dawn. The air was clouded with dust. Braying voices of athletes, both male and female, shouted encouragement to their candidates, now down to the final four. The noisy chaos of the scene provided perfect cover for the conversation taking place in the otherwise vacant stands.

Veronica and Athena sat in the bleachers. Tim perched on Athena's shoulder, his eyes closed to the morning sun.

The CEO of Olympus, Inc., listened intently to Athena's report. News from her trip to Washington D.C. was mixed. Veronica was alarmed Athena's true identity had been uncovered, though Secretary Chadwick had sworn the secret would accompany her to her grave. On the positive side, Chadwick had concurred with the benefits to be gained by populating the world's armies with a majority of women soldiers and officers. She was skeptical, however, about overcoming cultural norms and persuading other world leaders to commit to a process that would take, in the Secretary's informed opinion, one or two centuries.

"Which leads me to conclude," Athena said as she returned a salute from the final four charioteers who galloped past in an exhibition lap, "that military reorganization must begin immediately, and from the top."

Veronica nodded and swallowed hard. She'd suspected from the start that changes must be made by the Gods, first, to properly inspire the mortals. The dirty job of removing Ares—a task she'd grown to think of with a mixture of cold fear and dark excitement—was the first step.

"What do you recommend?"

Athena's eyes glowed sorrowful and hard. "Imprison Ares at the first opportunity."

An icy finger stirred Veronica's soul. Did any history book hold the story of a Big-G God going to prison? There was a high-security cell block deep underground at Olympus, Inc., headquarters. Dad had shown it to her when she'd started as Vice-CEO. She didn't recall seeing any prisoners on the tour. Had the facility ever been used?

Veronica's head began to pound.

"He won't be easy to catch," Athena continued, her voice barely audible over the stamping of hooves, the groaning of chariot wheels, the lusty cheers raining upon the drivers as they queued at the start line. "It's as I said before. We need to recruit someone in his confidence, someone he trusts implicitly, to lead him into the trap."

The ache in Veronica's head spread through her body. Deception, she realized, was an indispensable tool for capturing Ares.

"Suggestions?" The only being she could think of who was close to Ares and might be powerful enough to trick him was Dad, and she wasn't even certain about that.

"Everyone has their weaknesses," said Athena. "Someone will be able to lead him to us. We need to stay alert. Read the social column in the *Olympus Times*. Listen to office gossip. We're looking for someone who has enough control—any type of control—to be persuasive, someone who has a grudge to settle."

Veronica shivered involuntarily.

"I've never liked this part of strategy," Athena said, "but if we're serious about reducing the waste and carnage of mortal warfare we have to be tough."

A thunderous cheer erupted as an Athens U finalist and one from Athens Tech crossed the finish line at the same time. The two were mobbed with hugs and cheers from their new teammates. The chariot drivers who finished behind them pulled up, turned and trotted toward the stable. Veronica watched their retreat with grim understanding. There was no second place.

David

David Bernstein's head was crammed full of a new world, and what a cool world it was!

The City of Mount Olympus was way different than Seattle. Instead of a bus system, transportation was by chariot, except for an awesome black motorcycle and a golden stretch limo, both of which he'd seen as he hoofed it around town.

There were lots of great places to eat. He'd tried a dozen restaurants, thanks to the Bank of Olympus debit card Veronica had sent to him at the hotel. She'd enclosed a note reminding him to keep current on entries to the transaction register on his digital pad. When he'd opened the app to take a look he'd nearly choked at the beginning balance, thoughtfully expressed in Euros, US Dollars and the local currency. David keyed a quick note on the memo pad, a reminder to ask Veronica how long he was supposed to make his money last.

He'd strolled the Athens U campus every day this week and had met with his advisor, Dr. Alyssa Andreas, a stern, practical woman of, he guessed, about five millennia. She shepherded him through registration, gave him a print-out of his schedule and presented him with a thick leather-bound book, *The History of Athens University*.

"Yours to keep," she'd said gruffly, "and you'd be wise to read it in its entirety before the start of the term. Orientation for new students and a tour of campus housing is two Mondays after next."

David prayed to—Heaven and Earth, like a true Olympian—he would have his own room and not be saddled with a roommate, especially not a roommate like Michael in Seattle or the loathsome Pan.

Pan was the one downer of David's Mount Olympus experience. It made him feel bad, too, because his foster parents, the Bernsteins, had raised him to be compassionate toward those less fortunate. As crude and irritating as Pan could be, David recognized Pan suffered from rejection. If he'd met Pan when he was growing up in Salt Lake City, Utah, Thelma Bernstein would have made him befriend Pan because none of the other kids would.

He'd only seen Pan once this week. The God of Shepherds and Flocks had led him on a tour of Mount Olympus bars. The tour ended in the wee hours with David packing his guide into a for-hire chariot and praying Pan wouldn't puke on the driver (who seemed to know Pan and accepted the fare with reluctance). When the rig departed, David keyed another memo into his pad, a reminder to ask Veronica if he could please, please have a different mentor.

Besides strolling campus, eating and avoiding Pan, David had spent most of his time reading. For two hours each day he'd labored through *The History of Athens University*, a dry, scholarly work that coughed up a worthwhile fact approximately every fifty pages. Even the section on building the model of the Acropolis was dull.

To counter the deadening effects of *The History*, David also read from his paperback copy of *The Gods of Today: Contemporary Lives of Zeus, Hera and Their Offspring*. In the forward, Herodotus Jones confessed his volume was unauthorized but asserted he'd written unvarnished truths about the Greek Pantheon's First Family. David flipped quickly to the index and looked for "Bernstein, David" but found no entry. He felt a mixture of relief and disappointment. Flipping to the front of the volume he looked at the copyright date, MMIX. In 2009, even he hadn't known who he really was.

This gave rise to a third question for Veronica—why, since they were Greek, did the Olympians use Roman numerals?

Chapters of *The Gods* were titled by person, starting with Hera. The author indelicately pointed out that the Goddess of Marriage came first, by age, covered the usual history of Hera's unhappy marriage to Zeus and made a snide remark about Veronica being a "surprise" baby. David winced—what would the author have written about him, had the truth then been known? He read and reread a brief passage starting in 22 BC, when Hera had left Mount Olympus for several decades. She'd traveled with a small retinue (perhaps Thelma and Milton Bernstein, David wondered?) in what some mortals referred to as The Holy Land. Hera had returned home in 30 AD, without an explanation. Jones credited her mysterious absence to "women's problems."

David scanned the chapter on Zeus, the God who'd been cuckolded when he, himself, had been conceived. In the long section about Zeus' extra-marital offspring there was a weird part about Aphrodite. Was Zeus really her father (he would have only been fourteen hundred at the time)? Flipping ahead to Aphrodite's chapter, David read about the Goddess of Love, Beauty and Sexuality. Though she succeeded in hiding it with spells, great make-up and a killer personal trainer, she was five thousand years old. The golden stretch limo he'd seen belonged to her. The cool black motorcycle belonged to her estranged husband (who was also her half-brother if Zeus was really her father), Hephaestus. She was also the mistress of Hephaestus' brother, Ares.

It was a lot like reading the Hollywood gossip magazines David had perused at the U-District Laundromat in Seattle. Recognizing the similarities, he tried to temper Jones' allegations with a grain of common sense. It wasn't really true Ares pulled the wings off of flies for a hobby, or Ilithyia was an eco-terrorist—was it?

By noon, Saturday, he'd read the last chapter, "Veronica Zeta." Jones had speculated the now-CEO of Olympus, Inc., would either launch a career in academics, like Athena, or take over the Department of Home and Hearth from her Aunt Hestia (who was the Olympian equivalent of a Vestal Virgin). David laughed at the author's lame prediction. It was time for a reality check in this strange new world. First thing on Monday he'd pay a visit to Olympus, Inc.

Clifford

Clifford Essex spent Saturday evening soaking in a hot tub at the neighborhood health club. He hadn't intended to join, let alone sign a 24-month membership agreement with dues due the fifth of each month whether he used the facilities or not, but he was desperate.

Every muscle in his body ached. He'd faithfully followed the workout routine outlined in the instructions that came with his new weight machine, except for the paragraphs about taking a day off between sessions and limiting yourself to fifteen minutes per session for the first month.

He scratched his bum, the bright red flesh of which was covered by plaid swim trunks. The tanning salon manager had been quite apologetic when he'd explained to Clifford that a very, very small percentage of people were allergic to artificial UV rays when applied to skin that had rarely seen the light of day. Thank goodness he'd opted for the disposable tanning thong to cover his—he shuddered, imagining the agonizing discomfort he would be experiencing right now if he hadn't.

A few health club members came and went from the swimming pool, but none of them deigned to share the tub (which was just as well, as he preferred privacy). Doubtless they wanted to stay clear of a man with an orange-tinged complexion, the present color of his face, chest, arms and legs. After the allergic reaction, he'd switched from visiting the tanning salon to applying a cream that promised a natural bronze hue. The achieved pigment had fallen gruesomely far from the anticipated result.

Another solitary Saturday night, alone and aching and orange and for what? He could have saved himself time, money and agony by taking long walks in the evenings and on the weekends. The activity would help him maintain muscle tone, and, as sun was in the forecast, his face might obtain some human-looking color.

Clifford repositioned himself in the hot tub to take simultaneous advantage of as many jets as possible. Tomorrow he'd start walking for exercise, provided he could get out of bed.

SUNDAY

Candy

The gods slept in on Sunday, except for Candy.

She was wide-awake, in bed alongside Jim. Jim! What could she think of to make Jim's day even more special than Friday or Saturday had been? Ever since she'd left Aphrodite's mansion late Friday morning it had all become so simple, so obvious. Jim was what mattered most in the world, and of course darling little Titus mattered most in the world, too!

Jim was really surprised when she'd thrown herself into his arms the instant she'd entered their suite at the Mountain High Plaza Hotel after her visit at Aphrodite's. It was so cute the way he'd shrieked, almost like he was alarmed, and how much more perfect could his response have been? And the way he'd looked like a scared rabbit when she'd begged him to tell her what she could do to make him happy, right now, this instant. Oh, how wonderful it all was! He'd said what he'd like best would be to go on a long family hike on the trail that circled the City of Mount Olympus, the entire trail from beginning to end. It was so funny and perfect the way he'd said it, like he was making it up on the spot out of desperation. Who could want a better husband? She'd never be able to go back to work on Monday when he offered a life like this!

The hike had taken the rest of the day and half the night, and Jim had blisters on his feet when they got back to the hotel. Titus, the perfect little angel, had cried most of the way and kept throwing his teething ring off the trail, so Jim kept having to crawl through the brush to get it. Candy's face was sore from smiling even now, just thinking about Friday night when she'd helped Jim into the bathtub to soak away his aches and pains and he'd said thank you. Thank you, and to her!

She absolutely lived to make Jim happy, and Saturday had been even more wonderful because he wanted to sit in front of the big-screen television and watch mortal baseball games for the entire day! It was so cute the way he'd look up at her every five minutes when she was standing behind him with a cold beer and a bowl of chips in her hands, ready to serve him. He'd even said it wasn't necessary for her to hover like that—what a clever use of words!—said she could leave the beer and chips (his favorites she'd ordered from room service) on the coffee table, like she had something better to do! And Titus sat on the couch, right alongside Jim, fussing about his teeth. The little cherub let her feed him zwieback by hand! Candy knew Jim loved her because he kept looking at her like she was crazy and asked her if she didn't have some shopping to do today. The shopping part worried her for a moment, until she got up the courage to ask Jim if he didn't like her in red anymore and he quickly assured her he loved her in red. He loved her in red! How much better could it get!

Candy was so excited about the day her fingers and toes wriggled under the sheets. Jim would tell her what he wanted to do and she'd do it, right along with him! It just didn't get any better than that!

Week Three - MONDAY

Jim

James A. Smith paced the length of the sitting room, his arms filled with a fair-haired toddler.

"Easy, big guy," he coached, bouncing his son ever-so-slightly as he walked. Titus, red-faced, sniffled from the pain of cutting his fourth tooth. It was a welcome relief from the bawling that had thus far punctuated the morning. Titus' eyelids fluttered, promising a nap. Jim needed one, too.

Since Candy had come back from her mysterious Friday morning rendezvous—at Aphrodite's mansion, as the detective he'd hired had reported—their married life had taken its most bizarre twist to date. Candy had nearly knocked him down with the force of her homecoming embrace, the usual fire in her eyes dulled to something soft but relentless. She wouldn't tell him about her meeting, had said it wasn't at all important compared to making him happy, and wouldn't leave him alone until he, in desperation, closed and locked the bathroom door between them. Thus sequestered, he'd tried to figure out what was wrong with her. Had work demands pushed her to a nervous breakdown? Had she somehow gotten hooked on mortal mood-altering drugs?

It wasn't just the way she behaved toward him, either. She'd clung to Titus, too, and wouldn't acknowledge she'd come to Mount Olympus on business. With difficulty and tears (Candy's), Jim had finally pried her arms from around his neck this morning and demanded she keep her appointment with Hera.

"Are you absolutely sure it will make you and Titus happy if I go?" she'd asked, her cheeks streaked with mascara.

"Please," he'd said wearily. Jim could still feel Friday's hike in his sore calf muscles and tender feet, lower back pain from spending Saturday as a sports couch potato and a dull headache from Sunday's tour of Mount Olympus wineries. For the past three nights Candy had pounced on him as soon as Titus had fallen asleep. They hadn't had so much sex since he'd agreed to start a family with her several years ago and this, too, was wearing on him.

"Okay, sweetheart," Candy had said, her eyes half-averted with wanting to please. "If that's what you really want I'll go see Hera."

She'd repaired her makeup and fluffed her hair, her expression oddly vacant. Would she ever tell him what had happened at Aphrodite's? He was so tried he hardly cared. And now, at last, she was gone for a while and he could get some rest.

Jim looked down at Titus who snored softly in his arms.

"Thank Zeus," he murmured. He laid his son on the bed and settled beside him.

Jim closed his eyes to review recent life and consider the warning signs. He inhaled and exhaled to the count of ten and relaxed into the memory foam. They'd been through so much lately, and it wasn't all Candy's fault. He'd resisted her pleas to accompany her on business trips. He'd grown irritated when she'd pointed out he was dragging his heels about improving his work connectivity skills, a change that would free him from doing all his work in Seattle.

"Fighting technology," Jim muttered sleepily. Clifford had mentioned this, too, in an advisory memo weeks ago. Jim was supposed to be communicating with his boss through the wretched digital pad but he'd made no attempt to do so. What was he, Jim, trying to prove? Did his reaction against the digital pad share a common root with dressing Titus in a clashing outfit the day they'd met Candy at the airport? He dozed, the image of the track shared by Athens U and Athens Tech drifting into his mind. The track was filled with competitors, some of whom he recognized. Candy, surrounded by fans, thrust a javelin high and far, all the way to the sun. Clifford raced alongside Hermes and Veronica, the three of them driving chariots at break-neck speed. Jim looked for himself in the scene; he was sitting in the bleachers.

His eyes popped open.

"Benched," he muttered, still half-way in the dream.

Benched, but who'd put him there? Jim stirred to full consciousness feeling anger. Old anger. More than a century ago Candy's aggressive and too-public remarks about how she'd like to destroy mortals on a large scale had gotten him bounced from Continental Manager of Australia and landed him in a low-ranking position in the Pacific Northwest. It was now clear she'd suffered from severe hormonal imbalance at the time, something he could have paid more attention to, including her longing for a baby. They'd both suffered, but Candy had morphed into a mortal media star while Jim was stuck in the rut of middle management. At least when he'd started his Pacific Northwest assignment the structurelings had really needed regular counseling sessions. Now, with architectural support for mortal structures facilitated by small-g operated computers, jobs like Jim's were quickly becoming an obsolete box on the Olympus, Inc., organizational chart.

Jim's muscles tensed. His stomach soured. He sat on the edge of the bed and rested his head in his hands.

"It takes balls," he grumbled to the floor. If he applied his PhD in behavioral sciences to himself, he'd be forced to admit he was resisting change and was growing increasingly passive-aggressive in his professional and personal interactions.

He glanced over at Titus, who snored around the thumb in his mouth. Jim shuffled to the bathroom, switched on the light and looked in the vanity mirror. He contemplated his long, pale face, receding hairline and watery blue eyes behind thick lenses. Ever since college, ever since he'd crashed his chariot at the track-and-field meet in his senior century, he'd adopted the guise of what 20th century mortals called a nerd. He was forty-six hundred years old, well-educated, married to a beautiful and talented goddess and father of a big, healthy boy.

"There's nothing wrong with you," he whispered to his reflection, then paused and swallowed hard. "Not if you get your act together."

Jim silently imparted a self-improvement list to his new client, Jim. Start with simple changes, some on the inside, some on the outside. Figure out what you need from Candy, from Clifford, from your work, and ask for help to make those changes. Make an appointment with Apollo to see if you can improve your vision and ditch the glasses. And for right now—

"Stand up straight!"

His mother's admonishment called across the centuries from his youth. She'd nagged at him to stretch his spine, to feel as if his head were held up by a string with his vertebrae falling neatly into alignment underneath. He was a son of Poseidon, half Big-G God. He had every right to stand his full six-foot-eight, even if the newness of good posture made his neck and shoulders ache.

The man looking back at him in the mirror *did* look more secure, more confident than the fellow who'd been there before. "A symbol, a promise to myself," Jim said out loud, his voice pleasingly resonant.

"Stand tall," Jim said to Jim. This would be his mantra if he got off track with getting his life in order.

The phone in the sitting room rang. Jim reached the receiver in four long strides.

"James A. Smith speaking."

"Jim, my boy!" boomed a hearty male voice. "Hera told me you were in town. This is Zeus."

"Zeus." Jim knew the Ex-Lord of the Universe, of course, but they'd never been close and he could count on one hand the things they had in common, including being blood relatives. "What a pleasant surprise," he stalled, waiting for inspiration.

"I meant to call you sooner, but Aster keeps me so busy I hardly notice when the sun and stars trade places these days."

Aster. In a few beats Jim attached the name to an e-mail announcement about Hebe's new baby.

"I know the feeling," Jim concurred, wandering back into the bedroom to peek at Titus, whose chin was encrusted with drool.

"Well of course you do, my boy, of course you do with that fine boy of your own." Zeus sighed. "You young fathers are lucky, having the opportunity to help raise the little ones with no one thinking it's strange."

Jim caught a note of wistfulness in Zeus' voice.

A short chuckle rumbled across the connection. "That's why I'm calling, in fact. I'm inviting you and Titus over for a play date."

Jim's jaw dropped. Socializing with Zeus? *Stand tall*, the new Jim coached.

"As a matter of fact," Jim said in a tone he hoped sounded casual, "we have some time open this afternoon—"

"Splendid!" Zeus boomed. "I'll send my driver for you at one on-the-dot. Don't bring a thing, we've got diapers, toys, teething crackers, the works. This is gonna be some fun!"

The call ended without a goodbye. Jim replaced the receiver and tiptoed to the bed. He gently shook Titus awake.

"C'mon, big guy," he said to his son. "Time to put on your best duds. You're going to meet the Biggest of Big-Gs."

Hera

Candy Smith had been biting her nails.

Hera noted the jagged tips of red tapping nervously on the clipboard identical to her own. She'd organized their meeting with care, with plenty of documentation to keep them on track in case Candy still suffered from exhaustion and burn-out after a long weekend off. Things were not moving forward as she'd planned.

She tried again.

"Let's look at page one again," she said, struggling mightily to keep irritation out of her voice. "Our focus for next quarter, now that the book tour is done, is to update the Marvelous Marriage seminars with topics from *The Best Thing in Life is We*. The core concept is the Connubial Retreat—"

Though Candy's fingertips continued to drum the clipboard she was staring into space again, as she had during Hera's previous attempts to get the conversation moving. Hera reached over the table between them and snapped her fingers in Candy's face.

"Candy? Hello?"

Candy sighed and stopped drumming long enough to flick her hair behind her shoulders.

"Oh. Sorry."

"Heaven and Earth!" Hera swore in frustration. She tossed her clipboard to the floor and strode to the mini-bar. The hour hand on the clock above her cache hadn't reached X but this was an emergency. She wrenched open the door and liberated a bottle of Chardonnay. Two goblets completed her arsenal. The Goddess of Marriage returned to her chair and uncorked the wine with a flick of her finger. She cascaded a healthy pour into her employee's glass and an even larger one into her own.

"Drink!" Hera ordered as she raised her goblet and took a gulp.

She peered over the edge of her glass at Candy. The small-g's hand trembled as she picked up her goblet, took one shallow sip and returned her drink to the table. Her fingers resumed their clipboard tattoo.

"Talk!" Hera commanded. Immortal Resources would write her up if they found out about her brutal approach but she was beyond caring.

"It's…" Candy's eyes wandered around the room like a stoned version of the motion-tracking security camera Hermes had insisted Zeus and Hera install outside their condo.

Hera slugged down another exasperated swallow.

"Spill it, Candy!" she snapped. "This program can't afford PR problems."

"Oh," drawled Candy, her dreamy tone out of sync with her violently drumming fingertips. "It's not really a problem. It's just that I need to spend all my time with Jim and Titus. That's all I want to do."

Hera slammed her goblet on the table so hard Chardonnay slopped over the sides. Her media star, who'd expressed frustration about her husband not supporting her career just five days ago, had swung 180 degrees on the marriage vs. work compass. True, Candy's was an extreme personality, but this shift was too much to be believed. It might be drugs, it might be a spell, but Hera was certain—someone had tampered with Candy.

"How interesting, dear," Hera said with ice in her voice that

Candy seemed incapable of detecting. "And how lovely you've all come on this business trip so the happy little family can be together. It must be difficult for you to leave them for even a moment, but you're such a celebrity now. I'm sure some of the other Olympians have wanted to meet you."

Candy's eyes flickered for a few seconds as if she might recover, but she sank back into her stupor and muttered, "The tone of her upper arms is incredible."

Hera contemplated the non sequitur—or was it? She smiled bitterly when realization struck. Yes, she knew just who Candy was talking about, and the attack was not so much on Candy as on herself.

"Have some more wine, dear," Hera urged, topping off Candy's nearly full goblet, "and tell me all about your wonderful visit with Aphrodite."

David

This morning, his second Monday in the City of Mount Olympus, David donned a fresh toga, tucked his digital pad and Edith Hamilton's *Mythology* into a pouch slung around his shoulder and caught a chariot to Olympus, Inc., headquarters. Time to see actual people instead of reading about them!

He rode the elevator to the sixth floor and wandered the halls until he passed Veronica's old office. David knocked on the half-open door, telling himself he didn't really care if he got another look at Cleo—he just wanted to make an appointment with Veronica. He stuck his head around the door.

Cleo was at her desk but she wasn't alone. Some guy who looked like a middle-aged surfer dude stood behind her, leaning over her shoulder and tapping a lightning-quick finger on her digital pad.

"Just a few strokes and it's done," Surfer Dude said, his slick tone insinuating a double-meaning. *Gag me* thought David when Cleo giggled in response.

"Excuse me," David said. They both looked up.

"Hello, David." Cleo blushed. "Hermes was showing me a new app." She looked from David to Surfer Dude. "You've met each other, right?"

"Not *the* David?" Hermes said. He extended his hand and simultaneously tossed his head back to get the hair out of his eyes. "Welcome to Mount Olympus, cousin. Ronnie's told me about you. Starting at Athens U this semester, right?"

"In the master's program," David said, his voice pitched low in an effort to sound manly, but it made him sound like a complete and total idiot.

"Anything I can do for you, David?" Cleo asked, a half-smile playing on her lips.

"I need to make an appointment with Veronica," he said in his regular voice.

Hermes grinned. "Later," he said, waggling his eyebrows at Cleo.

She watched stroll him out the door, sighed and looked down at her digital pad.

"Let's see," she said, tapping her fingers on the screen. "Veronica...she's busy up to and through lunch. Let's look at the afternoon." Cleo swiped the screen with her fingertip. "Hmm. I see a fifteen-minute block at two-thirty." She looked up at him with her huge, gorgeous eyes. "Is fifteen minutes long enough?"

"Uh, yeh, sure. Sure," he faltered, "fifteen minutes is fine."

"Okay," Cleo said, "just let me verify." She tapped out a message; soon there was a responding chime. "Two-thirty works fine. She'll meet you down here if that's okay?"

"You bet," he said with more eagerness than was cool.

Cleo laughed. "I don't blame you a bit. Who'd deal with Stella if they didn't have to?"

Good—Cleo hadn't caught on that he was eager see her again. He recklessly blurted, "I don't suppose you'd—" but stopped himself before he asked her to meet him when she had a coffee break.

She looked at him with charitable pity.

"Sorry. Really busy today," she said and returned to tapping on her screen. "See you at two-thirty."

David smiled and nodded, masking his humiliation until he reached the hallway. He strode to the elevator, silently chastising himself for being such a social geek. Of course tall, beautiful, somewhat older Cleo didn't have time for a guy like him. She wanted some worldly big-shot, like Hermes. Why should he even try?

He entered the first available car, empty but ascending, and pushed all the floor buttons. A man got on at the seventh floor and off at the eighth. A trio of women boarded on the ninth. On the tenth floor the doors rolled open, revealing Candy Smith and Hera. Candy looked weird, kind of dazed but also like she was about to cry. Hoping to avoid them, David tried to slink off behind the three women without being seen, but Hera spotted him.

"David," she commanded with the power accorded a birth-mother.

Trapped, he stood up straight and stepped forward to meet his fate. Candy set a foot in the elevator but drew back instantly when Hera said, "Wait, please, Candy."

David hadn't seen Hera for a year at least, when she'd taken him to dinner during a business trip to Seattle. Her appearance hadn't changed, but there was something about her—he couldn't describe it exactly—but there was something weird about Hera, too.

Hera put her hand on David's shoulder. "Candy's not feeling well," she said in a low voice. "Do me a favor and make sure she gets into the chariot I called from the Mountain High Plaza Hotel."

David took Candy's arm and escorted her into the elevator. As the doors rolled closed, Hera said, "Come back at noon, David. I'll take you to lunch."

"Great," David said, feeling the opposite. He didn't dislike Hera but he didn't entirely trust her, either and only accepted her invitation out of courtesy. From the corner of his eye, he could see Candy was shivering.

He turned to her. Her lips were pressed together and her eyes were wide.

"You okay?" he asked with genuine concern.

David had spent quite a bit of time with the Smiths since he'd learned he was half Big-G God. He had weekly counseling sessions with Jim, an opportunity to ask questions and receive guidance about being immortal. Jim had given David flying lessons and taught him level-one cloaking (strong enough to conceal himself from mortal view). Their sessions often ended with dinner. While Jim cooked— he was especially good with pasta—Candy would corner David and ask him a bunch of embarrassing questions, like did he have a girlfriend.

"I need to get back to Jim and Titus," Candy said through chattering teeth.

Whatever was wrong with her, David hoped it wasn't catching.

The chariot driver kindly offered Candy a blanket and waited while David settled her into a seat. "Hope you're feeling better soon," he said as he tucked the blanket around her shoulders. "Say hi to Jim for me."

His head ringing with the warning voice of Thelma Bernstein, David returned to Olympus, Inc., located the nearest Men's Room and washed his hands with plenty of soap and hot water. It would suck to get an immortal cold or the flu. How long would that sort of illness last—weeks, maybe, or years?

When he returned to the lobby it was barely 10 AM. He studied the directory in front of the atrium, in search of something to do until his command lunch date with Hera.

The Technical Development Department and Laboratory, fourth floor, sounded cool until David noticed Hermes was the department director. There were two sub-departments, Digital Devices and Robotics. Hephaestus was listed under Robotics, which seemed odd—shouldn't he have his own department?

Hera had the entire tenth floor, Department of Marriage and Family. She, like Hermes, was a director and had a deep listing of assistants for everything from Marriage and the Media to Family Celebrations.

Continental Managers had offices on the ninth floor. From what David understood of the job (through Jim's reminiscences about being Continental Manager of Australia), these immortals rarely visited Mount Olympus but when they did they brought an entourage. The Weather Department, third floor, was where Candy had trained to be a Rain Goddess, her job before she became the Marvelous Marriage spokesperson.

David suddenly felt guilty. He didn't live in Seattle anymore. With Candy traveling all the time, what would Jim do for company while David spent 200 years at Athens U?

He powered on his digital pad and sent a message to Jim, though it was probably futile to communicate this way as Jim was notoriously bad with technology and might never pick up the message. David sent his best wishes for Candy's speedy recovery and invited Jim to meet him some night at the Campus Pub.

At 10:15 employees trickled, then swarmed up and down the gold-railed staircases. Break time, David supposed, as he watched from a bench near the directory. Cleo passed by in a group of young women, smiling and laughing. At least she wasn't with Hermes. A guy dressed in black motorcycle leathers limped down the stairs and stalked out the main entrance to light up a cigarette. From what he'd read in the Herodotus Jones book, David was sure this was his half-brother, Hephaestus. Common sense coached him to wait for an introduction, rather than intrude on the dark figure.

In twenty minutes or so the crowd had cleared. He stuck his nose in *Mythology* to brush up on his other half-siblings in case they crossed paths today. According to the directory, Hebe, Ilithyia and Ares had offices on the eighth floor, but it was weird—none of them had staff listed for their departments (Youth, Childbirth and War, respectively).

Restless, David tucked the book back into his pouch and climbed the nearest staircase. On the mezzanine he peeked through a carved archway at the employee cafeteria. Tables and chairs, sparsely occupied, seemed to spread to infinity. The aroma wafting in the air verified the word written on the daily special board—pizza.

David's stomach growled. He checked his watch (it looked stupid with a toga but he couldn't bring himself to give it up yet). Nearly an hour to kill. He sighed, approached the elevators and pushed the "up" arrow. An empty car arrived instantly. David pushed the fifth floor button and rode to the Department of Architectural and Computer Services with the uninspired plan to say hi to Clifford. This was a bust, as Clifford was in a meeting. His executive assistant, a tall young man with a German accent, chatted politely with David for a few minutes but soon excused himself to work on a complex drawing displayed on the biggest desk-top monitor David had ever seen. He opted for the stairs instead of the elevator, climbed to the seventh floor and strolled the halls of Immortal Resources, a buzzing hive of offices and conference rooms. He skipped the eighth floor, reluctant to meet Hebe, Ilithyia or Ares on his own, and checked out the ninth, which was decorated with art and artifacts from around the world. Every continent was represented, and it was great stuff, like what he'd seen in museums.

He arrived on the tenth floor two minutes before noon. The reception area was staffed by a woman named Gilda, who vigorously shook his hand and called him "young David." She then bounded to a door on the far wall and knocked to summon Hera.

"Back in an hour," Hera said to Gilda as she took David's arm and steered him to the elevator. They rode to the mezzanine and entered the employee cafeteria.

"You don't mind informal dining?" she asked, but it wasn't a question. Hera ordered a goat cheese and spinach pizza for him, a diet plate for herself and a glass of Chardonnay for each of them. The concept of wine with lunch startled David. He forced a smile and tried to take it in stride. Hera led the way to a table for two in an alcove near the back of the dining room. For a moment he wondered if she didn't want to be seen with him because of his origins. The wine arrived as soon as they were seated, in large glasses filled nearly to the brim. David took a sip to brace himself.

"How fortunate we bumped into each other today," Hera said. She sipped deeply from her glass. "Pardon my bad manners for not seeing you before now, son." She said the last word with emphasis. "I've been fighting fires in one of my programs."

"No problem," David said. He took another sip.

"Look," she said, tilting her head toward the entrance.

David turned around and strained his eyes to bring the distance into focus. "What?"

He started to turn back but she said, "No, keep looking, just past the archway. I'm sure I see someone you should know out on the mezzanine."

David looked for several seconds. "I don't see anyone except the cashier and two guys placing an order," he said, turning back.

"Probably doesn't matter," Hera said. She was looking down into her spoon. After a moment she tisked and set it aside. "I've told Ronnie more than once the cafeteria needs a new dishwasher. This spoon is so spotted it's a disgrace."

David thought he saw a wisp of steam rise from the utensil. He blinked his eyes and looked again. The steam, if it had ever really been there, was gone.

"Not that dishwasher spots are a big issue," Hera said. She smiled and raised her glass. He reciprocated. They drank. The wine had a tartness to it, an edge he hadn't noticed on his first sip. His taste buds getting acclimated, he guessed.

"It's Candy I'm really worried about," Hera said. "You like Candy, don't you, dear?"

His teeth clenched when she said "dear."

"Yes, I like Candy. Jim, too."

"Well of course you do. We're family."

Talk about family made him tense. He took two more sips. The tart edge to the wine was gone. A new smoothness filled his mouth and set him at ease.

"But enough of that," Hera said. She reached across the table and patted his hand. "Tell me, David, how was your morning?"

His wine-loosened tongue let slip his unsuccessful attempt to ask Cleo on a date.

"Cleo," said Hera, her voice a wise purr. "She's lovely, dear, perfect for you though a bit wiser in the ways of the world. You said you don't have much experience with girls?"

Had he said that? He didn't remember saying that, but he must have.

"That's right," he agreed.

Hera put her elbows on the table and leaned toward him.

"David, if I were you, I'd get some advice about women."

"You would?" he said, gratitude surging in his chest.

"I would. And I know just who I'd ask. She's a cousin of yours. The best person for romantic advice is Aphrodite."

"Aphrodite," David repeated dreamily.

"That's right, dear. Why don't you call Aphrodite or send her one of those digital message things? I'm sure she'd make time for you, and when you meet with her you could do me a very small favor."

David smiled and nodded at the simple, simple task Hera asked him to do. Draining a large glass of wine in the middle of the day was much, much easier than he'd thought it would be, and the pizza was delicious, best he'd ever had. David thanked Hera for lunch.

"It's been a pleasure," she said as they rose to leave the cafeteria.

In the archway they passed Veronica and a pudgy, red-cheeked woman in a pink toga trimmed with pearls.

"Hello, girls," Hera said.

Veronica, who looked preoccupied, nodded in acknowledgement. The pudgy woman glared at David and said, "Hello, Mother."

"Your sister, Hebe," Hera explained as she led David toward the gold-railed staircase. "Now, run along, dear, and make your appointment with Aphrodite."

"Aphrodite," David repeated.

"And remember, David, what Mother asked you to do."

"Yes, Mother," said David with a smile. He drifted down the stairs and hailed a chariot, proud Hera needed his help, even in a simple, simple task.

Hebe

Hebe, Goddess of Youth, was having a rotten string of days.

When she'd dropped in at Olympus, Inc., last Friday to pick up her paycheck there was a note from Ronnie (she refused to call the little brat Veronica) in the envelope. It was an order, not a request, to meet her for lunch at the corporate cafeteria (posh—not!) the following Monday.

This irritating news was followed by a miserable weekend. Aster had kept her up every night, fussing and feverish with emerging teeth. Hebe had placated her as best she could by rubbing wine on Aster's angry gums, wine borrowed from her own glass or two of self-medication. Heracles was no help at all with the children, especially when they were babies and needed 'round-the-clock attention.

"I'd just as soon eat 'em," he'd said, jokingly. Hebe had assumed he was joking, though his filicide record from earlier marriages was less than stellar. She tried not to dwell on it. Dwelling on unpleasant thoughts accelerated wrinkles and she had plenty to worry about besides a husband with murder in his past.

For example, what was she thinking when she'd gotten pregnant again, and at four thousand? She'd been stupid to fall for Heracles' charm, especially since he wasn't the one who'd be stuck at home for another round of parenting centuries. No, he was too busy guarding Mount Olympus (or so he said). She'd been so close to being free of mothering! The boys, Alexiares and Anicetus, were nearly out of the mansion and for the first time in her adult life she'd faced the prospect of having worry-free time to herself, time for liposuction and collagen lip treatments, time for securing a personal trainer and getting her abs into a condition that didn't mimic partially set gelatin.

Today, so far, sucked even worse than the weekend. Ronnie had intercepted Hebe the moment she entered the lobby, like she was some kind of security risk instead of a Big-G Goddess. They'd climbed the staircase to the mezzanine instead of taking the little freight lift Hebe favored. She'd been hot-faced and winded when they arrived at the cafeteria. As an added insult, they passed Mom and her bastard son no one had bothered to introduce her to, not that Hebe cared. The wild-haired little shrimp was slack-jawed, probably mentally deficient since Mom had been forty-six hundred when she'd made that mistake.

Ronnie had ordered two "health plates" at the cafeteria counter, then walked as fast as she could to a booth in the back. Hebe hated her sister for making her sweat, especially since the pink silk toga she'd worn for the occasion had to be dry cleaned. The fabric stuck to her clammy back, making it difficult to slide onto the padded bench opposite Ronnie. Hebe glanced at the table top to see if it was clean. It was. At least the Olympus, Inc., cafeteria had cloth napkins.

Hebe fiddled with the white linen square alongside her bread plate. A wait person delivered their order with brief, pleasant remarks and scampered away. Ronnie didn't say anything, just sipped from her goblet of pure spring water and stared at Hebe as if she were measuring her both inside and out.

The Goddess of Youth knew her deficiencies. Reality was taking its toll on her face, the last battlement of fast-fading freshness. Youth, by definition, did not include tits that sagged to the knees. The last time Hebe and Mom had had a real heart-to-heart (it seemed decades ago), Mom had offered useful advice on slimming foundation garments; she'd also said Hebe seemed to be applying makeup with a trowel.

Hebe picked at her lunch, an appallingly healthy heap of field greens with low-fat goat cheese dressing, half a pita bread and a small dish of grapes (not that a large dish of grapes would be an improvement). Thank Dad Ronnie had never served as Cupbearer to the Gods, as Hebe had in earlier centuries—she probably would have refused to serve ambrosia because it was too caloric!

Why did Ronnie have to come along, anyway?

Hebe ruminated bitterly as she tore her pita into small pieces, stuffing them one by one between lips the Mount Olympus sculptors portrayed as plump and pouty, though fine, vertical lines showed when her lipstick wore through. Ronnie had been born just in time to steal Hebe's figurative thunder, just as she'd reached the age of fourteen hundred and was see-sawing between childhood and becoming a young woman. She'd needed Mom's attention, needed her advice about boys and what clothes to wear to enhance her budding figure. Then the stupid baby came along. Now the stupid baby was in charge of everything!

Hebe's musing broke at the sound of Ronnie clearing her throat.

"Thank you for meeting with me today, Hebe."

Ronnie's voice sounded cool and neutral but Hebe didn't trust the tone. She looked up. Her eyes (made dazzling green with the aid of contact lenses) looked into her sister's, dark as ever but there was something new, something chilling, almost, in their expression. Ronnie was going to bring up the damn evaluation again, she was certain of it.

"Sure. Whatever," she said, with a sideways look at the grapes. Would it hurt the bitch to give her a real dessert before raking her over the coals?

Ronnie rested her elbows on the table and laced her fingers together. "I need to talk to you about your last evaluation, Hebe."

Hebe leaned back and folded her arms beneath her underwire-supported bosom but offered no reply. Ronnie was going to rant about the health and fitness thing again, like that had anything to do with youth!

"The goals we set," (we? thought Hebe), "were straight-forward. I asked you to work on a solution to the childhood obesity epidemic in first-world countries and develop a program to reduce teen pregnancies."

"Bo-ring!" announced Hebe with a roll of her eyes.

Ronnie leaned forward, her expression grim. "You're the Goddess of Youth, Hebe. You're supposed to protect and enhance the lives of young mortals, not behave like you're one of them."

"Get a life," Hebe said under her breath.

"For centuries you've had the easiest job on Mount Olympus and you've made a hash of it. I pulled your original job description from the archives." Ronnie bent sideways to extract something heavy from her briefcase on the bench alongside her. She set a marble tablet on the table with a *thunk* and barked a short laugh. "I still can't believe how long it took Dad to convert to papyrus," she muttered. Ronnie glanced down at the tablet, then up again. "Your only job responsibilities were looking young and helping Mom into her chariot."

Hebe heaved a disgusted sigh. She'd loathed helping Mom into her chariot, a service Mom hadn't needed until she was pregnant with Ronnie.

"So?"

Their eyes locked.

"So," Ronnie said, "if you were receiving five drachma a week for a child's allowance instead of drawing a full Big-G salary for doing virtually nothing, maybe I wouldn't expect more from you."

"You think you're so hot, just because Dad left you in charge!"

Dark eyes flashed back at green.

"You don't have a real job, Hebe, you never did have a real job and you know it. I hoped to get you pointed in a meaningful direction by asking you to set up some projects to help the youth of today's world, but you didn't even try." Ronnie leaned back in her chair, her eyes narrowing to slits. "Hebe, you're fired."

"You can't fire me, you little bitch!" Hebe said. She laughed nervously. "Dad won't let you!"

"Dad has nothing to say in the matter."

Ronnie raised her right hand and made a swirling motion, forcing Hebe to sit up straight and plant her plump, pedicured feet squarely on the floor.

A chill of disbelief and something worse rushed through Hebe. "He gave you The Power?"

Ronnie rose. "I'll see you to the door."

Hebe, for once, moved faster than her baby sister. She hoisted herself out of the booth and bee-lined for the exit, passed through the archway and trotted as fast as her weak legs could carry her, down the staircase and out into the street. This was some kind of mistake! Dad had to get her job back, at least get her salary back? Hebe hadn't told Heracles about the charges she'd run up for Aster's baby things or the down payment she'd made to a plastic surgeon. If the old stories were true, he'd killed his first wife for less! She'd watch the mail for their Bank of Olympus Platinum card statement and hide it from him, maybe sell some jewelry to make the minimum payment until she figured out what to do.

But first she'd hail a chariot and go straight to Dad.

Aphrodite

When the Goddess of Love had a telephone installed in her boudoir she'd had a premonition she was making a mistake. Today, the premonition came home to roost.

Aphrodite, relaxing on a chaise lounge as much as today's irritating circumstances would allow, raised her index finger and tapped the voice messaging "repeat" key. The ruby-encrusted frames of her readers slid down her nose as she shook her head in disbelief.

It was a message from someone calling himself David Bernstein, a halting, boyish message asking for advice on wooing the girl of his dreams (or, as he'd so lamely put it, "getting her to go out with me"). He was willing to pay for Aphrodite's services (hah!) and would very much appreciate meeting with her sooner rather than later.

Aphrodite snorted with disdain. Who did this David Bernstein think she was, an agony aunt who answered letters for a lonely hearts magazine?

The name sounded familiar, though. David Bernstein. Had she heard it or read it somewhere recently? There'd been a Milton Bernstein at Olympus, Inc., centuries ago, a runty, balding man who'd prepared bi-decade income tax returns for everyone in the Pantheon, but he hadn't been around since…sometime around when BC had switched to AD and everything was confused for a while…

This had to be a crank call, probably Ares disguising his voice, trying to make a fool of her because she'd stood him up a couple of nights ago, for which she felt not a jot of remorse. All he ever talked about was faster jets and bigger military appropriations. He'd been a real pill since Veronica had taken over, now that he didn't get everything he wanted just because he asked for it.

"Boo-hoo, baby," she sneered at his gold-framed picture that grinned at her from the vanity table across the room.

That was it!

Aphrodite sat up so abruptly she knocked the carved ivory princess phone off the side table. She'd read about David Bernstein in last week's Sunday edition of *Mountain High Times*. He'd been the subject of Mount Olympus gossip a few years back when word leaked out about Hera's young son—but not by Zeus. In fact, no one seemed to know the father's identity. Last week's newspaper article said David was enrolled at Athens U and would be in town for a couple of centuries. When she'd scanned the piece it had seemed unimportant, but now, as she and Hera were tacitly at war…

She retrieved the phone from the floor, listened again to the message and selected the call-back option. Setting her voice to purr mode, she was poised to pounce when he answered.

"David Bernstein," she cooed after he said hello. "This is Aphrodite. Thank you for the lovely message."

She winced when he said, "No problem."

"No, I wouldn't think so," she said, the honey in her voice unaltered. "I'd be delighted to meet you—hmmm, let me look at my schedule." Aphrodite counted to five. "Oh, how fortunate. I have some time tomorrow afternoon, three-ish?"

"Sure. Okay. No problem."

Aphrodite felt a sudden rush of sympathy for the poor girl who was the object of David's desire. Aside from covertly pumping David for information to use against Hera (especially about his father—how laughable if it really were Milton Bernstein!) she would definitely lecture him on vocal tics.

"I'll send my limousine if you'll tell me where you're staying," she said silkily.

"Cool," he said and gave his hotel address.

"Perfect. See you tomorrow."

She cut the connection before he finished saying goodbye.

Aphrodite cast a scornful glance at Ares' photo.

"And it wouldn't hurt one bit if you heard about his visit," she said to the black and white image, a satisfied smile curving her lips.

Veronica

It was 1:17 PM when Hebe waddled out of the employee cafeteria in a cloud of fear and face powder. Veronica, head throbbing, was glad the Goddess of Youth had run away. Excused from escort duty, she lowered herself back into the booth and rested her head in her hands until the black feeling started to lift.

Her head still ached when she arrived at her sixth-floor office.

"Hi," said Cleo, looking up from a copy of Veronica's memo to the Continental Managers she'd been proofing. "You okay?" she said, on her feet and offering a steadying hand when Veronica slumped in the doorway.

"Fine. I'm fine." She'd meant to sound reassuring but her voice came out angry.

"You've got some time before your two-thirty appointment," Cleo said, guiding Veronica to the inner office. "Why don't you lie down for a while? I'll buzz you when David gets here."

Veronica didn't argue. She curled up on the sectional sofa and closed her eyes. It was good to be here, hidden away in her old office, the one corporate-paid extravagance she had allowed herself since becoming CEO. How could she have survived the past year, without this hide-out and without Cleo? Young and smart, Cleo could easily have been assigned to another department (Hermes had inquired about her more than once) but she'd agreed to stay on as Veronica's extra eyes and ears. An assistant could go places a CEO couldn't, could take the pulse of employee sentiment without being obvious.

She couldn't sleep, not after the rush of firing Hebe and the sickness induced by exercising The Power. Veronica felt worse than she had after she'd demoted Hef, though she'd feared Hef's reaction much more than she had Hebe's. Did using The Power have a cumulative toxic effect? Dad could tell her, if she saw him anytime soon.

Veronica rose and crossed to the colorfully framed mirror in her private bathroom. She splashed some water on her face and smoothed her hair. Her stomach grumbled. The Power must have accelerated her metabolism and burned through lunch already. After she saw David she was due at her top-floor office, to set priorities with Hermes and Clifford for the coming month. There wouldn't be enough time in between to go back to the cafeteria and snag a cookie.

A soft chime sounded, activated by a button under Cleo's desk. Veronica squared her shoulders and strode to door, stopping to slide up the dimmer switch to brighten the room. When she grasped the doorknob it felt warm in her hand—or was her hand unusually cold?

"Hello, David."

David straightened up from where he'd been leaning over Cleo's desk, a stunned, goofy smile on his lips—no surprise as Cleo had mentioned his earlier attempt to ask her out.

"Uh, hi."

Praise Dad, David wore a toga and sandals instead of his mortal get-up. Not that she, Veronica, had given his acclimation much thought since she'd seen him ten or twelve days ago. For an instant she felt guilty for neglecting him.

She smiled weakly and swept her arm toward her private office. "Come in."

The usual bounce was missing from David's step, perhaps an adjustment from tennis shoes to sandals. They'd set no agenda—in fact, she now realized she had no idea why he'd wanted to meet with her. She pointed him to the sofa instead of the guest chair at her delicately carved cherry wood desk.

David plopped down on the sofa. He wrestled with the hem of

his toga and, eventually, crossed his legs.

"So," she said, once he'd settled. "What can I do for you today?"

"Oh."

There was something different about him. A slack version of his nice-young-guy smile propped up his lips. Probably he was worn out from assimilating Mount Olympus life. He reached into the pouch slung over his shoulder, took out a digital pad and powered it up. "I just wanted to ask you a few questions."

The first one was easy. The Olympians started using Roman numerals instead of Greek numerals millennia ago because Roman numerals were easier to carve on sundials. This once-practical custom became tradition for use in timepieces and numbering years, but it was a messy system for most modern applications, in which case Arabic numerals were used.

David looked a bit sheepish when he asked how long his debit account funds were supposed to last.

"My intention was to provide enough to get you started," she said, probing.

He shrugged, looking confused.

"Seven or eight years, I was hoping? Ten if you can make it last but let me know if you can't. It's from a trust account I had Mom set up when I—" she chose her words carefully "—found out about you."

"Mom," David said, his face brightening.

Strange. Veronica was pretty sure David's feelings for Mom were neutral, at best. But she'd seen them leaving the employee cafeteria together this afternoon. Maybe they'd come to a new understanding? She hoped so, anyway.

"Anything else?" she asked as she peeked at the clock on David's digital pad. They'd eaten up all but five of their fifteen minutes.

David bit his lip and sighed.

"It's—" His words stopped, his face contrite.

"What?" She struggled to mask her exasperation. What kind of trouble could he have gotten himself into in ten or twelve days? Was her half-brother going to turn out like her full siblings? She prayed to Heaven and Earth that, aside from Ares, no more corrections requiring The Power loomed on the horizon.

"It's Pan," he said. "I don't like to say anything bad about anybody, but he's—"

"A jerk?" she supplied, more quickly than was kind.

"Well—yes!" David slumped with relief. She gave him a few

seconds to recover. "Is there—" he started again, timidly. "Is there anyone else you can assign me to? I mean, I know you're really busy and I feel really bad asking you to do this but the stuff Pan's showing me, it—I don't think it's what you brought me here for."

"I'll see what I can do." She thought of Clifford, would have asked him in the first place but he'd been scheduled for vacation the day after David arrived. "Can you meet with a new mentor tomorrow evening?"

An abrupt look of concern swept his face. "What time?"

"Seven?" she offered, wondering what had just happened to him.

"Sure," he said, looking relieved.

"Okay," she said. "I'll message you as soon as it's confirmed."

"Thanks."

David rose quickly. They passed through the outer office. Though Cleo was gone, the goofy, dazed smile returned to David's lips. Strange, Veronica thought as she accompanied him to the elevator. He pushed the down arrow. She waited with him until the elevator arrived, then pressed the up arrow for her trip to the top floor. The one positive side-effect of The Power was the ability to withstand the lightning-fast ascent to the CEO suite without discomfort.

Stella, praise Dad, was out. Clifford, five minutes early, stood waiting by the reception desk. It was the first time Veronica had seen him since he'd returned from vacation. His skin was an odd hue, like a ripe apricot. Probably the reflection of Stella's bronze-colored desk.

"Welcome back," she said, extending her hand.

Clifford raised his arm slowly, as if in pain. They shook hands. "Glad to be back."

She gestured for him to enter her office, surprised at his stiff gait as he approached his usual chair. Though concerned, Veronica's policy was to avoid asking personal questions of her directors. If Clifford wanted to tell her why he was impaired—and why, as she could now see, his skin truly was orange—that was his prerogative.

"I need to ask you a favor," she said when they were seated.

The hope in his eyes gave her a twinge of guilt. She swallowed the feeling and proceeded to recruit Clifford as David's new mentor. He agreed at once.

"And if you could let me know," she said, leaning forward and lowering her voice, "I saw David today and he seemed—not his usual self."

Clifford, too, leaned forward, his elbows on the desk. "You wish me to report if I notice anything odd about him?" he said, resting his orange chin on his orange hands.

"Exactly." His skin, Veronica now realized, was the same color as Bill Gates, Jr.'s, fur. She bit her inner cheek to stop herself from laughing.

Zeus

The Ex-Lord of the Universe grinned from ear to ear. Not only were the little ones, Aster and Titus, friends from the moment they'd set eyes on each other, but Jim had hinted he might enjoy a game of *Stratego* if the toddlers could be persuaded to take a nap. It was a jolly afternoon, the best he'd had in months, the sense of camaraderie was like a tonic, he—

"Da-a-a-a-a-d!"

Zeus leapt from the floor, where he was building a palace of blocks with Aster and Titus.

"Damn Me!" Zeus growled. He looked at Jim, who was seated in Hera's Barcalounger. "I wish that girl would take the herbs her mother gave her for mood swings!"

Jim returned a sympathetic gaze.

"Be thankful you have a son and not a daughter." Zeus rolled his eyes and called out, "We're in the den, Hebe."

The front door slammed. Heavy footfalls approached from the condo foyer. Hebe stormed in and flopped down in Zeus' Barcalounger. Her face was swollen with tears.

"You never call me Princess anymore," Hebe lamented, either oblivious to the fact visitors were present or simply not caring. "Ever since that little bitch Ronnie came along—"

Zeus covered Aster's ears with his hands. The baby cast her eyes toward Hebe, piped "Ma-Ma" and returned her attention to Titus and the blocks.

"Language, Hebe."

"I'll 'language' you, Dad!" Hebe squinted, her face contorted in misery. "The little bitch fired me!"

"Heaven and Earth," Zeus said under his breath. If Hebe didn't have a job, even a bogus one that required no effort on her part, she might realize she didn't need a babysitter. His days with Aster would be no more!

Hebe thrust her bulk forward in the chair and wagged her finger in Zeus' face. "You gave her The Power, Dad!"

"Hebe!" warned Zeus. He nodded toward Jim. "Not in front of—"

"How could you be so stupid?" she barked, missing his cue to stop talking about The Power, until now a secret within their immediate family. "Can't you see she's going to ruin everything?"

"Settle down, just—" Zeus paused and carefully chose his words. "Settle down, Princess." Hebe sneered at him, amplifying her growing resemblance to a toad with a turned up nose. "Are you sure you've got it straight? I know she demoted Hef but he still has a job."

But in his immortal gut Zeus suspected Hebe had not misunderstood. Heaven and Earth, why hadn't he taken care of this problem himself, centuries ago? He'd created the Goddess of Youth position as a temporary fix to make Hebe stop feeling sorry for herself when she was going through an ugly adolescence. Zeus ground his teeth with remorse. He'd been lax in his supervisory role, had neglected to find Hebe a more appropriate job as she aged, and now the problem was tenfold worse.

"She was practically laughing at me, Dad." Tears streamed down Hebe's face. "She said I didn't have a real job, that I've never had a real job!" She choked on a sob. "No one but me remembers what a pain in the ass it was to help Mom into her chariot when she was pregnant with that brat. Ronnie cut me off without a drachma, Dad, and I've got bills to pay. She's evil!" Hebe shouted at Zeus, then turned to Jim and yelled, "She's evil!" as if this proved her assertion.

Hebe lunged to the center of the room where the little ones were playing and snatched Aster from the construction site. The violent sweep of her toga tumbled the teetering assemblage of blocks. The toddlers wailed.

"We're going home," Hebe announced coldly. "Do something about Ronnie, Dad, before my hair turns as white as yours!"

The former Goddess of Youth spun on her heel and stormed from the room. Aster looked over her mother's shoulder, wide-eyed with fright, and shrieked, "Ba-Pa!"

The Ex-Lord of the Universe crumbled to the floor amidst the blocks. A tiny hand tugged at his toga.

"Ba-Pa?"

Titus held out a building block, a puzzled but hopeful look on his cherubic face. Zeus took the block from Titus and muttered, "Thank you, child." His head sank to his breast.

Silence sat heavily on Zeus. He'd meant to ask Jim's advice about Veronica and Athena's plot against him, but the humiliation of Hebe airing a heap of the family's dirty laundry made him feel an undeserving fool. His life was as big a jumble as the building blocks strewn across the floor. Slowly he raised his head and sat back on his heels, eyes staring at nothing. Jim's voice intruded on his zombie-like state.

"If you want to talk, Zeus, I'm here to listen."

Tuesday

Aphrodite

Through her most powerful readers, Aphrodite took a good, hard look in her heart-shaped vanity mirror. The fine lines she'd been dismayed to discover two centuries ago had deepened and today she almost—almost—didn't care.

She glanced in the waste basket beside the vanity table. It overflowed with makeup remover wipes and a recent copy of a mortal aging magazine. A huge bulge in the mortal population had hemorrhaged into middle age this past decade and the magazine promoted the ardent belief that growing older was somehow sexy. The smiling movie star featured on the cover was ravishing, of course, but Aphrodite was wise to the photographic technique called airbrushing and the new digital method, Photoshop.

"Fools."

Her reflection was proof enough even she couldn't hold back wrinkles. Wouldn't it be nice, she thought, to be free to throw on any old midi-toga and not worry about the hair, the nails, the makeup?

But public image was paramount in her job. With an irritated sigh the Goddess of Love arranged the paint pots and cosmetic brushes on the vanity table and began her daily ritual that required increasing artistry. Today might yield something of interest, even if it meant entertaining Hera's bastard son. Aphrodite flipped up her lenses, one at a time, and applied bold strokes of black eyeliner to create an upward-tilted frame for her legendary violet eyes. Today she'd dress as a harem girl (a failsafe in her wardrobe of seduction as long as her abs stayed firm) and entertain her guest in the Sheik Room.

The Sheik Room was one of two counseling chambers she still maintained in the upstairs hall. There used to be a different exotic setting behind every door, doors that appeared to stretch into infinity, thanks to a trick with mirrors. She'd been especially happy to shut down the Marie Antoinette Room—doing the hair was a bitch and a half. Now it was just the Romance Room, where she'd entertained Candy Smith, and the Sheik Room, a setting mostly, but not exclusively, reserved for men.

Her pupil in romance, David Bernstein, arrived at the appointed hour. She watched from a peek hole as her butler, Eros (dressed as an Arabian prince instead of in the gold thong he'd worn for Candy's visit) answered the door. Aphrodite was disappointed in David's appearance, had expected more from someone half Big-G. He looked very young and fairly silly, his pale arms and legs sprouting from his toga, his head of black curls nearly as untamed as Pan's.

From her hiding place she made a soft tsking noise and shook her head. Aphrodite drew back from the peek hole, two eyeholes skillfully hidden in a tapestry hanging in the grand entryway, and crept quietly up a concealed staircase to the second floor.

She made her usual grand entrance, aided by subtle, theatrical lighting operated by Eros from a control booth across the hall.

David Bernstein sat against the pile of cushions, facing the door. The Goddess of Love had planned to grill him about his father's identity but, seeing him at close range, she gleefully realized this wouldn't be necessary. Hera wasn't the only one who'd traveled in and around Jerusalem a couple of millennia ago. Aphrodite, too, had visited that city and met a notable citizen who, but for his coloring, was a virtual twin to her pupil. If she imagined the boy's dark hair as light brown, his skin ruddy instead of pale, blue eyes replacing black—it was too, too easy. Aphrodite's lips curved in a sinister smile. Wouldn't it be fun to give him a make-over and send him back to Hera, looking just like—

But no, that would be showing her hand. Bluffing might prove more advantageous.

She swept the sheer pink veil from her face and cooed, "David Bernstein."

"Hi." He scrambled to his feet. "Aphrodite," he added, turning scarlet to the ears.

"So." She fixed her eyes on his and spread her arms wide to indicate their surroundings. "What do you think?"

David glanced around the room at the potted palm trees, the Persian rugs covering a floor laid with golden sand, the glow of oil flame from ornately etched brass lamps. "Neat." He eyed the hookah on the low brass table between them. "Is that real?"

"Yes." His eyes shifted to her cleavage, well-sculpted by her bejeweled bra. "All of it's real."

He cleared his throat and stiffly sat down.

Aphrodite suppressed a smirk and sat opposite him. "You've come to talk to me about romance, about a girl you'd like to—date?"

The word, a mortalism, was strange. How was romance like a dried fruit? She'd have to ask Apollo sometime when he was in a poetical mood.

"Uh-huh," he said, as forthcoming as an oyster.

She tried again.

"Tell me what's happened so far."

"Not much." He laughed nervously. "I mean, she figured out what I was going to say and cut me off before I could say it."

Aphrodite leaned forward. "Tell me what you tried to say."

He blinked. "Okay, I said, 'I don't suppose you'd—'"

"No, no, no!" she shook her head in dismay. "Never sound vague and groveling when you ask a girl out! Women prefer men who sound confident."

His forehead furrowed. "But I'm not."

"You can learn." She reached across the table and slapped her palms lightly on his cheeks. "And if you sound confident, you'll become confident. But there's more to it than that. How well do you know this girl? Does she have any hobbies or special interests?"

"Hermes," he said gloomily.

"Ahhh." She leaned back against her cushions and tried not to smile. "Yes, he can be a problem. Such a flatterer." She'd succumbed to his charms in ancient days, before she'd married Hef. Hermes had declared her the most beautiful of the Goddesses and managed to father two of her children before she realized she was only one consort of many. It seemed funny, now, that she'd been so naïve.

"He's old enough to be her father," David complained.

"But he's one of Zeus'. Your girl wouldn't be the first to fall for his Big-G charm. Of course…" She paused to study her pupil. A few more centuries and he'd grow into his strong-featured face, would lose the half-formed, chick-without-feathers appearance. "You're half Big-G, too. Does she know that, this girl?"

David hung his head. "Yes."

"Trust me," she said, "it will work to your advantage one day. Now, here's what you must do."

He pulled a digital pad from the pouch at his side.

"No, no, no! Put that away, David. You need to remember this with your heart." She traced a heart shape on her chest, his eyes following. "This may sound strange, but the very first thing you need to do is forget what this girl looks like on the outside. Do everything you can to learn what she's like on the inside. Then you'll know how to reach her."

"But how do I—"

"For Zeus' sake, use the head on your shoulders and think! A girl, no matter how beautiful, is just like anyone else. She has friends, a home, a family, ambitions. The next time you see her, look for clues. Now," she rose, the golden coins on her belly dance belt tinkling, "go forth and conquer! My limo's waiting for you in the driveway."

Aphrodite tossed her platinum blonde tresses over her shoulders and strode grandly out the door. In the interest of maintaining a regal appearance she ignored the motion detected in the corner of one eye, of David reaching past the low brass table for something, but she couldn't imagine what. A few minutes with the ignorant whelp, no matter how useful he might be in her war against Hera, was as much as she could tolerate in one sitting.

Clifford

Clifford strained his ears against the din of Open Mic Tuesday. The Campus Pub was jammed, the air hot and stuffy. The venue was not his choice, but that's where he'd agreed to meet with David Bernstein and the loathsome Pan.

The toneless thud of an electric bass, turned up to 12 on a scale of 10, throbbed underfoot. A guitar with an effect that made it sound like a dentist's drill screamed a non-melody. Clifford's eyes narrowed with dull, nauseated pain.

Pan's mouth seemed to flap non-stop. Clifford was just as happy he couldn't hear what the horny little git was saying (especially after Pan had dubbed him the Jolly Orange Giant), but he did want to keep up with David. After all, Veronica had asked him—it had been more like an order, really—to take over from Pan as David's mentor. Though Veronica hadn't been specific, she'd asked him to report anything odd in David's behavior.

Clifford half-smiled. It would be hard to judge anything David said or did as odd when compared to Pan. Still, reporting what David did or didn't do provided an additional opportunity to communicate with the woman he loved. Veronica had mentioned she suffered from a headache the last time they'd spoken. It worried him. No one seemed to be looking after her these days, not that she'd let anybody near. Except, possibly, Hermes.

The thought of his smarmy rival made Clifford clench his jaws, but now was not the time to dwell on it. Now he must facilitate an orderly transition and replace Pan as David's guide in the City of Mount Olympus. It wasn't so many decades ago that he, himself, had completed his PhD at Athens Tech. He'd show David the more refined aspects of student life—debating societies, concerts in the Great Hall of Music. Perhaps the two of them could persuade Veronica to join them on a cultural outing?

The electric guitar sent out an ear-splitting shriek, the noise as chilling as fingernails on a blackboard. Clifford drained his second pint. He rubbed his temples in rhythm with the electric bass and shouted to his companions "I'm stepping out for a bit to clear my head."

"I'll come with you," David mouthed.

The two of them rose and waded through the crowd toward the door, leaving Pan in his current frenzy of bobbing his head from side to side, pounding his empty pint glass on the table and shouting cheeky remarks at the nearest bar maid.

"Whew! That's enough of that," Clifford said as they ascended from the basement to the sidewalk. He leaned against the display window of the wine shop upstairs from the pub and savored the relative quiet of the city street—the clip-clop of hooves, the conversations of passersby, the faint notes of swing music wafting toward them from the Plaza Fountain. David stood several feet away, as he often did to see Clifford's face without wrenching his own neck in a sharp, upward angle.

"Until last week I always thought it would be cool to go to a tavern," David said, "but after hanging out with Pan I don't care if I ever go to one again."

Clifford chuckled. "I think your sister will be glad to hear that." Maybe David had been hung over the last time Veronica had seen him? That would be one explanation for odd behavior, anyway.

"She's kind of different now." David said, looking thoughtful. "The first time I saw her here, up in the CEO office, she was kind of—I don't know—cold, I guess."

"Ms. Zeta doesn't have much time for pleasantries these days," Clifford said, "but she is concerned as to whether you're managing all right."

He decided not to mention Veronica's headache yesterday, didn't want to worry David unduly. Likely she'd been staring too long at paperwork in her miserably dark office.

"Oh sure, I'm doing fine," said David with a grin. "I've spent a lot of time looking around campus and stuff."

There was something a bit wonky in David's smile. Clifford sensed the word "stuff" concealed information of interest. But was it worth mentioning to Veronica? Surely David was entitled to his own privacy. Clifford balanced the observation with the trust Veronica had placed in him.

"Mount Olympus is quite different from Seattle," Clifford said, hoping to draw David out. "Did the chariots surprise you?"

"Yeah, the chariots are cool." David looked around and stepped closer. "And today I got to ride in a stretch limo," he said in a lowered voice.

"I say!" Clifford looked at David with new respect. There was only one stretch limo in the City of Mount Olympus. How had this pup become acquainted with Aphrodite, a formidable woman he, himself, would never dream of approaching? Had the Goddess of Love enchanted his young friend? That might explain the odd behavior Veronica had observed, and Clifford was confident the CEO of Olympus, Inc., would be more than interested to learn about David's new friend.

"Perhaps we'd better get back to our companion," Clifford said, nodding toward the pub steps. He'd make his excuses to Pan and hoped David would prove more than gormless and do the same. One of many things he didn't need was an all-night piss-up with the God of Shepherds and Flocks. Once he saw David back to his hotel he'd spend the rest of his evening organizing his thoughts about the lad in a message to Veronica.

Wednesday

Jim

James Ares Smith watched his son, Titus (slathered in sunscreen), roll down the Knoll at Athens U. The little boy shrieked with laughter as he ran up the incline and threw himself down again. The knees and elbows of his play clothes were covered with grass stains and stray green blades had woven themselves into his curls.

Jim relished the moment. There'd only be another century or two of toddlerhood to enjoy. *Doctor Apollo's Baby Book*, Jim's gift to Candy on her four-thousandth birthday, had explained early immortal development concisely and clearly. For the first year, immortal babies aged at the same rate as mortals. It was an evolutionary necessity, as a small degree of self-sufficiency had to be gained to keep the parents from going mad keeping up with a helpless infant's needs. By their fifth year, immortals gained the abilities of mortal two-year-olds. The long trek toward turning the equivalent of three mortal years stretched on for a century and a half; everything evened out to one "year" per century by the time the child was five hundred.

The sun warmed Jim's shoulders. Though it was still morning, the air temperature rested comfortably in the mid-70s and the sky was clear blue. A wonderful world, he decided, though far from problem-free.

A short man, white-haired and dressed in a toga like nearly everybody in the city except Jim and Titus, came into view on the walkway between the Admin Building and the Knoll. Jim raised a hand and waved to Zeus, who immediately veered course and cut across the lawn.

The City of Mount Olympus was at its best in early summer and Zeus had agreed instantly when Jim suggested they hold his first official counseling session out-of-doors. The Ex-Lord of the Universe seemed eager to get away from his penthouse and had chosen the Knoll for their meeting place.

Zeus extended his hand to Jim, patted Titus on the head and said, "Good morning, gentlemen." His white locks were snarled, his beard stained with a dribble of coffee. His shoulders stooped, strange for the God who always stood tall and square as if to dismiss his short stature. Zeus kept looking from side to side, as if he feared someone was following him.

No question Jim's client was troubled. He had his own problems, too. In order to free up his morning he'd had to negotiate with Candy, had assured her the best thing she could do to make him happy was to set a mid-morning appointment with Hera.

"Your career is important, Candy," he'd said over her sniffles and protests, and he meant it, though he felt somewhat guilty about making today's arrangement. The last time Candy had met with Hera, she'd come home ill and shivering. That time he'd persuaded her to take a sleeping tablet and go to bed, fearing Candy had exhausted herself in her new and disturbing compulsion to cater to his every need. Thankfully, she'd fallen asleep by the time he and Titus left for their play date with Zeus and Aster and was still dozing when they'd returned. Jim couldn't figure out what was wrong with her. She hadn't experienced the ups and downs of intoxication and withdrawal, so he'd ruled out drugs. Whatever it was must have happened at Aphrodite's mansion, but he couldn't ask Candy directly without revealing he'd hired someone to trail her there.

Zeus cleared his throat. Jim's face felt momentarily hot when he realized his client had caught him in a daydream.

"I can still raise a basic sound barrier," Zeus said as he turned in a circle, surveying the area around them. "Small-gs won't be able to hear what we're talking about no matter how close they get but I—I can't mute my voice from Big-Gs."

Zeus pointed an index finger skyward and made a circling motion. Jim sensed the natural sounds around them—calls of birds, the rustling of a copse of nearby ash trees—growing dim, as if a volume control had been turned down a notch.

Jim scanned the area. The only human figure besides themselves was a female don in a traditional black toga who bustled down the Admin Building stairs and turned away, toward the campus gate. His client was exercising a disproportionate need for privacy, but why?

"Let's sit," Jim suggested.

Zeus chose a seat facing the Athens U and Athens Tech common areas—the track, the library, the model of the Acropolis, the provost's house. Jim set Titus alongside his client. Titus leaned toward Zeus, face beaming.

"Ba-Pa!"

"Oh my." Zeus patted the boy's head but looked away, his other hand rising to catch the tear cascading down his cheek.

Jim waited for Zeus to compose himself. "What would you like to talk about, Zeus?"

"Where to begin." Zeus shook his head and looked down.

Without seeming to notice what he was doing he pulled Titus onto his lap. "I observed some mortals in high places go into retirement this past century to get some idea of what it would be like. I knew it would be a difficult adjustment going from, well, having the power to oversee the entire world to becoming a—" he winced before he could speak the words, "a lesser deity."

Jim, too, winced, chastising himself for succumbing to sympathetic body language as he did so. There was no couching the issue; the Big-G God he'd admired and feared since boyhood was, in truth, no longer Lord of the Universe.

"Tell me what that's like," Jim prompted after a pregnant pause.

Zeus took a deep breath, seemingly oblivious to Titus tugging on his beard. "It's all so different, it feels so different without having—" with effort, his spoke eerily endowed words, "—The Power."

Thunder clapped in the clear summer sky. Zeus glanced up. When he looked down again his eyes were somber.

"I trust your professionalism, Jim. I know you'll keep this confidential, but I must warn you, any mention of this matter outside of our conversation is likely to have dire consequences for Olympus, Inc., as well as for yourself."

The sky rumbled again, sending a chill down Jim's spine. He glanced at Titus to assure himself the boy was safe in Zeus' arms

"I understand. Please, go on."

The Big-G God let out a breath. "All those millennia I was living as half a being. The Power," he said in a whisper, "it ruled my emotions, blocked me from being anything but a tyrant, even in my benevolence. It overbalanced me, I can see that now. I never questioned the rough handling I gave to Hera and the children, never wondered why I didn't care about anyone's happiness but my own. You know I killed my own father to rise to the top."

Jim nodded. The history of Zeus conquering Cronus was nearly as old as time.

"I can at least blame that on being a hot-headed youth," Zeus continued, shaking his head. "But looking back, I think that's where the—You-Know-What—"

The Power, thought Jim and nodded again.

"—I think that's where it started." Zeus' chin dropped to his chest as if the confession had exhausted him.

Jim watched and waited until Zeus looked up again.

"What happened to the—to the—You Know?" Jim asked.

Zeus blinked. "I passed it on to Ronnie when she took over as CEO. Hera and our children know how it's deployed." He demonstrated by fanning the fingers of his right hand in an arc. "I used a watered-down version of it to punish the children when they were naughty, the equivalent of a spanking. Heaven and Earth," he swore, "I never would have made the transfer to Ronnie if I'd realized how it would harden her. I'm—"

Zeus trembled. Titus patted Zeus' chest. "Ba-Pa?"

"I think she and Athena are plotting to get rid of me," said Zeus. "Get rid of me for good."

Jim sighed. Zeus had willingly handed over leadership to Veronica. What would be her motive to get rid of him?

"Can you tell me about that?" he said.

"I stumbled on them over there," Zeus said, pointing toward the Athens U Rose Garden on a twin rise nearby. "They didn't see me," he continued in a hoarse whisper, "but I overheard their plans. They're going to imprison me, at the very least!"

Jim wondered how two powerful Big-G Goddesses could have failed to detect Zeus' presence near their alleged cabal but chose not to pursue this question. His client might have misunderstood something he'd overheard, or perhaps imagined the scene. Geriatric psychology wasn't Jim's area of expertise. Perhaps he'd collar one of his former professors after his session with Zeus and inquire about the indicators of senility in immortals.

Zeus wiped a tear from his cheek and hugged Titus close. "I should have spent more time with the children when they were growing up."

Jim nodded. Guilt was definitely at the root of Zeus' fears.

"I shouldn't have roamed from Hera every time the chance presented itself," he continued. "Now she's totally absorbed with her career. Who could blame her?"

"Have you talked to her about your feelings?" Jim asked.

The expression in his client's eyes turned mournful.

"What good would it do? Why should she listen to me? I can't make her listen to me anymore, now that I've given up—my rank."

"She might surprise you," Jim said, planting a seed of hope before shifting the conversation. "Has retirement brought you any positive experiences?"

Zeus offered a flat smile. "One, anyway. My dear little Aster. But now she's gone." He tenderly patted Titus' head. "You have no idea how lucky you are, Jim. No idea at all."

Jim swallowed the lump in his throat. He wondered how vengeful Hebe would be, wondered how long she would withhold Aster from Zeus. "Sometimes when one door closes, another one opens," he said, hating the mortal platitude but it had its uses. "Now that you're free of—" somehow, saying 'the P word' felt beyond silly, "—your job, maybe you'll find some new work that satisfies the God you are today. I'd like you to think about that, Zeus, before we meet again."

Zeus nodded.

Jim extracted his digital pad from the pocket of his chinos. He powered it up and poked the icon for the scheduling feature he'd been making himself use for the past three days.

"Let's set a time next week, if you're available, and we'll talk some more."

With great concentration and only a couple of false starts Jim entered the agreed-upon time on the agreed-upon date.

Zeus pointed his index finger skyward. With a quick shake he restored the volume of birdsong and rustling leaves. He patted Titus' head and set him on the grass alongside Jim.

"Good job, buddy," Jim said to Titus as they watched Zeus' retreat, his shoulders perhaps a little more square than when he'd first arrived.

But there was more, much more, to do. Jim fiddled with the digital pad to bring up an address for Clifford, remembering to push "send" on the second try after his first attempt failed. This puzzle was larger than the woes of a former CEO; Jim must, hopefully with Clifford's help, investigate what changes were happening in Veronica, too.

Veronica

Ilithyia slouched in a purple bean bag chair at Isle of L Coffee House. She glared belligerently at Veronica (seated opposite on a lipstick-red bean bag) and made sucking noises with the straw in her nearly drained iced latte.

The Goddess of Childbirth was long and lean. She wore tight denim jeans, knee-high black leather boots and a matching leather vest. Small silver rings pierced her right nostril, both shaved eyebrows and her left earlobe. The hot pink tips of her buzz-cut hair crowned the look.

Veronica shifted in her bean bag and tugged at the hem of her toga, not an overly short garment but short enough to concern someone who was not keen for all of Mount Olympus to know the color of her underwear. She never would have come here but Ilithyia had refused, flat refused, to meet at Olympus, Inc., headquarters.

The cave-like atmosphere of the coffee house—shades drawn

against the early afternoon sun, walls painted black, an air freshener emitting an invisible cloud of patchouli and wild roses—dulled Veronica's senses. The task at hand was to reassign Ilithyia to work that would do the world some good. Unlike hot-headed Hephaestus or lazy Hebe, Ilithyia had demonstrated both personal initiative and concern for the mortals. But over the centuries the methods she used to carry out her mission had degenerated into almost complete inefficiency. She was a kook, but her heart was in the right place.

"So what's your plan, Baby Girl?" Ilithyia snarled. She raised one bald, pierced eyebrow in a disturbing arc. "Gonna fire me or just demote my sorry ass?"

Baby Girl. The pet name, even when used harshly, drew Veronica back two millennia and more to when she was a little kid and Ilithyia was the only one of her siblings who'd paid attention to her. "Gotta look out for you, Baby Girl," Ilithyia used to say, "'cuz no one else in this Dad-forsaken place will." When Hef and Ares were busy exploding and maiming and Hebe was bemoaning a new zit, Ilithyia had taken Veronica on hikes, taught her how to ride a pony, acted out funny stories about things the family had done in centuries past (she did a brilliant imitation of Dad).

"No, Elle," Veronica said. The shortened name she'd called her big sister when Ilithyia was too hard to say softened her voice. "You're not getting fired or demoted. I know you're trying to do a good job, but mortal-made drugs for women in labor have taken a lot of the purpose out of your work."

"Ya think?" Elle smiled a little but looked sad. She set her empty glass on the table alongside her beanbag, sat up and wrapped her sinewy arms around her knees. "I tried to talk to Mom about how childbirth has changed, figured she'd be interested since she's the Goddess of Marriage, but no. All she wanted to talk about was how I need to look more feminine if I want to catch a husband!" Elle's nose rings quivered with a snort of disgust. "What would I want with a husband after helping all those women get through their labor pains?"

Veronica laughed out loud. Elle's eyes widened as if startled before she joined in the laughter, too. For minutes they couldn't look at each other without sparking a new burst of giggles and guffaws. Veronica's side started to ache.

"Wow." Veronica wiped a happy tear from her cheek as their merriment crested. "I can't remember the last time I laughed so hard." She took a sip of bottled water and dabbed another tear.

"But seriously, Elle, it's not about a demotion or getting fired." She waited a few moments until Elle looked her soberly in the eye.

"What I need you to do is make a lateral move, to a new job that I hope you'll find satisfying. No loss in rank or pay."

Elle raised her chin, looking "all ears." By Veronica's assessment, the Goddess of Childbirth had wasted a century or more trying to do a job the mortals had made obsolete. Elle had tried to change with the times and work as an advocate for women's new concerns through protest rallies and lobbying. Veronica had recently monitored Elle's work, had watched her struggle to make her voice heard in reproductive choice and women's health. But the mortals in power had shied away from these issues to woo and win their wealthier, more conservative bases of support. Elle needed a position of greater authority, not some old-world adjunct to Hera's work that even Mom no longer cared about.

"No loss in rank or pay," Veronica repeated, "but you won't have complete autonomy."

Elle's glittering eyebrows raised.

Veronica leaned forward and lowered her voice, just in case the sprinkling of other patrons chose to eavesdrop. "You'll be working with Athena. I can't go into specifics yet, but it's to do with women's health and welfare."

Elle tugged on one of her earrings. The expression in her eyes betrayed thoughtful interest. "Okay," she said, "I can work with someone I respect."

"Good," said Veronica. "We can meet again next week to go over the details. Can we get together in your office at corporate?"

Ilithyia narrowed her eyes. "Do I have to wear a toga?"

"I'd appreciate it if you did," Veronica said, reluctantly setting aside a lesser battle to win the important one, "but I won't force you."

"Okay," Ilithyia said with a grudging nod.

"Good. Stop by before then if you want. I'll have Cleo sort out your office and find you an assistant."

Veronica felt a cold tug inside. A silent voice said, "Use Me." Veronica fought to keep distress off her face as she said goodbye to Elle. She pushed the voice down in her consciousness while she waited for a chariot in front of the coffee shop and silently told The Power it wasn't needed in this instance. By the time she'd paid the driver and alighted in front of Olympus, Inc., the voice had quieted but its spirit housed itself in her temples, a dull, cold throb to remind her it was with her always, and waiting.

ThURSDay

Aphrodite

On Thursday evening The Goddess of Love sat at her vanity table and studied the weary face in the heart-shaped mirror. Yesterday's miseries looped in her brain, stealing the sparkle from her fabled violet eyes.

By Zeus, she'd slept poorly. Last night she'd overheard the conversation of a couple at Club Dionysus, at the table next to hers and Ares'. With fingers entwined and a regular punctuation of kisses, the couple had gabbed on and on about Hera's Marvelous Marriage rubbish and their own plans to renew their wedding vows. Aphrodite chugged her wine, bitterly apprehensive the spell she'd put on Candy Smith had been too little, too late, and left the Club in a huff. Ares stayed behind to join an old Athens U fraternity brother he'd spotted at the bar. Once home she told Eros no one, especially Ares, was to be admitted until she said otherwise. Safe in her boudoir, she rubbed her aching temples. The phone chirped, signaling she had a message so she punched "play." That was another mistake.

"Hey, Aph."

"Arrrgh!" She nearly launched the phone across the room when Hef's surly tones played back, but her curiosity after decades without hearing from him quelled the impulse.

"I'm, uh, sorry."

She snorted dismissively at these words. Had he ever apologized once, during three millennia of marriage?

"Sorry I haven't been in touch lately. Damn Ares, he…but maybe this isn't really about him, huh, Aph? Maybe it's because… because I was too busy with my work and didn't pay enough attention to you."

"Drunk!" she snapped at the recording. "You're drunk!"

"I, uhm, Aph, I'd like to try again."

"Shit!"

This time she did pitch the phone across the room and pelted it with pillows. Hef droned on until the 60-second limit cut him off. But message after message followed. She retrieved the phone and listened until Hef finally got around to saying he wanted to see her Thursday evening, wanted to take her out to dinner, for Zeus' sake!

Last night his offer had been too much to contemplate.

Miserable Hef and his grumpy attitude. No fun Hef and his workaholism. Gimpy Hef and his crappy self-image.

But by morning, curiosity overcame common sense.

She'd had Thalia, her confidential secretary, call Hef to accept his invitation, with the provision Aphrodite would arrange her own transportation to and from Club Dionysus. The Goddess of Love had felt giddy all day—not that she wanted to see him or gave a hoot about his desire to try again.

Now, two hours before their date, Aphrodite faced the challenge reflected in her mirror. She picked up a brush and started piling on the paint. Sure, Hef sounded repentant the five or six times she'd replayed his messages, but she'd had all day to recall his past slights and could hardly wait to give him a piece of her mind. How dare he miss her birthday every single year for the past millennia? How dare he tell her, when they'd last talked face to face, that he didn't care who she slept with as long as she didn't apply for a divorce, in which case Zeus would force him through the inconvenience of remarrying? Hef had never given a shit about her, about the Goddess she really was aside from all the work—yes, work!—she'd had to do over the centuries, inspiring sexual love in everybody from Ares to the lowliest mortal. She'd busted her perfect ass for everybody but herself and she was by-Zeus sick of it! If she hadn't just finished applying her eyeliner she would have cried.

"No love for Aphrodite," she said into the mirror. She was getting older with nothing to show for it, if you didn't count fame, power, wealth and aging but extreme beauty.

"I'll show him!" she spat through hot pink lips. With a boiling temper and a cold heart Aphrodite resolved to make Hef, fool though he was, love her again.

Jim

Jim waited for his party at the head of the Campus Pub stairs. He bounced Titus on his hip and grinned. Using the digital pad wasn't hard at all, once he'd gotten the hang of it. When he'd sent his message to Clifford yesterday, Jim had received a message from David sent two days prior. Since Jim wanted to see Clifford and David wanted to get together, too, Jim had messaged *both* Clifford and David at the same time and invited them for a Thursday evening beer.

David and Clifford arrived together. David had mentioned Clifford was his mentor while he got acclimated to Mount Olympus.

Good thing, thought Jim. From his own experiences with David, Jim knew him to be smart and capable, but also impressionable and a little naive.

"Nice toga," Jim said when he and David shook hands.

"Going native," David said, grinning. "Hey, big guy," he said to Titus.

"A pleasure to see you, Jim," said the boss-man, offering his hand. Clifford wore a sports jacket and trousers, echoing Jim's own decision to stick with chinos and a plaid shirt.

"Likewise," Jim said with a relaxed smile.

Jim led their party down the cellar steps. Their hostess, a pretty girl in a simple toga with hair pulled back in a ponytail and no makeup, guided them to the dining area. Jim pointed to a vacant booth where she seated their party and returned with a high chair for Titus.

Clifford raised an eyebrow at the diaper bag slung over Jim's shoulder and the toddler cradled in his arms, but David seemed eager to visit with Titus. He sat opposite Jim at the open end of the booth, the high chair between them. Clifford had slid into the booth ahead of David. He sat so close to the exposed brick wall a puff of mortar dust bloomed on his shoulder. Jim glanced down at the tabletop. His index finger traced the indentation of a name—not Candy's—he'd wistfully carved during his freshman century.

Poor Candy. She'd practically turned herself inside out when he'd told her he really, really wanted to treat her to a full spa session tonight, like the one Hera had given her last week.

"Oh Jim, are you sure?" she'd said, tears welling in her eyes. "Will it really make you happy if I'm away from you and Titus so long?"

He'd felt terrible about the obvious emotional pain she was feeling but he had to follow up on the problem Zeus had identified with Veronica and—he hated even to think the words—The Power. He'd placated Candy by promising they could spend the whole day together tomorrow. It would be awkward, taking Candy and Titus to his appointment with Professor Anastasio, the geriatric psychology specialist at Athens U who'd been out of the office yesterday, but why worry about it now?

The waitress arrived with a pitcher and three chilled pint glasses. Jim, as host, poured for his guests and raised his full glass.

"To old friends."

The three men sipped. David laughed when Titus reached for the pitcher.

"Not yet, dude, not until you're old enough to read the menu."

David proceeded to make funny faces at the toddler. When Titus cooed and clapped, David beamed.

"Here, David," Jim said, digging in Titus' diaper bag for a tippy cup and a can of apple juice. "You can be the bartender."

"Cool," said David.

Jim sipped his beer and studied Clifford. The new Jim, the one who stood up straight, noted Clifford's preoccupation with his fingernails. The young British immortal had always been socially reserved, but to Jim this behavior looked like avoidance. Was a global management position wearing down the brilliant former structureling? Being in charge of an exciting special project, as Clifford had been when he'd freed structurelings from molecular dispersal and marched them into the digital age, was different than being behind a desk in an intense administrative role. So much young blood at Olympus, Inc., these days. There couldn't help but be some cases of burn-out.

"So good to get together without a business purpose," Clifford said stiffly. He looked from Jim to Titus and back again. "Fatherhood seems to agree with you, Jim."

Clifford's eyes held a trace of melancholy. Personal regrets, perhaps? His own fatherless childhood gnawing at him, or maybe fear of the future? Or maybe he wasn't feeling well? Maybe it was an effect of the dim pub lighting, but he looked a little jaundiced.

"Being a parent is like a missing piece of the puzzle falling into place," Jim said. "All those centuries I was afraid to be a father, not knowing who my own was." He shook his head, musing briefly and bitterly on his one meeting with Poseidon. He'd found the God of the Sea a macho, pompous boor. "My boy, here," Jim said, gazing at Titus who was playing peek-a-boo with David, "he's the one who's taught me what a father should be."

David stopped his game and looked up. They'd all had the same experience, David, Clifford and Jim. David still didn't know who his father was.

"Having my own family has erased so many fears. Now I understand I can be counted on to raise my child," Jim said, looking at both the young men. "We were all raised in the dark about our own fathers but that's the past, guys, not the future."

David nodded solemnly. Clifford sighed. Jim had heard the rumors—Veronica's friendship with Clifford had cooled. A few years ago everyone had been speculating not if, but when, the two of them would marry.

"Funny how shifts in life can wreak havoc on our plans," Jim said. "Sometimes personal issues, sometimes work."

He let the thought sit and sipped his beer until the glass was half empty.

"People change, sometimes, with a change in circumstances," Clifford said quietly, his jaw tight.

"Yeah, like Veronica," David chimed in.

Jim noted the widening of Clifford's eyes.

"We were talking about her a couple of days ago," David continued, nodding toward Clifford to indicate the other half of "we." "She's not friendly like she was in Seattle. I mean, she's serious, sure," David leaned across the table toward Jim, "but it's like she's, I don't know, distracted all the time, almost kind of mean in a way." He turned toward Clifford. "Right?"

Clifford shrugged his shoulders. "To be honest, Jim, I'm worried about her." He, too, leaned across the table. "I think she might be headed for a breakdown. She doesn't confide in any of her directors anymore—well, possibly Hermes." The name came out with an edge. "When she was working alongside Zeus she had the world by the tail, overworked, yes, but happy too. Enthusiastic about leading Olympus, Inc., into a new age and all that. But now…"

The Power. The words, as spoken in Zeus' tremulous voice, chilled Jim's spine.

"We were thinking," David shot a quick glance at Clifford, "we were thinking maybe she needs some kind of intervention or something? You know about that kind of stuff, don't you, Jim?"

Jim turned the proposal over in his mind, thinking back to the one time he'd counseled Veronica. It was years ago, when he'd first suspected she was Zeus and Hera's child. She'd seemed a normal, capable, frustrated young person who wasn't being given the responsibility she'd been promised. But now there was the issue of The Power.

Jim looked at Clifford.

"Can you arrange a meeting with Veronica and include me? You could say it was about," feeling daring, he threw the idea out as nonchalantly as possible, "restructuring my job, maybe having me reassigned to Immortal Resources."

Clifford cleared his throat. "She's really hard to get to these days," he said, his words more clipped than usual. "Stella guards her appointment calendar like it's a treasure hoard."

"Maybe she'd see me?" David said. "I got an appointment with her through Cleo this week." He turned scarlet to the tips of his ears. "I mean, Veronica said we should get together for coffee sometime. Maybe I could lay on some little brother guilt-tripping, tell her I need advice that only she can give or something?"

Clifford looked doubtful, and Jim couldn't picture how he, himself, would barge in on a brother and sister get-together to see what he needed to see.

"Let's try Clifford setting up a meeting through Stella, first," Jim said. "We'll try the coffee angle if that doesn't work."

He looked down at Titus, whose eyes, the same color as Candy's, seemed to fathom the gravity of the situation. Deep in Jim's immortal soul he feared intervening between Veronica and The Power, but if he ignored the challenge something worse might happen. Olympus, Inc., itself might crumble and if it did—he shivered to think of it—the Earth and the Big and small gods who kept it running might be out of business for good.

Aphrodite

The Club Dionysus wasn't Aphrodite's first choice for dinner because she'd been there twice in recent weeks, but she quickly realized the advantage of being seen.

With unanticipated good manners Hef held out her chair at the secluded corner table some patrons referred to as "the" table. He must have tipped the maître d' big-time to get it. It was where everyone looked when they entered the restaurant, curious to see who was romancing who. No one like the Olympians for gossip, and once Ares got hold of the latest...

Hef took the chair on the adjacent side of the table. He sat so close his foot brushed hers under the floor-length tablecloth. The glow and shadow of candle light emphasized the scar on his cheek, a contrast to his uncharacteristically warm smile. His eyes, solemn beneath his dark, continuous eyebrow, held a glint of worry. A lifetime of reading faces told her Hef was in agony, hoping to impress her. She was tediously used to men vying for her love, but her estranged husband trying to do so amused her so much that she snickered.

Blood rushed to Hef's cheeks. He cleared his throat, his gaze fixed on hers, and said, "You look beautiful tonight."

"Well of course I do," she blurted, annoyed when her heart raced.

"I mean it, Aph." He took her hand in his, a strong, calloused hand that electrified her lotion-pampered flesh. "I've never seen a woman more beautiful than you."

Heaven and Earth, she was melting! By the grace of Zeus she

stopped herself from telegraphing this disastrous condition. The Goddess of Love, five thousand years wise, felt as helpless as a milkmaid in the wake of simple flattery from a man she no longer cared about, had never cared about in the history of their arranged marriage. What did she want with this—this tinkerer? He'd always been more interested in his volcanoes and his metalwork and his robots than he'd been in her. That was why Zeus had arranged the marriage in the first place. Hef was the only Big-G God who wouldn't mind, would barely notice a philandering wife!

Hef signaled Ganymede, who was across the room taking an order from a noisy party of naiads celebrating a birthday. The cup bearer nodded to Hef, finished with the naiads and strode to the bar. He arrived at their table moments later carrying a wine bucket and two fluted glasses.

"Champagne," announced Ganymede, deftly twisting the cork from the bottle with a faint "pop" and half-filling a glass without raising foam. "For Madame's approval," he said, setting the flute before Aphrodite.

In spite of the rush she felt inside she managed a haughty smile. She looked from Ganymede to Hef as she raised the glass and sipped.

The sparkling liquid passed her lips and tickled her tongue. By Zeus! Hef had ordered Soul of Dionysus 1730 AD, a sublime vintage everyone said didn't exist anymore. She hadn't tasted Soul 1730 since the last time she'd dined with Napoleon, and he'd been dead for...

Her smile softened as the champagne danced down her throat. Heaven and Earth, Hef looked good tonight. The streak of gray in his wild, dark hair bespoke a man of experience who would know how to please a woman.

"Does it suit?" Hef asked as he nodded to Ganymede to top off her glass.

She was poised to enthusiastically reply when an armor-clad figure swaggered into the room.

Like everyone who entered Club Dionysus, Ares glanced casually at the corner table. He froze mid-stride. He stared at her, then glared at Hef. Aphrodite squeezed Hef's hand but he withdrew it and rose from his chair as Ares advanced.

"Whoo-hoo!" shrieked one of the partying naiads. "Who hired the stripper?"

The speaker lunged at Ares, grabbed the stupid, short cape hanging from his shoulders and pulled him off-balance. The God of War fell backwards and crashed onto the table. Goblets and birthday packages flew in every direction.

The deterrence lasted only a few seconds. Ares was on his feet again, ignoring the complaints of the naiads. His long, coal-black locks made Aphrodite want to vomit. How had she ever fallen for a man who died his hair?

The brothers squared their shoulders in hostile greeting. She'd forgotten how much taller Hef was than Ares, how strong and sinewy Hef's arms were from working at a forge.

She leaned forward and peered up into their faces, their identical eyes locking upon each other. For a moment all was silent.

"Whaddaya doing with my girlfriend?" Ares slurred.

Hah, drunk already, Aphrodite thought with an inward sneer.

"Is there a law on Mount Olympus that says a husband can't take his wife to dinner?" said Hef with steely calm.

"My law!" bellowed Ares, leaning in to Hef's face. A vast cloud of ale-breath assaulted Aphrodite's nostrils.

"Let's settle this outside," Hef growled. "You've done enough damage in here." He placed his broad hands on Ares' shoulders and turned the God of War around. Giving a firm shove on Ares' back, Hef propelled his brother toward the exit.

"Fight! Fight!" squealed the naiads in chorus as the sons of Zeus and Hera left the room. They stampeded behind the combatants, through the front door and into the chariot lot.

Aphrodite, too, started to rise but Ganymede appeared suddenly at the tableside.

"Monsieur anticipated this incident and has requested Madame not trouble herself with the unpleasantness outside," Ganymede said as casually as if he'd been talking about the weather. A box covered with silver paper appeared from behind his back. "A gift from Hephaestus to help you pass the time," he said.

The *Dilettante Chocolates* logo arrested her attention. How did Hef know? They hadn't spoken since the confectioner had started business late in the twentieth century. He would have had to travel off Mount Olympus to get them, at least as far as the United Kingdom where Eros traveled once a month to purchase Aphrodite's home supply.

The cheers of naiads rose outside.

"I'd hate to miss the floor show," she said to Ganymede.

Aphrodite grabbed the box of chocolates and the champagne bottle and raced for the door, heart pounding for her hero, her husband, her very Hef who, she was quite certain, would rise victorious from the Battle of The Ages.

FRIDAY

David

The Thursday night get-together with Clifford, Jim and Titus had ended early, which was a good thing because David had to work on the task Aphrodite had set for him—learning about Cleo as a person so he'd have something to say to her.

He'd tried to see Cleo on Wednesday, on his way to give Hera the strand of Aphrodite's hair. It was a weird request Hera had made, but he'd plucked a platinum blonde strand from a cushion Aphrodite had leaned against in that Arabian Nights kind of room without hesitation.

David stopped on the sixth floor first and peeked around Cleo's open office door. She wasn't at her desk. Though he'd felt guilty for snooping, he'd tip-toed in to hunt for clues about her interests. He'd never before noticed the three-shelf bookcase to the left of her desk, the bottom shelf filled with business and office management texts, the middle hosting an interesting looking assortment of pots. Several small, framed drawings and photos stood on the top shelf. The drawings depicted different buildings carved into a cliff. A sepia-toned photo showed an archaeological dig. The young woman in the photo, Cleo, wore a pith helmet, long-sleeved shirt and split skirt. There was a color photo of Cleo and Veronica standing side by side in front of the office, both of them smiling and pointing toward the gold "Veronica Zeta, Assistant CEO" placard fastened to the door. With this intelligence, David crept out of the office and continued to the tenth floor for his business with Hera.

After he'd given Hera the strand of Aphrodite's hair (which he'd been pleased to deliver but his euphoric state evaporated the instant he left Hera's office), David caught a chariot downtown. He returned to the bookstore he'd visited a couple of weeks ago and bought every title on 19th and 20th century archaeology. After hours of flipping through pages of photos and illustrations he found Petra, a city established in the 6th century BC in present-day Jordan. There was a picture of the Treasury, an impressive multi-columned building carved in rock which was the subject of a drawing he'd seen on Cleo Petra's bookcase.

Encouraged, David had returned to the bookstore the next day and purchased books on ancient pottery. He didn't remember the details of Cleo's pots as well as he'd remembered the drawings of the buildings, but after scanning through the books he figured one of the specimens was probably Cretan. Absorbed in study, he'd forgotten about Thursday night drinks with Jim and Clifford until his digital pad chimed—Clifford paging him from the hotel lobby.

But that was yesterday.

Today David strolled into the Olympus, Inc., lobby in his best toga, head high and shoulders back in an imitation of manly confidence. The stairs to the mezzanine teemed with immortal worker bees, bound for the elevators and their office cells in the corporate hive.

A fortyish woman with hot-pink buzz cut hair stood out in the crowd, her expression as dark as her black leather pants and vest. Ilithyia, he guessed from the description in Herodotus Jones' book. He tried not to stare at her, tried not to count her ear, nose and eyebrow piercings. They ended up in the same elevator. Ilithyia punched the 8th floor button. She raised an eyebrow at David but didn't say anything when he pushed the 6th.

The elevator stopped on every floor, most employees getting out on the 3rd floor for the Weather department or the 5th at Architectural and Computer Services. David felt like a dolt, standing there with his forced he-man posture and not saying anything to his half-sister like, "Hi, I'm your brother. Nice to meet you." When the car stopped at the sixth floor he faced another dilemma—much as he longed to see Cleo, he was scared.

In the polished metal of the elevator doors he studied the idiotic posture he'd adopted for this encounter. He looked like a comic military figure in one of those Gilbert and Sullivan operettas of which Milton Bernstein, his foster father, was a fan.

This is hopeless said a voice inside him. David pushed the down arrow and waited for the first car out of there. But in moments he was trapped. The doors in front of him slid open and revealed Cleo in all her tall, beautiful glory.

"Hi, David," she said. "Busy morning. I was just getting an assistant settled in for Ilithyia. She hasn't used her office in decades." She stepped aside and waved a hand toward the vacant elevator car. "Going down?"

Her friendly smile gave him hope. Scared though he was, he righted himself and said, "I was, but now that you're here there's something I want to ask you about. Something I noticed in your office."

"Sure," she said with a quizzical glance. He followed her down the hallway.

He asked first about the drawings of Petra. She described it as "the old family place" and laughed when he asked her about the archaeological expedition.

"I wasn't there in an official capacity," she said, "just tagging along, trying to find a bracelet I'd lost on vacation a couple of centuries earlier."

When he changed the subject to ancient pottery David realized he knew more about it than she did.

"They're all from Veronica," Cleo said apologetically. "She collects this stuff and gives me one every birthday, one for each year we've worked together." David counted five pots. "She'd love to know you're interested. You should tell her the next time you see her. She could use a break from thinking about work all the time."

David was stunned by his own stupidity. How could he have overlooked the one thing he and Cleo had in common?

"I'll do that," he said. Talking about Veronica with Jim and Clifford last night had fueled his own worry. "And you're right, she's serious all the time now. I used to see her a few times a year, when she was still monitoring things in Seattle. We'd get together for lunch or something and I could always make her laugh, but now—I mean, I don't know her like you do, but…"

They looked at each other for a long moment.

Cleo shrugged her shoulders. "Maybe we can put our heads together and think of some way to make her lighten up. The stress is really getting to her. She seems to have headaches all the time now."

"Coffee sometime?" he asked without thinking.

"Okay," she said. Cleo tapped the digital pad on her desktop. "Today's bad, but how about—" she drew a finger across the screen to change dates, "—ugh, she needs me all day Monday, but could you make breakfast? Cafeteria at eight?"

"That'd be great," he said in spite of his suddenly dry throat. "See you then."

"Thanks," Cleo said. She reached out her hand and they shook on it.

David kept his composure all the way to the elevator. The descending car was empty. He could barely wait for the doors to roll closed before he punched a fist in the air and shouted, "Yes!"

Saturday

Clifford

Clifford Essex was taking a walk. He breathed deeply and enjoyed the changing scenery, something he'd missed during his stint as an old-style structureling, imprisoned fifty-plus years in Seattle's Space Needle. Certainly his muscles and limbs enjoyed this exercise more than lifting weights, though he persisted in the new regimen on a sensible scale. Better still, the effects of the wretched tanning cream had faded and his skin, at last, was its normal hue.

He'd walked half the neighborhoods of Mount Olympus—the university district, downtown, the industrial area where goat cheese and other goods were made. He now strolled through New Mycenae, known for luxury condos and high-end specialty shops, including an artisan cheese store he patronized. He'd nearly turned in to Aristaeus' Cheese-And-More when he spotted Veronica. She was half-a-block ahead of him and carried something large and heavy. He quickened his pace.

"Good morning, Veronica," he said as he overtook her. She jumped. Knowing her as well as he did, he assumed she'd been concentrating so hard on something she'd momentarily forgotten the world around her. "Sorry to startle you. May I offer assistance?"

She stopped walking and smiled mechanically. "Thanks," she said, and burdened him with a vast bag of cat litter. "It's just a few more blocks. Warm this morning, isn't it?"

"Indeed," he answered, looking at the darkening sky. He'd watched a lot of weather when he'd been stationed in Seattle. The cloud formation looked predictive of a thunderstorm. They resumed walking. Clifford adopted her quick pace. Sweat formed in his armpits from the exertion of hefting thirty-five pounds of clumping sand. "I thought you had just the one cat?"

"Yes, just Bill Gates, Jr.," she said, her smile warming. "I've been so busy at work lately I haven't paid much attention to him." She smoothed a hand over the front of her embroidered denim toga, which, Clifford noticed, sported several snags. "I've been forgetful about stocking his supplies, so I've started buying econo-sized everything to keep from running out."

"You have today off, at any rate."

"Not all day," she said in a wistful tone. "There's a—"

She cut herself off as if she'd almost said something she didn't mean to.

"I have a big project next week. Personnel," she said quickly.

He'd seen the memo about Hephaestus' reassignment to Hermes' department and heard the water cooler gossip about Hebe getting sacked, had been introduced to Ilithyia at a senior staff meeting yesterday afternoon. If it was something to do with Veronica's siblings, that left Ares. But that was sheer and utter nonsense. Who would take on the God of War?

The sky above them rumbled. Clifford tried not to regard it as an omen.

Veronica looked up and issued a mirthless chuckle.

"I wonder if Dad's upset about something," she said.

Her own beautiful face reflected the pent-up energy of the blackening sky. Veronica's pace slowed. She stumbled and raised a hand to her forehead.

"Are you ill?" Clifford shifted the load of sand to one hip to free up a hand to steady her.

"I—no, I—I'll be fine." She squared her shoulders and started walking again. "We're nearly to my condo. I'll lie down for a few minutes before I go to the office."

Her face was chalk white.

They turned down a side-street to a four-story structure, the entryway faced with Doric columns and "Olympus Arms" carved in the pediment.

"Shall I call a doctor?" said Clifford. "I believe your family uses Apollo?"

"No," she said harshly, then, "no thank you, Clifford," in a softer tone. "A little rest and I'll be fine. Really."

She patted his arm as if to reassure him, but her face remained chalky.

Instead of going through the main entryway Veronica turned left and led him to a ground-floor unit with a small front garden and its own exterior door. The roses had faded and the grass around the edge of the bed needed trimming. She drew a key from a side pocket in her toga and unlocked the door. He held his breath, anticipating his first time in her flat.

"Hey, kitty boy," she cooed in a voice Clifford had never heard her use. The scent of cat and decaying plants tickled his nostrils.

"Mrah," a feline voice groused somewhere inside.

"Sorry the place is such a mess," she said, ushering Clifford in. He glanced at the bust of Queen Elizabeth I and the yellowed, shedding fern alongside it. "I haven't had a chance to clean for a while."

A fat, striped collection of ginger fur slunk into the hallway and moved in a sinuous figure-eight pattern around Veronica's ankles.

"There's my pretty boy."

She bent down and collected the scowling, flat-faced creature in her arms.

Clifford sneezed.

"Forgot you were allergic," she said apologetically while she and the cat touched noses. Feline claws kneaded the embroidery on Veronica's chest. "Just put it down anywhere," she said.

Clifford leaned the bag of sand against the wall and dusted off his hands on his trousers.

"Are you sure you'll be all right?" he said, feeling another sneeze building.

She shifted her weary, dark-rimmed eyes to his. "I'll be fine after a nap. Would you like that, sweetheart?" she said, looking back to the cat.

Feeling a third wheel, Clifford said, "Cheerio, then. See you Monday," and eased outside, closing the door behind him. The sky had lightened from black to gray but the air retained a heavy, charged density. It was common knowledge Zeus' emotions could rule the weather. Clifford wondered if Veronica, as successor CEO, now held such power.

Jim's request to schedule a meeting with Veronica struck him with new urgency. Clifford hurried home with long, purposeful strides. As soon as he reached his apartment he'd power up his digital pad and message Stella to make the necessary arrangements.

SUNDAY

Veronica

The gods slept in on Sunday, except for Veronica.

Her eyes snapped open before daybreak, the instant the Sunday *Mount Olympus Bolt* hit the condo door with an authoritative thud. All week she'd scoured the daily newspaper (her favorite for local news, even though they refused to go digital) for a hint to point her toward an ally against Ares. Somewhere in the City of Mount Olympus there had to be someone close enough to him to gain access who also had an axe to grind.

Bill Gates, Jr., meowed in complaint as Veronica slid him off her chest and untangled herself from the sheets and comforter. Her nightgown was made of thin fabric and last night's rain storm had left a lingering chill in the air. She grabbed a shawl from the bedpost, wrapped it around her shoulders and padded to the front door. The cool marble under her bare feet made her shiver.

The Sunday edition of the paper was loaded with advertising circulars and a weekly lifestyle section she usually ignored. She retrieved the log-sized roll of newsprint from the welcome mat and continued her route to the kitchen to brew the morning caffeine. The cat wound around her ankles, screaming protests of starvation.

"Okay, okay," she mumbled to the insistent pile of orange. Veronica set the paper on the dining nook table and punched the espresso machine button programmed for tall skinny double mocha with cinnamon. She scooped up Bill Gates, Jr., and crossed the threshold to the guest bedroom, better known as the kitty habitat.

The cat jumped from her arms and trotted indignantly to the automatic feeder. He glared at the empty clear plastic cylinder and the empty dish attached to it, shot her a reproachful glance and shouted, "Myaaaa!"

Looking around, Veronica could see his point. The room was a disaster, even though she'd changed the cat box before going to work yesterday. Veronica did her own cleaning, hadn't hired a maid since she'd adopted Bill Gates, Jr., because strangers upset him. The woven carpets on the floor were barely visible under clouds of cast-off orange fur, the curtains were half-off the rods and scarred with claw-pulled loops of thread, the floor-to-ceiling scratching post had been loosened from its pedestal and leaned against a wall at the same angle as the famous tower in Pisa.

She sighed, unscrewed the kibble cylinder from the automatic feeder and toted it to the pantry for a refill. Bill Gates, Jr., followed at her heels, bawling a continuous series of instructions. She filled the cylinder and screwed it back on the feeder, waited while the mechanisms reset and watched a load of kibble tumble into the dish. The water bowl alongside it was nearly empty, a light ring of scum made from dust and cat hair glowing at the water's edge. Veronica wrinkled her nose and carried the disreputable vessel to the kitchen sink for a hard scrub. The scent of mocha, steaming from the espresso machine, teased her nostrils as water filled the clean dish. She delivered the water to the kitty habitat and promised Bill Gates, Jr., she'd vacuum as soon as she got back from another Sunday of catching up at work.

But now, to business. Veronica retrieved her mocha, settled at the dining nook table on a cushioned straight-backed chair with one foot tucked beneath her and removed the rubber band from the burgeoning newspaper. She tossed the advertising circulars on the floor and scanned the news section (which included a daily round-up of news from the mortal world), the sports section (the feature article was about the new chariot team recruits at Athens U and Athens Tech), the business section (renovation of the Mountain High Plaza Hotel in the coming year promised a spike in construction employment but a downturn in the service sector). Nothing on the pages involved Ares, except a blurb in the mortal world section about a new model of jet to be used in military applications.

Veronica made another mocha. While she waited, she scanned the lifestyle section, which she usually ignored because who had time for interior decoration tips or the latest look in togas? But today she even read the "Around the Town" column on page 2, a column she loathed as it often caused embarrassment for someone in her extended family. Hopefully the gossip columnists had missed David's visit to Aphrodite, as Clifford had reported to her last week. She read the first paragraph.

"Oh shit!"

Last Thursday night her two older brothers had been in a fist fight in the parking lot of Club Dionysus. The event had drawn a crowd. The reporter, hiding behind the pen name Nose for News, shared the number of blows and the content of insults exchanged. There was also a quote from an enthusiastic spectator:

> "You should have seen the look on Ares' face when he saw Aphrodite sitting at the corner table with

Hephaestus," said Bernice Johnston, employee of Olympus, Inc., Weather Department, Floods Section. "There was cold-blooded murder in his eyes!" Aphrodite, wife of Hephaestus and romantic gal pal of Ares, was also on the sidelines, cheering for her estranged hubby and offering to cold-cock Ares with a bottle of champagne. This reporter dares to ask: are the tides of passion turning for the fiddle-footed Goddess of Love?

"What in Heaven and Earth?" Veronica said out loud, her face hot. This was the icing on the by-Zeus cake, her brothers brawling in public over Aphrodite! Had the Greek Pantheon gone mad? Everyone on Mount Olympus knew about the millennia-old triangle but the principals had mostly managed to keep their personal doings out of the papers. The exploit must have made the Olympus, Inc., water cooler gossip, at least in the Weather Department.

Veronica ground her molars. Already the balance and dignity she'd started to restore to the family business by variously reassigning and firing her siblings was being undone by unforeseeable events. The children of Zeus and Hera would be subject to more ridicule than ever, her own position as CEO made a topic of editorial cartoons! Why did this have to happen now, when she was so close to settling Ares, once and for all—

Sudden insight gave her pause. The parking lot brawl only looked like one of the worst things that could happen. Now, she realized, it might be a sought-for boon.

Bill Gates, Jr., emerged from the kitty habitat, sated and affectionate. The brush of his fur around Veronica's shins barely registered as the cold voice in her head said, "At last."

Week Four - Monday

David

David Bernstein woke before dawn, wild with nerves. Why on earth had he thought meeting Cleo for breakfast was a good idea? They'd made a date. A date! No way was it going to turn out good, but it was too late to cancel. She expected him at the Olympus, Inc., cafeteria at 8 AM.

David looked in the bathroom mirror. The guy reflected was a pale, twentyish specimen with a mop of black curls and just enough stubble to make shaving optional—or not. He picked up the electric razor and set it down again, stalled by the fear he'd somehow manage to make a complete idiot of himself and all but throw Cleo into Hermes' arms.

Thus prepared for failure, David picked up the razor once more and turned it on. How could shaving make the situation worse? He plumped out his right cheek with his tongue to smooth a scar he'd picked up some time in his early centuries, a token Thelma Bernstein had told him came from a truculent playmate with a sharp rock. The area around the scar was tricky. It took him three tries to fell some stubborn bristles. He rejected the hotel-provided aftershave when a test-sniff nearly knocked him down. David fanned the air, praying the scent wouldn't cling to his toga. Who could stand to eat around a guy who reeked of musk?

Further agony arose when he passed the gift shop in the hotel lobby. Too early for it to be open, but maybe he should have bought Cleo a present? Would she expect him to pay for breakfast? Would she be insulted if they didn't go Dutch?

By the time the chariot dropped him in front of Olympus, Inc., he'd worked himself into a tizzy. David tried to calm himself—it was just breakfast, not a life or death situation. His stomach churned all the same. He was fifteen minutes early, how lame was that? David leaned against one side of the cafeteria archway, trying to not look like a stalker. People passed in and out. Eight o'clock arrived. He was on the verge of chickening out when, three minutes later, Cleo bustled out of the elevator.

"Sorry!" she said, smiling too wide. "I got caught in a little war with Stella." Her nose wrinkled when she named Veronica's executive assistant.

139

"No problem."

They each took a tray from the stack at the start of the line, breakfast being served cafeteria-style only. She chose a blueberry muffin, a bowl of fruit topped with yogurt and an empty coffee cup. Regardless of his nerve-roiled stomach, David helped himself to a large serving of scrambled eggs, four pieces of sausage and three triangles of toast. The cashier peered over the top of her reading glasses.

"These together?"

"Yes," said David without thinking.

"Thanks," said Cleo. "I owe you."

"No problem," said David as he slid his debit card through the reader with a barely shaking hand. The first daunting bridge of the event had been crossed without incident. Maybe he was the only one who'd considered this a date? The thought came as a huge relief.

Cleo filled her mug from a pump pot at a station that also held condiments and cutlery. David had forgotten to pick up a mug. When he looked back, the cafeteria line was at least fifteen people long. He followed her into the sea of tables and chairs.

"This okay?" Cleo asked, stopping at a two-top.

"Sure." They were out in the middle section where anyone could see them. What had he been thinking, that he was going to kiss her? Well, sure, he'd thought about it and who could blame him? But this was better. Now he was free to just—talk. His empty stomach shifted from churning to growling.

"So, problems with Stella?" he said, pleased with himself for remembering the first thing Cleo had said to him this morning.

"Oh!" Cleo threw her hands up and rolled her eyes. "She's such a dragon about Veronica's schedule, has to be in complete charge of it. Veronica linked my scheduling software to Stella's so I could set up appointments through the sixth-floor office when needed, like I did for you." She smiled and spread her hands, palms up, as if to say "ta-da!"

"Sounds practical to me," David said between bites.

"Sure, to any sane person," Cleo said. "But this morning Stella threw a by-Zeus tantrum about some hours Veronica asked me to block out for her on—Wednesday, I think it was. She was screaming—screaming!—about chain-of-command and all that garbage. Veronica only keeps her on because of a promise Zeus made. That whole top-floor cave-of-doom suite gives me the creeps. Sometimes I wonder if there's some chemical in the paint or flooring that Veronica's sensitive to. All year she's been complaining about headaches and lately it's been worse. Much worse."

David looked from her full plate to his nearly empty one. "Don't you think you'd better eat?"

"Thanks," she said, picking up her muffin. "Sorry to unload all this on you. I've been doing all the talking. Tell me, what's it like in Seattle?"

He talked about the weather, the University of Washington and the landmarks the structurelings used to occupy while she nibbled her breakfast. The conversation returned to Veronica when David reminisced about how supportive she'd been and how he missed her sense of humor.

"I wish I could convince her to take some time off, even a week," Cleo lamented. "This week's worse than usual. She's involved in something so confidential even I don't know what it is. I'm thinking maybe it has to do with Ilithyia? I mean, she hasn't been at headquarters in decades and suddenly she's here. Nothing else makes sense."

The worry in Cleo's eyes was unmistakable. Without thinking, David reached across the table and set his hand on hers. "You okay?"

"Sure, yes, thanks, sweet of you to ask," she said, patting her other hand on top of his before she withdrew them both. "But I tell you, David, if things get much more stressful around here I'm going to kidnap Veronica and take her on an all-day spa break just to shake things up. She's always been an overachiever but she doesn't seem to realize she has limits. It's like she's sacrificing herself to the Olympus, Inc., monster."

David flashed on the old version of *King Kong* he'd seen in a film appreciation class, the scene on the tropical island when Fay Wray is about to be offered up to the giant gorilla.

"Let me know if I can help."

"You're sweet," Cleo said. She blotted her lips with her napkin. "Gotta go, I have a meeting at half-past eight. Sorry this was so short."

His heart fell at her obvious dismissal. "No problem."

"My treat next time," she said.

He stood when she did and watched her leave the cafeteria. David looked down at the ruins of their breakfasts, decided to get a cup of coffee after all. He was halfway down the cafeteria line when it registered, and it took every ounce of self-control not to cheer. She'd said there'd be a next time!

Veronica

Veronica had made the critical recruiting call from her condo Sunday morning, wary of being overheard or in some way hacked if she contacted Aphrodite from the office. The Goddess of Love had quickly agreed to betray her lover, Ares—almost too quickly for Veronica to trust Aphrodite's words. But the voice inside, The Power, counseled her not to fear.

This morning Veronica was on the ninth floor, meeting with Athena in the North American Continental Manager's office. She cast a spell on the entire floor to prevent anyone else from entering. They'd just discussed Aphrodite's role in the Ares sting.

"I rarely condone the use of sex as a weapon, but in this case I believe it's our best option," Athena said soberly.

Veronica almost smiled. For all her age and experience, Athena's notion of what constituted sex was, well—suffice it to say she'd taken after Aunt Hestia, the confirmed virgin.

The stares of the native masks that decorated the walls cautioned Veronica to stay serious. She'd barely slept the night before and impulses were hard to control. Already this morning she'd had to choke down the urge to reprimand Stella who'd been raging into her old-style rotary telephone, brow-beating Cleo about the schedule. Poor Cleo. She always made light of the misery Stella inflicted on her but today was worse than ever. Veronica promised herself she'd give Cleo an all-day spa treatment when the mess with Ares was resolved.

"Such irony, the miseries of love turning Aphrodite," Athena said. "Heaven and Earth have sent you the gift of an advantageous ally."

Tim, perched on Athena's shoulder, blinked and hooted as if to concur.

"There's no protocol for what I propose," Veronica said. Dad had never talked about deposing his father, Cronus, but everyone knew Zeus had committed patricide. The situation with Ares was less extreme—he would merely be imprisoned. Still, there was no precedent. The voice said, as it had all morning, that killing Ares was the safest choice. She'd lost her breakfast from the stress of perpetually refusing this advice. Once she'd vanquished Ares, she hoped the voice would go away.

"Your choice of venue is good," said Athena. "Ares will be entirely out of his element."

"That's my hope." Veronica took a deep breath and massaged her temples. "Do you have any recommendations for improving the plan?"

"Only that the words you speak to him be specific and exact. If not, the Olympian Laws might give him recourse."

Veronica nodded while thinking *blast the laws*, or was it the voice thinking for her? She'd studied Olympian Law in her undergraduate centuries, the laws Dad had set down to protect Big-G Gods from destroying each other as he had destroyed Cronus. Under the law, all Big-Gs were equal in rights and powers, but the textbooks did not mention that one Big-G—first Dad, now herself—secretly held The Power.

The laws don't apply to you rang in her head. Veronica shuddered.

Athena leaned across the desk. "Are you well, Veronica? You don't look well."

"Yes. Fine," she said, though perspiration beaded her brow.

"A warrior needs to take care of her health, sister. You must be fit for battle." Athena's eyes narrowed. "Promise me you'll rest and renew yourself before our proceedings on Wednesday."

"As much as possible," Veronica said. Piles of paperwork were stacked on the CEO desk, awaiting her review. As soon as Ares was contained she'd work on delegating some of the administrative load. But the voice urged her to take authority from her departmental directors—Hermes, Clifford, Hera, Euphemia in Immortal Resources and, soon, Athena—instead of giving them more.

"Buzz off," Veronica muttered.

The owl screeched.

"Talking to myself," she quickly assured Athena. Veronica rose. "We'll meet here, in this office, on Wednesday? The less Stella knows about our plans, the better."

Athena and Tim accompanied Veronica to the elevator. Inside the car she selected the sixth floor button; the paperwork could wait for half-an-hour more. She'd ask Cleo to get her a cup of tea and some toast from the cafeteria, rest while she waited, and, hopefully, manage to keep down a second attempt at breakfast.

Jim

Seated across a desk from Clifford Essex at Olympus, Inc., headquarters, Jim Smith tried to adjust the hem of his toga without being obvious. His formal toga was shorter than what he considered suitable for business wear, but it was the only one he'd brought with him.

Clifford was also dressed in accordance with the company code. He'd admitted to Jim some years ago, when Clifford's molecules were dispersed in the Seattle Space Needle and Jim had been his counselor, that wearing a toga made him feel like a sheep after shearing. They'd laughed at the time, and Jim had pointed out that freedom of dress was one tangible benefit of structureling work.

Those days seemed a millennium ago.

Clifford had just explained to Jim how the digital request he'd sent to Stella, his request to meet with Veronica, had gone unanswered. He was poised now to use the most reliable method of contacting Stella, but seemed to have reservations.

"What's our strategy?" Clifford said in respect to today's business. "We need to be prepared if the old dragon lets us in right away."

Jim smiled at this description of Stella, someone he'd encountered a few times when he'd met with Zeus as a Continental Manager. Her critical glares and barbed remarks had stung him at the time, but in retrospect he'd decided it was Stella's own defensiveness and therefore not valid. He almost looked forward to seeing her again, to verify she could no longer affect him. Sticks and stones.

"I think you should say we want to meet with Veronica to discuss my job and how it might be restructured."

Clifford's face tinged slightly red. "You think that will sound plausible?"

Jim nodded. He smiled a little. "Clifford," he said, his smile flattening with mixed emotions, "we both know my new position hasn't worked out as intended."

"Bull's-eye, old bean." Clifford leaned back in his chair and laced his hands behind his head. "I've been wanting to bring it up. Awkward, that, supervising a Big-G who used to be my counselor. I'm sure you understand the issues better than I do."

Jim kicked himself, again, for the time and opportunity he'd wasted, digging in his heels against digital technology. But there was more to it than that.

"It never was a good fit, now that I've had time to think about it," Jim said, "a counseling department reporting to Architectural and Computer Services."

"Veronica's notion," Clifford said. "One of the few mistakes she's made since I've known her."

Jim agreed with this assessment but didn't comment. "You'll be our spokesperson," he said. "You can say we want to run the idea by Veronica before we talk to Immortal Resources, to keep her in the loop. If you do most of the talking, I'll have a better opportunity to observe her behavior."

Not that Clifford would know he'd be looking for signs of The Power. Jim had told no one about the closely-guarded secret Zeus had confided in him.

Clifford cleared his throat and leaned forward, his hands resting on the desktop.

"And you're game to follow through on this, the job change you propose?" he said, eyeing Jim somberly.

Jim shifted in his chair, fiddled again with the hem of his toga. He'd given the matter a lot of thought over the weekend, had faced up to the fact he'd largely failed in his job for the past few years. If he wasn't part of the Big-G family he might have been fired by now. Counting this blessing, he'd determined to knuckle under and learn the latest managerial technologies. If the proposed change went through he'd probably have to come to Mount Olympus a few times a year to report in person to Euphemia, the IR department head— not his favorite destination but it would give him the opportunity to check in with his new client, Zeus. He'd tried to talk to Candy about his plan, but in her bizarre condition she'd merely applied a verbal rubber stamp. She seemed to be getting worse instead of better, was clingier than ever this morning and had refused to be left behind. She and Titus were waiting for him now in the cafeteria. Jim had made her an appointment with Apollo, but the doctor wouldn't be in Mount Olympus until Friday. If Candy didn't improve, she'd have to quit working and Jim's job security would be more important than ever.

"Yes," said Jim. "I'm game."

Clifford nodded. He picked up the receiver on a dial telephone, a model Jim remembered from the 1950s. He'd heard all the directors had these instruments, the only ones Stella would uniformly sanction for contacting her directly. Not equitable, Jim reflected, that Stella was coddled with outdated technology but then, who would want to argue with the corrosive old woman over something so trivial? Why she hadn't retired yet was a mystery. Jim supposed it was because work was her whole life. For a moment he felt pity.

A voice snarled over the receiver.

"Hello, Stella, Clifford Essex here," said Clifford. "Jim Smith and I have a matter we'd like to discuss with Ms. Zeta if she has time this morning? Oh." Clifford's brow furrowed. "Perhaps this afternoon, then?"

A long series of emphatic phrases, audible but indecipherable to Jim, filled the air.

"Yes, well, I see. Three o'clock Wednesday afternoon it is," Clifford said, raising an apologetic eyebrow to Jim. Jim nodded his assent. "Goodbye, then, Stella."

Clifford set the receiver back in the cradle. "She's enraged, as

I'm sure you've guessed, lathered on about Cleo fiddling with the schedule and no one showing her the proper respect. So."

The last word hung awkwardly in the air. Clifford's expression was strained.

"Well," said Jim, rising to close their meeting. "See you Wednesday."

"Yes," said Clifford. He, too, rose and walked around the desk toward Jim, hand extended. They shook. "Half-an-hour beforehand, if convenient?"

"That'll be fine," Jim concurred. He turned to leave.

"Jim."

Jim turned back. Clifford cleared his throat.

"I—I'm glad you saw a way to make your position work better. Should have been my job, but personnel management is a weak spot for me."

What it cost Clifford to admit this weakness was tangible in his expression—self-reproach, tinged with frustration.

"Thanks," said Jim with a smile and a nod. This time when he turned away he wondered if, when Veronica's issues with The Power were settled, he might find a way to coach Clifford in personnel techniques in exchange for a tutorial on digital technology.

tuesday

Zeus

The Ex-Lord of the Universe sat at his dining room table, chewing on the end of a quill. Zeus, though capable of running the world from behind-the-scenes, was not adept at homework. For almost a week he'd put off Jim's assignment to think about what kind of work he might do in retirement, work that would satisfy.

He studied the parchment, contemplating the short list of possibilities, each of which he'd crossed out. Daycare was his first idea, but did he really like toddlers, aside from Aster and Titus? Zeus didn't have the first idea of how to recruit staff to help him with a roomful of children. When he thought about all the building blocks and disposable diapers and nap times, he feared daycare's unceasing demands would suck him into Earth's surface and keep him there. The magic about caring for Aster came from his love for her—that's what made the experience transcendent.

Too many millennia had passed since he'd been Zeus the Thunderer, his main line of work before he founded Olympus, Inc., and appointed himself CEO. It would take years of weight training to achieve the fitness required to hurl lightning bolts from the sky as he once did, and besides, that job was now an entry-level position in the Department of Weather.

He'd jotted down "cooking school" on a whim. Acquiring culinary skill might please Hera, especially on Cook's night off. The notion was crossed out as soon as he'd penned it.

One idea, the first one he'd had but he didn't dare put it in writing, was advising Ronnie.

Zeus sighed and shook his head. "Too late," he said to himself. He'd lost his place in the company he'd founded, and now his successor was scheming to throw him in prison! Even leaving the penthouse to meet with Jim for Thursday's counseling session seemed like a risk, though that wasn't the worst of it. Something gnawed at Zeus' heart and mind, a strong sense that something was terribly wrong at Olympus, Inc., but the spectral notion wouldn't solidify.

He mulled this unhappy suspicion while the ink dried. Defeated, Zeus rolled up the parchment and tied it with a piece of string. It was the best he could do. He'd share his failed list with Jim, proof of how far the Ex-Lord of the Universe had tumbled from the sky.

Veronica

Veronica got home late, as usual. She'd particularly wanted to have everything in the CEO office in order before she left work, with notes for Cleo, Hermes and Clifford as to the status of important, unfinished projects they might need to take over in case of—she wasn't sure, exactly, but the bad feeling in the pit of her stomach wouldn't go away.

"Mrrrrrrrrrrrow!"

Bill Gates, Jr., greeted her the instant she opened the condo door.

"Hi, buddy." She reached down to scratch his head but felt too weary to pick him up for a cuddle.

The soft pad of tufted feet followed her to the kitchen. She set the deli bag of polenta and goat cheese, her go-to comfort foods, on the counter. Veronica took the opened but untasted bottle of Sauvignon Blanc from the refrigerator and retrieved a wine glass and a dinner plate from the cupboard, but she didn't want to eat. Not yet. Maybe not tonight.

"Mrrrrrow!" the cat implored.

"Okay, pretty boy."

She followed him to the kitty habitat, smiled for the first time today as his indignant hindquarters stomped ahead. Veronica replenished the food and water and cleaned his box. The room was in the same disastrous condition it had been in on Sunday but cleaning it seemed like a task for Sisyphus. The curtains, the leaning cat-post, the vacuuming would have to come—later.

Veronica shivered. Tomorrow she'd face the most frightening task of her life. She'd need to use The Power to take Ares down, and why wouldn't it extract a heavy payment to overcome this vicious mess? Dad could and should have handled the problem long ago, but it was too late to place blame, pointless to feel anger. She'd taken the job with open if inexperienced eyes.

Veronica paced to her bedroom, switched on the lights, searched the drawers of her desk for an envelope and a piece of writing paper. She sat at the desk and wrote instructions for the care of Bill Gates, Jr., how much and when to feed him, the name of his veterinarian. The instructions, tucked into the envelope and addressed to Ilithyia, were propped against a sickly looking begonia on the kitchen counter.

She cast a disinterested eye at the dinner makings, knew she should eat but couldn't make herself, not yet. Veronica wandered from room to room, looking at the few things she'd collected to make her condo a home. Not much, really. A few books and a couple of wall hangings. The bust of Queen Elizabeth I in the hallway wore its usual grave stare. Veronica wondered how many times this mortal woman had faced peril and the chance of death. Athena had known Elizabeth. Veronica meant to ask her about their acquaintance when the crisis had passed. At least, unlike Elizabeth, she was immortal and didn't have death to fear. Veronica wondered grimly if death wasn't the worst of it.

Sighing, she returned to the kitchen and poured herself a glass of wine. It wouldn't help to pass another night without food or sleep, to arrive at tomorrow's meeting place more weak and exhausted than she felt right now. Tomorrow's schedule, which she'd reviewed just before leaving the office, showed an appointment with Clifford Essex and Jim Smith at 3 PM, evidence life would march on after the confrontation with Ares. Athena and Aphrodite would face Ares with her, and with the force of The Power—

Sickened with a momentary, blinding headache Veronica set her glass down so abruptly the stem broke. The voice of The Power had been quiet today. That was what frightened her most of all.

WEDNESDAY

Aphrodite

Aphrodite drummed her fingers on a low table at the Isle of L Coffee House. She hadn't been in this hole for years. The only appealing aspect of the décor was the dim lighting, which eased her self-consciousness about the barely perceptible bags under her eyes. Screw the bean bag chairs! It was impossible to recline attractively in them. She hoisted herself up, selected a high, padded swivel chair at the bar and ordered an iced cappuccino.

Athena strode through the archway that led to the restrooms. Aphrodite watched in the mirror behind the bar as her warrior half-sister, with owl perched on shoulder, approached.

"If you sit here you'll need to distract Ares from seeing our reflections," Athena said, scowling.

"Not to worry." Aphrodite thrust her chest forward to make her point.

"We'll be waiting for you in the ladies' room."

Athena turned on sandaled heel and retreated to the named position.

Aphrodite sipped disdainfully at her beverage. Iced cappuccino was hardly champagne, but then, champagne had recently been used against her. The bubbly Hef ordered at Club Dionysus had been drugged. Why else would the Goddess of Love have cheered for him on the sidelines of a chariot lot brawl like a besotted schoolgirl? The entertainment had netted a split forehead for Ares, a fat lip for Hef, and a confession the love potion in the champagne had been provided by Hera.

This admission had come long after Aphrodite, still drugged, had fussed over Hef's injuries, loaded him into his chariot and driven his matched team of dapple grays to her mansion, there to kneel at her bedside and gaze upon him as she cooed nonsense syllables for his recovery. She'd awakened, after drifting to sleep while slumped against mattress and box spring, her mind sufficiently clear to realize she'd been duped. Her icy glare was all the prodding Hef needed to spill the beans. The one thing he couldn't explain was how Hera had made a love potion without a strand of Aphrodite's hair.

Aphrodite sucked air through her straw, her iced cappuccino drained to the dregs in frustration, and signaled the barista for another. Hef tried to apologize, he told her he wanted to reconcile after talking to his mother and giving her Marvelous Marriage campaign serious consideration.

"Why shouldn't I want to love you and share my life with you?" he'd said. "Does being the Goddess of Love and Sexuality necessarily have to conflict with, well, monogamy? We could work on our relationship," he'd said, hope kindling in his eyes, "find some things we have in common besides immortality and—"

There weren't enough heart-shaped satin pillows on her vast, round bed to pitch at him as he held his arms in front of his battered face and backed away.

"Just think about it, Aph. I'll call you in a couple of hours when you've had a chance to cool down."

Hef's behavior was bad enough, but Ares—hah! He'd acted like he owned her, the way he'd swaggered into the restaurant and challenged Hef. Aphrodite chastised herself for getting involved with Ares in the first place. Why had she ever been interested in such a blowhard?

She'd ignored calls and refused boxes of chocolates from both of the brothers, but the ignorant brutes persisted. When Veronica called on Sunday to recruit her in the campaign to depose Ares, she was more than ready to volunteer. At least one of those two idiots would be out of her life!

A sliver of afternoon light cut through the coffee house gloom and widened to a door-sized rectangle, throwing a carpet of light across the black-painted floor. Ares' jet black hair disappeared when the door swung closed, his faux-tan face with stitches in the forehead looking child-sized atop epaulet-widened shoulders. A bitter taste rose in Aphrodite's throat but she was the grand mistress of faking a sensual mood. A welcoming smile warmed her lips.

Ares sat on a stool beside her, his pupils sizing themselves to the darkness.

"What a dump," he snorted, frowning. "I thought only dykes came here. Trying to tell me something, Dite?"

She winced inwardly at this diminutive while raising a hand to his forehead and stroking his wound with salon-perfect nails.

"The conquering hero," she said with playful scorn. "You said you'd meet me anywhere, so I thought I'd make you prove it. Order yourself a something-or-other grande, big boy," she said, rising. "Ladies' room," she added, with a girlish wrinkle of her turned-up nose.

Her co-conspirators were leaning against the tiled bathroom wall across from a long line of toilet stalls. Athena sported charmed battle dress, her leather armor dull under vanity mirror lights. Veronica wore her usual white toga with gold trim, her arms crossed tight against her chest. Her dark eyes blazed, revising Aphrodite's opinion that her young sister-in-law was merely a book-smart milquetoast.

"Showtime," Veronica announced in a deep, echoing tone that bathroom acoustics didn't fully explain. The unearthly quality made Aphrodite shiver.

She watched the other Goddesses in the mirror as she freshened her lipstick and fussed with her white-gold curls to fill a realistic interval of time. Veronica stared straight ahead as if looking into the distance; Athena studied the younger Goddess out of the corner of her eye.

The Goddess of Love turned from the reflections, adjusted the front of her toga for maximum visibility of cleavage and returned to her seat alongside Ares. Somehow he'd managed to find a Bacchus Light beer. The brown bottle sweated with cold in his square hand.

"What's wrong, lover boy, afraid caffeine will stunt your growth?" she jibed and thrust her chest under his easily tempted gaze.

"Just what you'd expect from a bunch of lesbos," he growled.

The barista shot Aphrodite a sympathetic look and excused herself on an errand to the storage room, as Veronica had arranged in advance. Ares probably hadn't noticed there were no other customers in the coffee house, he was so absorbed with Aphrodite's cleavage. He didn't acknowledge the whoosh of the ladies' room door as it opened and closed, nor the Goddesses and owl who quietly positioned themselves in the gloom behind him.

"Ares, Son of Zeus and Hera," a dark, reverberant voice declaimed.

The glassware behind the bar rattled. Ares' shoulders squared. Aphrodite rose and took her place in the three-Goddess triangle, trapping him. Veronica gripped the back of Ares' chair and spun him around to face her.

"I, Veronica Zeta, arrest you in the name of Olympus, Inc., for persistent and prolonged crimes against the mortals you are honor-bound to protect."

Aphrodite blinked but failed to dispel what she'd hoped was a trick of the light: a dense, black mantle hovering around the young Goddess. She exchanged a quick glance with Athena, whose eyes reflected her own fear. There was something wrong with Veronica, something terribly wrong.

"The Power!" Ares cried. "Dad gave you the—you can't do this to me!" He sprang from his seat and bolted toward the door but Athena blocked his escape.

Veronica raised her right hand and fanned her fingers in an arc. Ares shuddered, his whole body vibrating. His legs slapped together. His arms clapped to his sides as if bound. Sweat sheeted on his brow.

"I hereby exile you to prison. Stripped of your powers but not of your immortality, you will be punished, to live forever in the pain and torture you've inflicted on mankind since time began."

Holy Zeus, Veronica was mad! She'd told Aphrodite about taking away Ares' powers, but torturing him for all eternity? Aphrodite tried to look in Veronica's eyes, but a searing beam of light shot back from them and momentarily blinded her. When her vision cleared she looked pleadingly at Athena. The Goddess of War and Wisdom raised an eyebrow and returned a solemn nod before she took Ares' elbow and marched him out of the Isle of L Coffee House like a vast mechanical doll.

Veronica stood so still she seemed made of stone. The black aura was gone. Aphrodite raised her hands to frame Veronica's face and focused all her power to break the trance. After several tense moments Veronica's eyes fluttered. Her head fell forward and she sagged into Aphrodite's arms. The Goddess of Love settled her sister-in-law on one of the bar stools with no idea what to do— except call Hef.

Jim

Jim hadn't seen Stella, executive assistant to the Biggest of Big-Gs, for more than a century. When he and Clifford had scheduled their appointment with Veronica, he'd thought of Stella with something close to amusement. But now the meeting was imminent. He coached himself to face her with a sense of professional curiosity instead of wincing at what he remembered of her abrupt and demeaning manner.

"Try to relax," Clifford said as they entered the express elevator to the executive suite atop Olympus, Inc. "She'll take you apart if she sees you're nervous."

Jim steeled himself against the cell-flattening ascent of the express elevator. Hermes had adjusted the speed ages ago at Zeus' command, and it proved an excellent deterrent to unnecessary meetings. But no preparation was adequate. Jim felt his stomach fall. The trip, though mercifully short, left him with sea legs.

"Some ride." He took a deep breath to ground himself.

"Steady on, old bean," said Clifford and stepped over the threshold. Jim followed. The elevator doors rolled shut behind them with the boom of a kettle drum.

Jim squared his shoulders and stood tall. It was ridiculous to be afraid of a crusty, sharp-mouthed assistant bureaucrat. Dealing with Stella was simply a necessary step in learning if he could help Veronica.

He'd never felt comfortable in the CEO suite, felt oppressed by the onyx walls and high ceiling that vanished in the gloom. A bronze desk lurked on the far side of the reception area. Stella sat behind it. Jim was startled by the poisonous green aura hovering above her, as if Stella, herself, emanated evil.

Clifford nudged Jim with his elbow. They approached Stella together. Jim noted the antiquated telephone and intercom box on Stella's desk, evidence of her need to exercise control over the changes happening at Olympus, Inc. It made him feel a fool for having resisted digital technology.

"Good afternoon, Stella," said Clifford in his most charming manner, though his mouth twitched. "This is James Ares Smith, Director of Immortal Resources for the A and C Department."

Stella raised steel-gray eyebrows. "A real come-down from Continental Manager," she snorted.

"We're here for our three o'clock meeting with Ms. Zeta," Clifford continued, irritation entering his tone. "Very kind of you to arrange it for us."

"She's not here."

They waited a few seconds for elaboration. None came.

"I'm afraid I don't understand," said Clifford.

"She called in sick," Stella said with apparent satisfaction. "That is, Hephaestus called in for her."

"Hephaestus?" Concern replaced irritation in Clifford's voice.

"I told Zeus centuries ago Hephaestus was the one for the job," Stella said. "That girl isn't strong enough to run Olympus, Inc., can't handle the stress. Couldn't even call in sick for herself when things got rough."

Jim wondered what Stella meant by this last phrase, but her mouth pressed shut like an oyster shell. Malice twinkled in her copper-colored eyes.

"Right. We'll be on our way, then," said Clifford, a slight tremor in his voice. "I'll call to reschedule when she's returned."

Jim and Clifford didn't speak until the elevator doors closed, sealing off the CEO suite. As the car drifted down, Clifford said,

"Something's wrong. Veronica is the healthiest person I know. She never gets sick."

"But you've seen it coming, you and David?" said Jim. "That's why you wanted me to meet with her today."

Clifford sighed, heaved his shoulders and nodded.

"It's not unusual for mental or emotional illness to manifest itself in physical symptoms," Jim continued gently.

"Veronica and Hephaestus have never been close, Jim." Clifford's forehead was lined with worry. "He's one of the last people I'd expect to take care of her in illness."

Jim nodded. Everyone at Olympus, Inc., knew Veronica's disdain for her full siblings, and he'd seen first-hand the effect she'd had on Hebe. Stella's apparent glee at the situation added one more unsettling block to the messy pyramid.

"Yes," said Jim to himself.

"What?"

Jim adjusted his glasses on the bridge of his nose.

"I think you're right, Clifford, something's wrong."

The elevator stopped. A chime sounded. The doors rolled open to the fifth floor. Clifford led the way toward his office while Jim puzzled over what he'd seen and heard. Something was definitely wrong, but what, exactly, and what were they going to do about it?

Clifford

Clifford Essex couldn't concentrate for the rest of the work day, he was so worried about Veronica. At five o'clock sharp he said goodnight to Heinrich, his executive assistant, and left Olympus, Inc., on foot, for home.

He couldn't have asked for a more perfect evening to take a walk, though he barely noticed the clear sky and the west-leaning sun that warmed his shoulders. Once in his condo he changed from toga to slacks and a sports coat and continued his stroll with no particular destination in mind. He ended up in the neighborhood of New Mycenae, in front of the Olympus Arms. To the left he spied the neglected front garden of Veronica's condo. A black motorcycle with a side-car was parked on the grass. Dim light glowed in the transom above the front door, likewise in a window, probably the kitchen.

For a moment he pondered whether he should look in on the situation. The clear presence of Hephaestus (for his was the only motorcycle in the City of Mount Olympus) decided him. Clifford strode to Veronica's condo door, prepared to fight his way in if necessary. He pressed the doorbell, alert to every sound beyond the two-tone chime. Footsteps approached on the other side of the door.

"Yes?"

Clifford gulped. The last being he expected to greet him was the Goddess of Love. He stared momentarily at the brevity of her hot-pink toga, the cascade of her platinum-blonde hair, her long and well-formed limbs.

"I'm here to inquire about Ms. Zeta," he said with barely a stutter.

Aphrodite regarded him with shockingly violet eyes. He felt as if she were reading his soul.

"You love her."

"Yes," he said, unable to halt this admission. "May I see her?"

"She's gravely ill," Aphrodite said, blinking.

Was she trying to stay a tear? Clifford's heart lurched. Veronica was immortal. Surely she couldn't die?

"Ilithyia's with her now," Aphrodite said. "She's hoping she can bring Veronica around. Please don't say anything about this to anyone, we haven't told Zeus and Hera yet."

"Tartarus," Clifford swore softly. "Can I do anything to help?"

"Pray to Heaven and Earth for her recovery," the Goddess of Love said, "and one thing more."

"Anything."

"When and if she recovers, tell her you love her."

The door closed quietly. Clifford, stunned, turned and started slowly back to his own neighborhood. As he walked toward the sunset, he vowed to step out of his comfort zone, to set aside his British reserve, to risk opening his heart to Veronica at the first possible chance, if only the chance would come.

ThURSOAY

Aphrodite

The first rays of sunrise sliced through the narrow rectangular window above Veronica's front door. Aphrodite acknowledged the new day with a glance as she paced the condo entryway. From the bedroom Veronica whimpered, "Elle! Help me, Elle! I can't see!"

She tried to distract herself from the cries by critiquing her young sister-in-law's décor. Aphrodite started with the living room—rigid blinds instead of softening drapes; angular arm chairs and a hard, matching sofa she'd uncomfortably napped on but not a loveseat in sight; throw cushions totaled zero. No wonder the young man she'd spoken with last night—someone important at Olympus, Inc., but she couldn't recall why—was reticent to declare his love for Veronica. This flat did not inspire romance!

"And too much beige—boring," Aphrodite muttered to herself.

But, try as she might, she couldn't detach herself from the crisis. Veronica had regained consciousness but couldn't speak. Aphrodite shivered. If Hef hadn't roared through the City of Mount Olympus on his motorcycle to help them, she wasn't sure what she would have done. He'd brought them to Veronica's condo, Aphrodite riding "bitch" behind him and steadying Veronica, still stunned, to keep her from tumbling out of the sidecar.

That was yesterday. They'd camped at Veronica's condo ever since. Hef had called Apollo as soon as they'd settled Veronica in bed, but Apollo's assistant said he was away from Mount Olympus until Friday. Next he'd called Ilithyia, in the hope she'd have the medical knowledge to break Veronica's trance. Ilithyia, who Veronica called Elle, arrived in minutes with an herbal paste that she applied to Veronica's forehead. She held Veronica's hand and waited. It was hours before the patient responded, weak and confused.

"It's so dark," she'd said over and over. "Elle, it's so dark."

Blindness had stricken Veronica a few minutes before sunrise. Aphrodite peered through the bedroom doorway. Veronica's cat had settled at the foot of the bed, hadn't stirred for hours. Elle sat on the far side of the bed, holding one of Veronica's hands; Hef sat across from Elle, holding the other. Aphrodite had never seen him so worried, even when he'd first suspected she was having an affair with Ares. His concern for his little sister, the one he'd been passed over for as CEO, touched the Goddess of Love in a small, unselfish chamber of her heart.

A tear streamed down her cheek. "Damn," Aphrodite muttered. She returned to the living room and paused in front of the mirror above the beige marble fireplace to check her mascara.

"I can't see!" Veronica cried weakly from the bedroom. "I can't see!"

The doorbell chimed. Aphrodite stopped fussing with the smudges under her eyes and paced to the front door. Through the peek-hole she spied Zeus and Hera. She opened the door and gestured them in. Hef hadn't called his parents until an hour ago, had wanted them to have a decent night's sleep before confronting the crisis. Their faces were drawn and pale.

"How is she?" Hera whispered.

"About the same," Aphrodite said. She nodded toward the bedroom. "They're all in there. Elle can give you the details. Can I—" she paused, irritated by the sympathy she felt for the Goddess of Marriage "—would either of you like a cup of coffee?"

Hera, her eyes filling with tears, nodded and tentatively approached the bedroom.

"Thank you. We both take it black," Zeus said and followed Hera.

Aphrodite hadn't made coffee for—well, she wouldn't count the centuries. Veronica's espresso machine had a host of icon-labeled buttons. After some experimenting, which cost her a broken fingernail and some mopping up when she failed to put a mug under the place where the coffee came out, she managed three cups—two for her in-laws and one for herself. It was a strange feeling, not entirely unpleasant, to do something kind for Hera. What worse could happen to a mother than for her child to suffer? Aphrodite approached the bedroom, two mugs in her hands. The door stood open. Hef had given his place to Hera, who held Veronica's hand in both of hers, and stood behind his mother with Zeus. Both men saw Aphrodite and joined her in the hallway. She handed each of them a mug.

"Thank you, daughter," said Zeus with a small, sad smile. Hef tapped a kiss on her forehead. The men passed through the front door. Outside, they started speaking, their voices low and unintelligible.

Aphrodite returned to the kitchen and lightened her coffee with cream from Veronica's refrigerator. She sat at the table, rummy from lack of sleep. Was it possible, she wondered, could Veronica actually die? What would happen to the world if immortals suddenly—

weren't?

She felt a compulsion to do something, even a small thing, to relieve the load on Hef's family. When a meaningful act at last occurred to her, she nearly laughed. Aphrodite held an imaginary thread between her thumbs and index fingers and snapped it in two. Now Hera, at least, would have one less worry.

Jim

Dark clouds were building in the sky as Jim strode from Athens U back to the hotel. Zeus had missed his appointment, set for 10 AM on the Knoll. After waiting twenty minutes Jim bagged the project. He'd unintentionally left his digital pad in the hotel suite. It would have been simple to send a message to Zeus and find out what had happened. Fat drops of rain splatted his shoulders. He'd get home to Candy sooner, anyway. She'd been a wreck when he'd left, upset he wouldn't take her with him.

Jim passed several eateries and high-end shops between campus and his hotel. Was it possible, he wondered, that Veronica was so ill Zeus had become involved? Distracted, Jim had to swipe his key card twice to get the door to his suite open. A toddler's wail pierced his eardrums upon entry.

Candy marched toward Jim, a red-faced Titus squirming in her arms.

"Where in Heaven and Earth have you been?" she barked, her eyes flashing. "He's teething again and we're out of zwieback!"

Hard-wired survival instinct made Jim draw back a step but he smiled, too. The cloying monster who'd possessed his wife for nearly two weeks was gone!

"Candy!" Jim said, giddy with relief. "You're you again!"

She threw back her mane of strawberry blonde hair and sighed in exasperation. "Of course I'm me, Jim, don't be stupid!"

As Candy thrust Titus into Jim's arms, Jim caught her chin and guided her lips to his for a resounding kiss.

"By Zeus, you pick the weirdest times to get romantic." She pulled away but the sizzle in her eyes suggested interest. Titus' wails mellowed to huffing sobs. "See if you can calm him down," she ordered. Candy spun away from Jim and grabbed her handbag from the entryway table. "*I'll* find some zwieback."

Candy slammed the door behind her. Jim caught his image in the hall mirror. He was grinning like a by-Zeus idiot he was so glad to see his volatile and impatient wife again.

"Mommy's back, big guy," he said to Titus' reflection in the mirror. He bounced the toddler in his arms until sobs subsided to sniffles. "That icky lady is gone."

"Da?"

Jim straightened his spine and stood tall. "I'm going to be a big guy, too," he said. "You and I are going digital, Titus. We're going to learn all about WiFi and Smart Phones and all that stuff, so we can travel with Mommy when she works."

For a moment Jim conjured the happy vision of trundling through airports in Candy's wake, a bag of baby supplies slung over his shoulder and Titus in his arms. Titus' eyelids began to flutter. Jim crept into the bedroom and put his son down for a nap. As he watched the child drift off to sleep, Veronica came to mind. Was her father watching over her, too?

He left the bedroom on tip-toe and closed the door all but a crack. Stella had offered no information about the nature of Veronica's illness. Jim reflected on some grave injuries he'd incurred years ago, injuries Hera had been able to cure with her Big-G healing arts and powers. Was she at Veronica's side now, working another miracle? How was it possible, he wondered, that a Big-G, the strongest of all immortals, could be subject to sickness in the first place?

"It doesn't make sense," he said to himself. Though he hated to intrude in times of trouble, Jim snagged his digital pad from the sitting room desk and started a message to Zeus.

Zeus

Zeus studied Jim as they stepped into the elevator, bound for the Olympus, Inc., CEO suite. His companion's brow was furrowed, as well it should be if what they'd pieced together could possibly be true.

"Don't look nervous, Jim. She'll tear you apart if you look nervous."

He wouldn't have brought Jim at all, but there was something the counselor had observed in the reception area—something odd but he couldn't recall what, exactly—that might have some bearing on the dire problem at hand.

Zeus pushed the elevator button and braced himself for the ascent. When he'd been the one with The Power he'd been immune to the effects of fierce upward velocity, but now he was as vulnerable as any other immortal.

The Ex-Lord of the Universe squared his shoulders when the car reached its destination, mustered the pride he'd built over the millennia before his retirement. This had been his office suite, damn it! He'd built this company from the ground up, and he wasn't going to let it crumble and take his favorite child as its victim.

Zeus stepped out of the elevator—alone. He turned. Jim, frozen in place, stared straight ahead.

"Jim?"

Zeus tugged at Jim's elbow, drawing him into the cavernous reception area.

"Brace up, man," he murmured as they walked through the gloom toward the bronze glow of Stella's desk. Halfway there, Zeus squinted. A heavy, black aura hovered around his former executive assistant.

The sight turned his stomach. He tightened his grip on Jim's elbow and lengthened his aging spine, sternum thrust forward, assuming a posture of command to mask his fear.

"Stella," he said.

"Zeus." Her eyes spoke poison. "You have no business here, you and your—" she studied Jim disdainfully, "bodyguard."

"Perhaps you're right." Zeus wished he could see her hands, resting in her lap and obscured behind the desk. "Perhaps I'm making a social call. Would you kindly buzz Veronica and see if she has a minute to spare her old Dad?"

Stella winced at the sound of Veronica's name, then stared at them incredulously.

"Didn't your friend tell you she's on sick leave?"

"You don't say?" Zeus motioned Jim to sit in the lone chair in front of Stella's desk. He put his hands behind his back and started pacing back and forth, his eyes riveted to Stella. "Did it ever occur to you that Big-G Gods don't get sick?" He stopped in front of the desk. "Not unless someone's been up to some kind of funny business."

"You're not in charge here anymore," she hissed, half-rising. "What's it to you?"

He braced his palms on her desktop and leaned forward until they were nose-to-nose.

"I don't know how you're doing it, or why, but you've been interfering with," he nearly trembled as he spoke the words, "The Power."

"Yes!" She chuckled malevolently. "And it only took you five thousand years to figure it out. Oh, well-done, my Lordship, well-done!"

"You admit it?" he said, stunned.

"Why not?" She smiled fiercely. "No one can stop me now! I've been waiting for my chance ever since you killed Cronus. All these centuries I've been watching and waiting to avenge the patricide."

She paced around her desk and stopped alongside Zeus. He turned toward her, studied her eyes that, he noticed for the first time, were at exactly the same level as his.

"He was—my father, too." A tear spilled down her cheek but she didn't seem to notice, didn't bother to wipe it away. "I was hidden from all of you because he wanted me to succeed him. Me!" She circled behind Zeus and leaned over the back of Jim's chair, her lips to his ear. "Now, what do you think about that, counselor? A bit of a Greek tragedy, isn't it?"

Stella swung around behind her desk, arms flung toward the ceiling. "I've ruined you all!" she cried savagely. "I made you a philanderer, dear brother, which made your wife, my dear sister, a shrew! And your children—hah! So easy to warp young minds with just a pinch of the Darkness—Hephaestus crippled and bitter, Ilithyia cast off and remorseful, Ares mindlessly arrogant and violent, and little Veronica, your princess, soul-sick and blind!"

"And Hebe?" Zeus said after a pause.

"Not my work, she's just your usual spoiled ninny," Stella said. "But now I'm in charge!"

She whirled behind the desk like a dervish. Darkness lowered over the three of them, threatening to extinguish the dim reception area light.

Zeus exerted all the concentration he possessed to turn his mind from the chaos and shuffle the bits and pieces he'd learned in recent hours into a plan of action. When he'd visited Veronica's bedside he'd attempted to take back The Power by reversing the process he'd used to transfer it to her. His attempt failed. That's when he began to wonder if The Power was actually manipulated by someone else. Stella, though in the reception area, was the only other person who'd been in the executive suite when the transfer was made. Was whatever Jim had observed on his earlier visit a part of it? If only he could remember—

"Does that mean you'll finally be converting to digital?"

Zeus, startled by Jim's casual tone, broke off his analysis.

"I beg your pardon?" Stella stopped dead. Her arms dropped to her sides.

"This intercom system, for example," Jim said. He pointed to the onyx box with vents and a few buttons that sat on a corner of her desk. "I'm terrible with new technology, can't even manage to set up a Facebook account, but this is a real old-timer. How does it work, anyway?"

He leaned toward the intercom, index finger poised above a button.

"Stop!" shrieked Stella. She charged for the box but drew back as Jim lowered his finger. "You don't know what you're doing!"

They were deadlocked, still as statues. A thundering revelation clapped in Zeus' brain.

"That's how you've done it!" he cried. "I assumed it was mere eccentricity when you insisted on keeping that old thing, same as you are with telephones." Zeus strode behind Stella and gripped her shoulders. "You must have used all kinds of hiding places, simple objects in plain sight, over the millennia."

"Let me go!" She twisted in his grip but he held her tight.

"Come along, sister," Zeus said and marched her toward the elevator. "Always a danger when you keep your power in some sort of vessel instead of within yourself."

"You think you can destroy me, but you're wrong!"

He could feel her strength fade as his own seemed to grow. Flooded with a long-absent sense of well-being, Zeus smiled to himself.

"What should we do about the intercom?" Jim called out.

"Get Hermes," Zeus shouted over his shoulder. "Tell him to bring the containment bag he uses for lethal charmed objects and put it in isolation until I have time to study it. Wait here for him. When you're done, I want both of you to meet me at the detention center on sub-floor seven."

He owed it to Ronnie and everyone else in his family to right this wrong—for good.

Bill Gates, Jr.

The big orange cat had moved from his place on the bed to the lap of the woman who smelled of leather. She'd been the one feeding him since Mom got sick. The woman didn't seem to notice (or, at least, not to mind) when he licked her vest, savoring the faint taste of bovine.

At first Bill Gates, Jr., had wondered if Mom had a hairball but he'd soon realized it was a more serious ailment. He'd head-butted her hands several times when they'd first put her in bed but she didn't return the merest, most casual scratch. He then opted to curl up near her feet, out of the way of the people who fussed around her. When she'd started muttering and thrashing, his patience was exhausted. That's when he'd taken his present position.

He was hungry again. Bill Gates, Jr., nipped at the woman Elle's hand. She patted his head but didn't recognize his "feed me" cue. Discouraged, he rolled himself up in a ball and fell asleep.

Mid-way through a dream about stalking a particularly fat mouse, a shriek woke him. It came from the oldest woman, the one with silver fur on her head.

"She's gone!" the silver woman lamented.

Bill Gates, Jr., focused his sleep-heavy eyes and looked at his mom. She was very pale and lay very, very still. Another woman and a man stood behind the silver woman, heads bowed.

Something dark throbbed in the middle of Mom's chest. Bill Gates, Jr., watched the mass surge against her sternum, like a caged crow beating its wings against the bars, trying to escape.

The woman Elle breathed in sharply and said, "Look!"

Bill Gates, Jr., honored the irresistible impulse to lunge at the blackness that shot from Mom's chest like a cloud of soot, but the cloud dispersed and vanished before he made contact. Elle's hands grabbed him around his prosperous middle and pulled him back to her lap before he landed on Mom. The silver woman and the other two people had eyes as large as saucers.

Mom's eyes fluttered open. She looked first at the silver woman, who said, "Heaven and Earth be praised!"

"Mom?" said Mom to the silver woman.

"Ronnie, sweetheart, can you see me?"

"Yes, I…"

Mom's eyes moved around to look at the others. She crooked her fingers and wiggled them at him, her signal for having a pet. He sauntered onto the bed and lay his head in her hand.

"Good boy," she said and scratched him behind the ears.

The other people started fussing. They asked Mom if she was hungry, if she was warm enough, if she could tell them anything about what had happened to her. Mom smiled a little, said maybe she'd like a double-mocha with cinnamon in a while but not yet. Elle and the silver woman lifted Mom's shoulders and propped some pillows behind her. The man and the other woman smiled and held each other's hands.

Mom pointed at a huge vase of flowers on her vanity table across the room.

"Who brought those?"

It was the man who'd brought the cat litter last weekend. Bill Gates, Jr., hadn't trusted him from the start, and the flowers he brought were suspicious, too. Someone had called them Birds of Paradise but they didn't look like any bird he'd ever seen.

"That guy from the office, Clifford Essex," said Elle. "He was here this morning. Just came into the hallway, didn't ask to see you. I think he has a cold or something, he couldn't stop sneezing."

Mom smiled weakly. "Allergies," she said, in a same tone she'd said "good boy."

Though it wounded Bill Gates, Jr., to hear Mom apply her special voice, used only for him, to the flower-bearing stranger, he was too exhausted to worry about it now. He snuggled into the crook of Mom's arm and purred himself to sleep.

FRIDAY

Ares

After a morning of pleading, Ares had finally persuaded the warden to arrange for a meeting between himself and Athena.

The strangest feeling had washed through him yesterday, had infused hope and eradicated anger and boredom as he sat slumped on his cell bed in the detention center. The glowing florescent tubes above no longer seemed depressing, though he longed to be outdoors and in the fields, a desire he hadn't felt in millennia. How could he have forgotten he was the God of Agriculture, as well as the God of War? The recollection had come to him as if created by lightning, a brilliant flash that showed so clearly how he would fulfill his true destiny.

It was past noon when a guard arrived.

"C'mon, mate," the small-g said. He unlocked Ares' cell door and signaled him to rise. Ares moved slowly, his hands and feet shackled with golden chains. How many times, he wondered, had he treated his own prisoners, soldiers of great valor and dignity, much worse?

The guard gripped his elbow and guided him down the narrow hallway. They passed through a series of heavy metal doors, each door unlocked with its own key. Ares was certain his days of mindless cruelty and bloodshed were over. He'd never be forgiven, that was more than even a Big-G could ask, considering his history. But he would convince the ranks at Olympus, Inc., of his life-altering repentance. *I can make good*, he thought. Tears of remorse welled in his eyes.

"Here we are, then," the guard said, unlocking the final door.

The visitation area was divided by close-set bars. The guard motioned Ares to sit in the lone chair on the prisoner side and took his own place in a corner. An identical chair stood beyond the bars, behind it a door with a small latticed window. Another guard looked through the lattice, grunted and opened the door, admitting Athena.

Ares' half-sister looked strong and composed, her chum the owl perched on her shoulder. Over her toga she wore a golden breastplate, emblazoned with rubies in the insignia of a general. A matching helmet rested in the crook of one arm. The guard on the visitor side pointed Athena to the chair and stood in a corner, a mirror of Ares' guard.

The Big-G Gods studied each other. Moments passed in silence.

"Thank you for coming to see me," Ares said at last.

"The warden told me you have something important to say." Her tone was neutral, her eyes questioning.

"I do." But how to start? He shifted in his chair, searching for the right words.

"You look different," she said, tilting her head toward the owl who hooted softly in agreement. Athena and the owl stared at him, gave him the uncomfortable sensation of being considered for dinner.

"I—I feel different, too," he stammered. Conversing with Athena, someone he'd been at odds with all his adult life, made him nervous. But, she, too, was a soldier, and he felt she would understand him better than any of the other Big-G Gods. "It came on me yesterday afternoon, the realization I don't have to be so bloody-minded—that I'm not bloody-minded! Why have I been such a brutal ass all my life? I don't understand it at all, not at all." Though afraid to ask, he said, "Do you think I'm losing my mind?"

Athena didn't answer at once.

"No, Ares, I don't think you're losing your mind. Other events corroborate what you say. Veronica suffered a dreadful illness after she confronted you. For a while we weren't sure she was going to pull through."

"But she can't die, she's immortal!"

"Just so," said Athena, her expression grave. "After your arrest she had a sort of break-down. No one's seen anything like it before. Yesterday afternoon—" she paused as if the timing should be noted "—she made a sudden recovery. She's still weak but is expected to return to full health."

"Zeus be praised." Ares leaned forward, intrigued. "You think her recovery and my—change of heart—have a common root?"

"It's too early to know for certain," she said. "There was an arrest yesterday afternoon. Zeus brought in the prisoner."

"Dad brought in the prisoner?" Ares said, astonished. "Who in Heaven and Earth would he…?"

"It might be coincidence," Athena said, "but around the same the time Stella was processed—"

"Stella?" Ares shuffled thousands of years of names in his memory. "The only Stella I can think of is Dad's executive assistant."

"That's the one," she confirmed. "Zeus said she'd absconded with something dangerous, some kind of device he and Hermes are trying to decipher. Now," she leaned back in her chair and crossed her arms, "let's hear about you."

"It's an idea I have about the military." He pictured millions of acres yielding wheat, corn, rice, beans. "If you work with me, do you think we can change military wars between mortals to a world-wide war against hunger?"

Athena listened to his plan to replace guns and tanks with plows and combines, to improve world-wide food distribution, to make famine extinct. He felt encouraged when she nodded her head as each point was made.

"Interesting," she said when he'd finished and offered a faint smile—not bad for someone he'd come to think of as Old Stone Face. She rose and brushed her fingertips on the owl's back. "It's Veronica's decision, but I'll present your proposal to her when she's stronger. And I'll have to explain it all to Secretary Chadwick."

"Who?"

"I'll tell you about it later."

Athena started for the door, then turned back. "Are they treating you decently in here?" she said, eyeing his guard.

"I'll be fine," he said, touched by her kind interest. He understood it would take time to get out of detention, but what was time to an immortal? "Maybe—" the request was so humble it seemed silly, but he continued anyway, "—maybe you could send me some books on agriculture? Anything from about, hmmm, Cleopatra's time forward would be news to me."

Her faint smile returned. "I'll see what I can do."

Saturday

Hera

For the first time in a long time Hera was home alone Saturday afternoon. She was stretched out in her recliner in the den, a spot she'd rarely occupied since Marriage and the Media had started demanding sixty-hour weeks.

Hera watched the seconds blink by on the home entertainment center's digital clock. She'd never been good at relaxing. After five minutes she kicked the footrest closed and wandered down the hall, going from room to room with no particular purpose. There was nothing to do—the staff kept the place spotless. Her only hobby was knitting, but she only liked knitting when she had a specific project to work on. The Goddess of Marriage was not one to mindlessly whip up dozens of potholders to sell at craft fairs.

It wasn't as if she'd been idle today. She'd been in the office all morning, meeting with Candy Smith. The Marvelous Marriage spokesperson had finally broken free of whatever charm Aphrodite had inflicted on her and was back to her normal, volatile self. At last they'd been able to discuss the new additions to the seminar series. They'd worked so intensely Hera realized, when noon arrived, she hadn't taken a sip of wine all day.

Without giving wine another thought she'd left Olympus, Inc., shortly after Candy. She'd hailed a chariot and given the driver Veronica's address. Hera was relieved to see her youngest daughter had color in her cheeks and was eating solid food. Ilithyia was staying with her for a few days to make sure she rested, and reported David had paid a visit this morning. A cheap "get well soon" card, signed with Hebe's childish scrawl, stood on the bedside table. The cat made himself useful by settling his considerable bulk on his mistress, making it difficult for her to get out of bed. Veronica was fretful about missing time from work. She messaged Zeus on her digital pad whenever she thought of something that needed doing. This happened four times during Hera's half-hour visit.

Hera smiled. Zeus had reported to Olympus, Inc., yesterday morning, filled with energy and enthusiasm for his temporary reinstatement as CEO. He'd called the department directors together and asked them to forward summaries of current projects, taking extra time to confer with Athena in her new role as Director of

Armed Forces.

Zeus was at headquarters again today, setting the agenda for the coming weeks and meeting with the plant supervisor about a remodel and redecoration of the CEO suite. He'd found a plan for this project in Veronica's desk and wanted to have everything ready when she returned from medical leave. In Apollo's opinion, Veronica was to rest and relax for one month, minimum, preferably two. Everyone was encouraging her to take a vacation. Ilithyia had offered to travel with her and was lobbying for several weeks on Tropicana Island, a vacation spot Zeus had acquired for the family long ago with white sand beaches and lots of sunshine.

Hera hadn't been to the detention center to visit Ares yet. Truth be it told, though she loved her son she did not like him. Word was circulating he had repented and reformed. She'd believe it when she saw it.

The discovery Stella had been manipulating The Power to her own ends for five millennia, plus learning Stella was Zeus and Hera's sister, was likewise difficult to absorb. Zeus had confided he wasn't sure what would become of Stella, who was currently undergoing physical and psychological evaluation, conducted by Apollo and Jim Smith. It was possible Stella, like Veronica, had been possessed and poisoned by The Power, possible her sociopathic behavior could be cured. Time would tell.

Hera found herself in the kitchen. She shook her head to clear it of all the changes and loose ends. Recent days had been grueling and she was suddenly ravenous. Cook wasn't in sight and didn't answer when called. Hera sorted through the refrigerator, took out the goat cheese and a jar of Kalamata olives. She made herself a snack plate and leaned against the kitchen island, munching. Cook's day off, she remembered. They usually went out for dinner on Cook's day off, but it had been such a hectic week and since Hera wanted something to do…

The pantry was well-stocked and she soon gathered the ingredients for Zeus' favorite meal. If Cook was making it, it would all be from scratch. Hera was just as happy to use the can opener as stand over a hot stove. The tomatoes and onions would have to be fresh, of course, and there were plenty of these in the tiered hanging baskets. For a beverage, wine would be the base—not her preferred Chardonnay, but a Spanish or Italian red, plus a few other ingredients. Hera searched the cupboards for a pitcher. She chopped, poured, stirred, set the result in the refrigerator and launched into preparing the entree. After additional chopping, grating, spooning, plating and wielding the can opener, she retired from the kitchen to put on a fresh toga, a filmy red one Zeus particularly liked, seeing as it was the butler's night off, too.

Now she felt like relaxing. Hera poured a half-glass of Chardonnay and sauntered to the marital suite. The maid kept it in perfect order though it hadn't been used for—well, why dwell on it? The afternoon was warm and the room felt stuffy. Hera opened the windows to let in a fresh summer breeze, setting the stage for romance. After she plied Zeus with nachos and sangria, he'd be putty in her hands.

SUNDAY

Aphrodite

The gods slept in on Sunday, except for Aphrodite.

Wide awake, she eased out of bed while Hef snored. She pulled on his discarded black tee-shirt as an impromptu dressing gown and padded to the master bath on bare feet.

Their reconciliation had been consummated Thursday night, hours after Veronica was freed from whatever dark force had possessed her. They'd gone to Hef's place, an impressive house with a sculpture garden and stables, and had fallen on each other like a pair of starving wolves. The weekend had proceeded in the same manner, with meals taken as needed, plenty of wine and exemplary chocolates.

The oblong beveled mirror in Hef's bathroom (the frame a masterpiece of intricate metalwork he'd fabricated himself) reflected Aphrodite's suspicion her hair and makeup was in a shambles. All she had to work with was a tube of hot pink lipstick and Hef's comb. She sighed and launched in on the reconstruction process, judging herself comical in Hef's black-framed reading glasses. At least her toga, cleaned and pressed by Hef's housekeeper and now hanging in his bedroom closet, looked decent.

It would be a by-Zeus miracle if she could get back home without the paparazzi spotting her. All of Mount Olympus would be talking about them by now, probably as much as they were talking about Veronica's near brush with death, the horrific deceit of Stella and the imprisonment of Ares.

Aphrodite grimaced at the thought of her ex-lover. It was now believed Ares had been enchanted for most of his life and was radically different since the spell had lifted. What a pain it would have been, to learn him all over again!

"Blast!" There was a bruise on the side of her neck, a hickey from Hef and there was no concealer to be had. Aphrodite couldn't bear thinking of the smug gossip that would circulate if word of his love bite got out. She'd call her chauffer and have him meet her behind the house, at the servants' entrance. The last thing she wanted was to provide fuel to her enemies, Hera chief amongst them. After the crisis with Veronica had passed, Hera had used her superior, tutting tone to say something very close to "I told you so" about Aphrodite and Hef reconciling. Yes, Hera had won the battle of Candy Jones through Aphrodite's brief and unwise dalliance with kindness. But she had not, necessarily, won the war. If the Goddess of Marriage continued to trample on the turf of the Goddess of Love, there would be Heaven and Earth to pay.

Aphrodite's freshly pink lips smiled wickedly. She still had her secret weapon—she knew who'd fathered David Bernstein.

ABOUT THE AUTHOR

S. D. Matley's short stories have appeared in *THEMA Literary Journal*, *GlassFire Magazine* and *Dark Pages* (Blade Red Press). Her sci-fantasy novella *Small-g City* is a WolfSinger Publications release. She lives near Walla Walla, Washington amidst thousands of acres of wheat (not hers!) with husband Bruce and many 4-legged kids. Learn more at http://susandmatley.com/.

Also by S.D. Matley

Small-g City

Seattle is on the brink of disaster, but nobody knows it! Nobody except Ralph, a "small-g" god from Olympus, Inc.

Ralph suffers from extreme job burn-out, and no wonder--his job is to reinforce Seattle's notorious raised highway, the Alaskan Way Viaduct, by disbursing his molecules throughout the unstable and hazardous structure.

But Ralph's molecules are feeling the pull of reconstitution. Will he survive one more agonizing rush hour without resuming his humanoid form and emerging from the viaduct, sending thousands of commuters to their deaths? And what about the familiar shadow hovering over him? If Zeus (Olympus, Inc., CEO and the Biggest of Big-G Gods) is spying on him, all Tartarus is sure to break loose!

Unintended Consequences – edited by Carol Hightshoe

For every action there is an equal and opposite reaction –
Newton's Third Law of Motion.

While Newton was talking about motion when he developed the above law, it can also be said that for every action or decision there is a consequence: sometimes good, sometimes bad.

Many times consequences can be foreseen and planned for. But there are times they are never seen. It is these unforeseen or Unintended Consequences that can have the biggest impact on individual lives.

An android working to pass as human.

A woman who loses her pre-destined 'soul mate' on world where they were marked at birth.

A Queen who uses magic to make her subjects more cooperative and helpful to each other.

A wife who authorizes a radical treatment for dementia to be performed on her husband.

And 16 more who will learn about the unintended consequences that will affect their lives.

Featuring stories by: Lyn McConchie, Alexandria Bellefleur, Michael Picco, Natasha Cage, Catrin Sian Rutland, DJ Tyrer, Dana Bell, Holly Riordan, Chris Dean, Guy Anthony De Marco, Andrew M.

Seddon, J.G. Formato, Michael W. Clark, S. D. Matley, Vaughan Stanger, Jean Martin, Edward Ahern, Glen Damien Campbell, Lyn Godfrey, and V. Hartman DiSanto

Get ready for more adventures with these fantasy books from WolfSinger Publications.

Fanny & Dice – Rebecca McFarland Kyle

"I'm leaving Hell for good, Eurydice…"

When she heard those words, Eurydice had a choice: remain in Hades' realm or escape to Earth with her kinswoman, Persephone.

She knew the Earth wasn't what they'd left. Demeter hadn't summoned Persephone to bring Spring for quite some time…and the last dead crossed the River Styx many years before. She hadn't expected to arrive in a world where trains rode across the prairie on metal tracks instead of chariots and men settled disputes with six guns instead of swords.

Eurydice will face perils both immortal and mortal, from gun and axe to her own heart…

The Lawman's Daughter – Paul Miller

Raine receives a final, disturbing message from her father. The problem is, it was written after he was supposedly killed in battle. Now she must join the ranks of the inhuman Rift Wardens to try and uncover the truth.

What she finds is a dark plot involving some very powerful people, and stopping it could very well cost Raine her life.

Or, even worse, it could cost her soul.

The Last Sorcerer – Felicia Cash

Throughout the history of time, a war has raged between the forces of light and darkness.

As the millennia passed the blood lines thinned and powers waned. One year ago, the last great sorcerer disappeared in the process of killing the last of the Dark Dragons, and now the world is in the hands of only the weakly magicked.

But can you ever really kill a dragon?

Twila Aurelius and Morgan Stevens are two girls who are thrust into this time-honored struggle, pitted against the dark forces. With wit and friendship, and a little bit of dumb luck, they set out to put the world right again, even if it means fighting off werewolves with no more than a stapler. Evil sorcerers aren't the only threat, especially when the girls learn more about their own histories and those of their families.

Can friendship overcome history?

Can two girls overcome evil?

Maya, Resurrected – Kimberly Todd Wade

859 A.D. Yohl Ik'nal ("Heart of the Wind Place") is alone with her two starving children on their drought-stricken farm. Her husband and two grown sons have been drafted to fight in a distant war. Will they ever return? Yohl can't afford to wait. Her hungry children must be fed. It's time to dig up Yohl's past, for her mother was a princess, her grandfather a king. She still has relatives amongst the Maya royalty. They are her best hope for salvation.

Follow Yohl and her children as they travel Maya causeways, highways of the ancient world, through ravaged jungle and depressed homesteads to the capital city, itself on the verge of economic collapse.

Can the religious spectacle of human sacrifice provoke the Gods' beneficence? If the Maya ceremonies and myths fail, Yohl has recourse to the older, deeper traditions of the forest people.

She'll do whatever necessary to survive.

The Moleskin Cap - M. R. Williamson

Helen is trying to get over the recent loss of her mother. Seeing the struggle, her father sends her to live with her grandparents.

Now among the forests her mother loved, Helen connects with her mother's hobby, photography. With her mother's first camera, an old Nikon, she snaps a shadowy figure in the early-morning shade of a fir tree.

The resulting friendship not only pulls her from the destructive depression she was sinking into, but leads Helen into a world of magic and adventure and gives her a new purpose in life and a new reason to live.

Necromantic Shenanigans –
J.A. Campbell & Rebecca McFarland Kyle

From building Towers of Solitude in Colorado's mountains to freeing a bestiary held captive by a demon-possessed Scottish Laird, Elise and Hagatha Macrow are on the case.

Necromantic Shenanigans is a lucky combination of thirteen stories detailing the escapades of two necromancers, who fight crime and normalcy without ever donning a cape.

Seventh Daughter – Ronnie Seagren

Some people are destined from birth to do great things.

Gil Orlov is born in the shadow of totality of a solar eclipse, the seventh daughter of a seventh daughter. She is the culmination of a carefully planned genealogy begun by her great-grandmother. Gil's purpose, the goal of her family—defeating a Vision of the world in flames, reduced to a lifeless cinder.

But the power she should have is muted or lacking. Gil and her six sisters begin an arduous journey to a place of power high in the Peruvian Andes known as Killichaka—the Bridge to the Moon. They must make it to this ancient temple in time to complete a ritual during the totality of the 1937 solar eclipse. If they are successful, Gil's powers should be restored—giving her the ability to prevent the global disaster her ancestors warned of.

To succeed they must first survive the journey and locate Killichaka. Against them is the environment, the elements, their own doubts and fears as well as the 'Other' and a force that would gleefully see the world fall into chaos—an entity known as Supay.

Find out more about these and our other books at
www.wolfsingerpubs.com